W9-AXM-862

WRANGLER'S RESCUE

Also available from
B.J. Daniels
and HQN Books

The Montana Cahills

Renegade's Pride
Outlaw's Honor
Cowboy's Legacy
Cowboy's Reckoning (ebook novella)
Hero's Return
Rancher's Dream
Wrangler's Rescue

The Montana Hamiltons

Wild Horses
Lone Rider
Lucky Shot
Hard Rain
Into Dust
Honor Bound

Beartooth, Montana

Fallen (ebook prequel)
Unforgiven
Redemption
Forsaken
Atonement
Mercy

B.J. DANIELS

WRANGLER'S RESCUE

Recycling programs
for this product may
not exist in your area.

ISBN-13: 978-1-335-00626-4

Wrangler's Rescue

This edition published by arrangement with Harlequin Books S.A.

For questions and comments about the quality of this book, please contact us at CustomerService@Harlequin.com.

www.HQNBooks.com

Printed in U.S.A.

This book is dedicated to anyone who has experienced the power and magic of true love.

CHAPTER ONE

ASHLEY JO "AJ" SOMERFIELD couldn't help herself. She kept looking out the window of the Stagecoach Saloon hoping to see a familiar ranch pickup. Cyrus Cahill had promised to stop by as soon as he returned to Gilt Edge. He'd been gone less than a week after driving down to Denver to see about buying a bull for the ranch.

"I'll be back on Saturday," he'd said when he left. "Isn't that the day Billie Dee makes chicken and dumplings?"

He knew darned well it was. "*Texas* chicken and dumplings," AJ had corrected him since everything Billie Dee cooked had a little of her Southern spice in it. "I know you can't resist her cookin', so I guess I'll see you then."

He'd laughed. Oh, how she loved that laugh. "Maybe you will if you just happen to be tending bar on Saturday."

"I will be." That was something else he knew darned well.

He'd let out a whistle. "Then I guess I'll see you then."

She smiled to herself at the memory. It had taken Cyrus a while to come out of his shell. One of those "aw shucks, ma'am" kind of cowboys, he was so darned shy she thought she was going to have to throw herself on the floor at his boots for him to notice her. But once he had opened up a little, they'd started talking, joking around, getting to know each other.

Before he'd left, they'd gone for a horseback ride through the snowy foothills up into the towering pines of the forest. It had been Cyrus's idea. They'd ridden up into one of the four mountain ranges that surrounded the town of Gilt Edge—and the Cahill Ranch.

It was when they'd stopped to admire the view from the mountaintop that overlooked the small western town that AJ had hoped Cyrus would kiss her. He sure looked as if he'd wanted to as they'd walked their horses to the edge of the overlook.

The sun warming them while the breeze whispered through the boughs of the nearby snow-laden pines, it was one of those priceless Montana January days between snowstorms. That's why Cyrus had said they should take advantage of the beautiful day before he left for Denver.

Standing on a bared-off spot on the edge of the mountain, he'd reached over and taken her hand in his. "Beautiful," he'd said. For a moment she thought he was talking about the view, but when she met his gaze she'd seen that he'd meant her.

Her heart had begun to pound. This was it. This was what she'd been hoping for. He drew her closer. Pushing back his Stetson, he bent toward her. His mouth was just a breath away from hers—when his mare nudged him with her nose.

She could laugh about it now. But if she hadn't grabbed Cyrus he would have fallen down the mountainside.

"She's just jealous," Cyrus had said of his horse as he'd rubbed the beast's neck after getting his footing under himself again.

But the moment had been lost. They'd saddled up and ridden back to Cahill Ranch.

AJ still wanted that kiss more than anything. Maybe today when Cyrus returned home. After all, it had been his idea to stop by the saloon his brother and sister owned when he got back. She thought it wasn't just Billie Dee's chicken and dumplings he was after, and bit her lower lip in anticipation.

SHERIFF FLINT CAHILL had been thinking about how quiet Gilt Edge had been lately, when a call was put through to his office. Before he could pick it up, the dispatcher appeared in his doorway looking worried.

Betty said nothing as he lifted the receiver, but he was already praying the call wasn't about the baby. He'd recently become the proud father of a baby girl who was the spitting image of her mother. But little Elizabeth, named after his sister, Lillie, had been small and he worried.

"Sheriff Cahill," he said into the phone and held his breath.

But it wasn't the voice of his wife, Maggie, on the other end of the line with the bad news.

"Sheriff Flint Cahill?" a man asked with a West Indies accent.

He glanced up to see that Betty was gone. He began to breathe a little easier. "Yes? How may I help you?"

"I'm sorry to be the bearer of bad news. Your brother Cyrus Cahill?"

"Yes." He sat up a little straighter, holding the phone tighter.

"He has disappeared and believed to have gone overboard."

"Gone overboard?" Flint repeated, thinking he must have heard wrong.

"Yes, he has fallen off the cruise ship he was on."

Flint shook his head. "I'm sorry, who did you say you were?"

"The police commissioner here on the island of St. Augusta in the Caribbean."

He felt a surge of relief. Was this some kind of scam call? "I'm afraid there's been a mistake. My brother is nowhere near the

Caribbean. Why don't you give me your number and I'll call you right back."

That usually took care of the scam calls.

"Of course." The man gave him a number, taking Flint by surprise. If this was some trick to extort money… He ran a quick internet search before dialing the number, which appeared to be from the island of St. Augusta in the Caribbean.

Flint couldn't imagine what was going on. Was it possible Cyrus's identity had been stolen?

The police commissioner answered on the third ring. "I know this must come as shocking news."

"Shocking yes, since my brother is on his way home from Denver, Colorado." Cyrus had gone down to look at a bull he was considering buying for the family ranch. "The last place he would be is on a cruise in the Caribbean. But if someone is using his name…"

"Perhaps this will clear everything up," the man said. "I can email you a photograph taken on the ship after the couple was married by the captain."

He almost laughed. There was definitely a mistake. Cyrus married—let alone on a cruise ship in the Caribbean? Flint gave him his email address and waited.

Moments later an email popped up on his computer. He opened the link from St. Augusta's Police Department assuring himself that this mistake would be rectified quickly once he… Flint felt all the breath rush from his lungs.

In the photograph Cyrus was wearing a tuxedo. He had his arm around an attractive blonde in an emerald green gown. Both were smiling at the camera. In the background was a turquoise blue sea. Closer was the name of the ship: *The Majestic Goddess of the Caribbean.*

CHAPTER TWO

"CYRUS ISN'T DEAD," AJ cried. "He's not." She would have felt it if that was true. But at the same time, she questioned why she wouldn't have also felt it when he'd married some woman he'd just met. She pushed that thought away. All she knew was that her heart assured her Cyrus was alive. "If he fell overboard, then he's still in the water? He knows how to swim, right?"

Flint nodded. He'd called everyone together at the Stagecoach Saloon his brother Darby and sister, Lillie, owned before it was to open for the day. Now it wouldn't be opening at all today.

Flint's brothers Tucker, Hawk and Darby were there along with Billie Dee, the cook, who'd become as much a part of the family as AJ herself.

"His fall was caught on a ship surveillance camera," the sheriff said.

"They're sure it was him?" Tucker asked.

"The photo is grainy, but it's him," Flint said.

She shook her head, fighting tears. This couldn't be happening. She'd been so excited about him coming back today. How could he have fallen off a cruise ship? He'd gone to Denver to buy a bull. What would have possessed him to take a Caribbean cruise—let alone get married? How was that possible? He hadn't been gone that long. Something was very wrong with all of this.

"What was he doing on that ship?" Hawk demanded. He and Cyrus worked Cahill Ranch together. "He's never talked about going on a cruise. Far from it. And to get *married*? I agree with AJ. Something's wrong with all this. Could he have lost his mind or… You're sure the wedding photo is real?"

Flint sighed. He'd made copies no doubt because he knew the family wouldn't believe it any more than he did. He handed them out, the room going deathly quiet.

AJ's hands shook as she took hers. There was no doubt it was Cyrus standing next to a tall, slinky blonde in an emerald dress. "Did your brother take his tuxedo when he went to Denver?" she asked.

"Tuxedo? He doesn't even own a suit," Hawk said. "This is Montana."

"Well, he seems to have found one," Darby ventured. "But look at his eyes. He's drunk." He tossed down the photocopy with disgust. "We all agree, something is definitely wrong. Cyrus never has more than a couple of beers at the most. This is all so out of character."

"You're forgetting the blonde with him," Tucker said. "Apparently she charmed him right onto a cruise ship and right into marriage."

The room fell silent again. AJ felt her face burning. They all knew how she felt about Cyrus. But she also believed that he'd cared about her. He'd promised to come back. Cyrus wasn't the kind of man who broke a promise.

"He doesn't love that woman," Lillie said, shaking her head. "Clearly she got him drunk or drugged, and dragged him to the altar."

"Whatever happened," Flint said. "He used his credit card

on the cruise. I don't think there is any doubt that Cyrus was on that ship. Or that he fell from it."

"What about this woman he married?" Tucker asked. "What do you know about her?"

"Nothing yet," Flint said. "But no matter who she is or why he married her, it doesn't change the fact that Cyrus went off that ship in the middle of the night and hasn't been found. Because no one apparently saw him fall off, no alarm was sounded."

"But you said he was caught on one of the surveillance cameras," AJ cried.

The sheriff nodded. "It wasn't seen until the next morning when Cyrus's…wife reported him missing. They had to go back through the surveillance videos when they realized he wasn't on board. But first they had to search the entire ship."

AJ covered her face, trying so hard not to cry. "So he was out there in the water all that time? How could his wife not know he was missing all night?"

"Apparently she had taken some seasick medicine that knocked her out," Flint said. "The seas were rough that night, according to the ship captain. He is sending me the report on the accident."

"I don't understand why he would have been outside at that hour on the ship alone to begin with unless he'd been drinking or regretting what he'd done and…" Hawk hesitated. "You don't think—"

"He didn't kill himself," AJ cried. "He was excited about coming home. Billie Dee was making chicken and dumplings. You know how he loves her…" She broke down unable to hold back the sobs any longer.

Billie Dee stepped to her to take her into her arms. "Oh, sweetie," she soothed. "We're all heartbroken and in shock."

No one was more in shock than AJ. She'd been so sure that she and Cyrus were getting close, that it was just a matter of time before they would be falling in love. Had she only dreamed the way he'd looked at her?

No, he'd cared. He'd almost kissed her.

But he'd married someone else—and in a heartbeat. The shy, aw-shucks cowboy who'd taken his time romancing her had met a woman, married her and taken off on a honeymoon cruise at the drop of his cowboy hat? How was that possible even if the woman had plied him with drinks and sexual allure?

Something was wrong. It's what her instincts had told her the moment she'd heard the news. These actions weren't those of the man she'd known for months. Cyrus Cahill was as solid as the stone of the old stagecoach stop where she'd been bartending since coming to Montana. After getting her law degree and advancing quickly at a prestigious firm, she had been pressured by her father to join the family business as one of his lawyers.

She'd put him off, knowing there was something she had to do first. She'd left Houston on a mission to help her friend Gigi reunite with her birth mother, Billie Dee, who'd been forced to give her up at birth. Mission accomplished, she'd realized she didn't want to work for the family business. She'd loved bartending and Montana. But the reason she'd stayed in Gilt Edge was because of Cyrus. She'd fallen for him. At twenty-six years old, she'd realized she'd never really been in love until Cyrus. She'd seen a future here with him.

"They're still searching for him," Flint was saying. "But the police commissioner told me that the search will be called off if he isn't found soon. After this many hours..."

AJ couldn't bear to hear this. She rose, excused herself and headed toward the apartment upstairs over the Stagecoach Saloon where she'd been living. Gigi was upstairs packing to leave as she walked in.

Her friend dropped what she was doing and hugged her. "I'm so sorry. I know you cared about him."

She'd had a crush on him for months. But in the weeks before he'd left, she'd fallen in love with him. From the beginning, she'd sensed something special between them. She hadn't imagined that any more than she was imagining he was still alive. She felt it, heart deep.

"I know that look," Gigi said, holding her at arm's length to search her gaze. "What are you planning to do?"

"It's just this feeling that I can't shake."

Her friend groaned. "Honey—"

"If they call off the search, I have to go look for him."

Gigi's eyes widened. "In the entire Caribbean? Do you have any idea how long that could take?"

She shrugged. "Good thing I'm rich, huh, and have plenty of time." She and Gigi both had come from wealthy families. She could live on the trust fund her grandmother had set up for her and never need to work a day in her life. Not that she'd ever considered it. She enjoyed working and making her own money. She had never touched a cent of the trust fund. But she would now if she had to.

"What about your job?" her friend asked.

"Darby will either give me the time off or accept my resignation."

"I wasn't referring to your bartending job, AJ," Gigi said impatiently. "You're a high-powered attorney and your father expects you to join the family business when you're done doing your thing here."

"I *was* a high-powered attorney. And I've told you, I don't want to work for the family business. It isn't where I belong."

"Your father might disagree," her friend pointed out. Gigi had met him so she knew how determined AJ's father could be.

"You know, I was never going back. I wanted to stay here." Her voice broke.

"And marry Cyrus. Oh, honey, what if he's gone?"

She shook her head. "I wouldn't be feeling the way I do if he was dead. I'm going to find him. As long as it takes. I have to find him. He's alive and—"

"Wouldn't we have heard from him if he was alive? If he'd been rescued?"

"Maybe not. Maybe he's somewhere where he can't get word out. I just know that I have to look for him. If I did nothing..." AJ shook her head. "I would never forgive myself."

"Give me a few days and I'll go with you."

"Gigi, you have employees waiting for you to get your restaurant open again." A fire in the building where Gigi had her Houston restaurant had caused fire and water damage. Now that the remodeling was underway it wouldn't be long before Gigi could get her business going again and her employees back to work. She shook her head. "I appreciate your offer, but I have to do this myself."

"Promise that you'll wait and give the trained personnel a chance to find him before you do anything rash."

AJ smiled at her friend. "Me, do anything rash? That is so not like me."

"Exactly. Then if he's not found..."

"I'll go look for him myself."

Gigi sighed, clearly seeing that there was nothing she could say to stop her. "Call if you need me. Seriously. I will drop everything if you do."

She hugged her best friend tightly. They'd been roommates at boarding school and looked enough alike to be sisters. From the moment they'd met, they'd been best friends and had gotten into all kinds of trouble together, AJ usually the ringleader.

"I'll keep you posted," AJ promised. "I'll wait. But if they don't find him and call off the search, I'm going to get on a plane to St. Augusta Island. Flint said the ship docked there to report Cyrus missing. Once I find out exactly where the ship was when he went overboard… I *will* find him." *If he is still alive.* Her heart told her he was. She had to believe it.

CHAPTER THREE

Juliette Cahill dabbed at her eyes as she was ushered through the crowd of reporters. She'd told her story a half-dozen times, first to security on the ship, then the captain, then the St. Augusta Island police commissioner and finally to an FBI agent. She couldn't go through it another time.

"What happened to your husband?" a reporter called to her. "Where were you when he went overboard?"

"Is it true you were newlyweds, married by the ship captain?" another one called out. "You must be devastated."

She stopped and turned. "I *am* devastated. It was...love at first sight. I'm not sure how I can go on without him." She broke down and had to turn away from the cameras as ship security helped her to the waiting taxi.

"Are you sure you don't want us to see you back to your hotel?" one of the security agents asked.

She shook her head and motioned for the taxi driver to hurry up as the car was quickly surrounded by news people and their prying cameras. As the taxi driver pulled away, she leaned back and closed her eyes.

The cruise ship line had booked her into the nicest hotel in Miami as soon as the boat docked. The captain had offered to fly her from St. Augusta Island, but the last thing she wanted was a puddle jumper to San Juan where she'd have to wait for a plane to Miami. She'd told the captain that she preferred to stay on the ship in her room.

"Whatever you want," he'd said. "I'll make sure you get whatever you need."

And he had. She ordered whatever she wanted and it was brought to her. She'd watched television and read, but had trouble concentrating on either. Mostly she stared out at the sea through the slider from her luxury cabin and just wanted for this nightmare to be over.

The taxi driver took her to her hotel. She checked in and waited until her luggage was brought up before she went down the elevator to two floors below. She tapped on the door. A dark-haired man with a mustache opened the door in nothing but a towel.

"You're late," he said and stepped back to let her enter.

FLINT HAD SPENT the morning trying to get more information on his brother and the rescue mission. It kept him busy, so he didn't have as much time to think about Cyrus being somewhere in the ocean. Cyrus being gone.

He'd just hung up from talking to the St. Augusta police commissioner when AJ appeared in his doorway. From the look on her face when she sat down, it was clear she'd hoped for some news of Cyrus.

Flint wished he had some. He knew that she cared about his brother and hated to see her even more brokenhearted. What he'd learned was anything but good news.

"They're still looking for him, right?" she asked, leaning forward in the chair across from his desk.

"They have air support and coast guard, also other ships in the area looking for him. If he's still out there, they'll find him," he said with more confidence than he felt. It had been too long already.

"I just don't understand," she said, voicing what the whole family had been feeling since getting the news. "How could he have fallen overboard?"

Being born and raised in Montana and having never taken an ocean cruise, Flint had never given any thought to overboard incidents. But since the phone call yesterday, he'd learned that it was rare given how many people took cruises each year. The chance of going overboard was 1 in 1,650,000 passengers.

But still, twenty to thirty people went overboard from a cruise ship every year. Most were either accidents or suicides. But a few were because of foul play.

The worst statistic was that only 22 percent of those survived and were rescued. If a person was stranded for more than three or four hours, their chances of surviving were extremely low. Cyrus would have been in the water far longer than that before they'd even begun looking for him. Flint couldn't imagine what it would be like to be floating in such a huge body of water and see the ship leaving.

"Apparently," he said, shaking off the image of his brother alone in the dark water, "it is incredibly hard for a person to fall off a cruise ship. From what I've read, the railings and guardrails are designed to prevent people from slipping, tripping or losing their footing and falling over them."

"Then how could this have happened?" she demanded, as if he knew the answer.

He was as frustrated by this as she was and having just as much trouble making sense of it. "Unfortunately, railings can't prevent accidents when passengers have too much to drink." Was that what had happened to Cyrus? He agreed with Darby. His brother had looked drunk in the wedding photo. Overly intoxicated passengers did stupid things like sitting on the railings, climbing over them, even trying to walk on them.

While he couldn't imagine his brother doing that, he also couldn't imagine him buying a bull, planning to come home the next day and then deciding instead to go on a Caribbean cruise and hell, why not get married while he was at it?

"He was on his *honeymoon*," AJ cried. "Why would he be that wasted unless..." She shook her head. "I can't imagine Cyrus being that drunk."

Flint couldn't, either. In the first place, Cyrus wasn't much of a drinker. Nor did he take chances. None of the Cahill offspring were drinkers because of their father, Ely. A confirmed mountain man who spent his days back in the hills trapping and mining, Ely only got into trouble when he came back to town and tied one on at the bar. So it was no wonder that his children drank very little alcohol or, like Darby, didn't drink at all.

But then again, Flint couldn't imagine his brother doing anything so impulsive as meeting a woman and running off to marry her on a cruise ship, let alone getting wasted and falling overboard.

Being a lawman, he couldn't help thinking there was more to all of this. If Cyrus hadn't accidentally fallen overboard or done something stupid while drunk, then there were only three other possibilities. That his brother had jumped. Or that he'd been pushed. Or that he might have been drugged.

"And why didn't someone see him?" AJ was asking. "What about his wife? She could be lying about taking seasick medicine. Doesn't it seem strange that she just happened not to be with him?"

It all seemed strange, but Flint had no answers. Since the police commissioner's call yesterday, he'd been sent the report from the cruise line. "According to his wife, she wasn't feeling well and Cyrus decided to go for a walk on deck."

"In the middle of the night?"

"Apparently there are parts of the ship that never sleep," Flint said. "According to the wife, he'd promised not to be long. She'd fallen asleep and when she woke the next morning, she realized he hadn't returned and set off the alarm."

"Too late. He would have been in the water for hours by then," AJ said, her eyes filling with tears. "You said they then had to search the entire boat first before they actually started looking for him?" She looked away, brushed at her tears. "More time lost."

"They can calculate where the ship was when he went overboard so they had a place to start. They consider drift and other factors and home in on that area." If Cyrus was out there floating in the ocean. "The ship was able to correlate the time-stamp images when Cyrus was last seen with the approximate location of the ship at the time he went overboard," Flint said. "But it's a big ocean." He wished he could give her more hope, but he was running out of it himself.

She pushed out of her chair and took a deep breath, let it out. "I'm going to fly down there and help look for him. Please don't try to stop me."

He knew he had to tell her the other bad news he'd gotten this morning. It had been in the report from the cruise line. "There's something you need to know before you decide to do that. Blood has been found on a lower deck railing. It is believed that Cyrus hit the railing before going into the water."

"What are you saying?"

"Often when someone goes overboard, they'll hit a lifeboat or another floor railing of the cruise ship before actually hitting the water. Injured..." He met her gaze, hating that he had to do this. She was already devastated. "Injured they often die within minutes. Most of the time, their bodies are never recovered."

AJ covered her mouth with her hand for a moment as tears welled and ran down her cheeks. "Are they sure it's his blood?"

He looked at her, understanding why she wanted to believe it wasn't. He felt the same way. "The FBI sent it to a lab to be tested against DNA taken from his cruise ship cabin. They will also run a toxicology report to see if he was on drugs at the time."

She nodded, but he could see she wasn't giving up.

His phone rang. She motioned for him to take it. He picked up. "Sheriff Flint Cahill." Silence. "Hello?" For just a heartbeat he thought it was Cyrus on the other end of the line. His pulse jumped. He realized he was waiting for his brother to speak, praying for a miracle. AJ was frozen in the doorway, no doubt praying for the same thing.

But when the caller did speak, it was a woman's voice. "Is this Flint Cahill?"

"It is. Who's calling?" He still held out hope that this call would be news of Cyrus. That he'd been found alive. Safe.

"Juliette. Juliette Cahill. I'm Cyrus's wife. He told me so much about you, all of you and about Montana and the ranch and his love for..." She seemed to break down.

He didn't know what to say. Disappointment filled him to overflowing. This was not the call he was praying for. "I'm sorry. We're still reeling here from the news of his death, let alone his sudden marriage." His gaze went to AJ. "He didn't tell us anything about you."

AJ seemed to crumble as she leaned into the door, her blue eyes wide and scared. On the phone Juliette seemed to pull herself together. "Of course you're reeling. I'm the same way. I still can't believe it. How does something like this happen?"

That was the question, wasn't it?

"As for keeping our marriage from his family, Cyrus wanted

to surprise you. We both did. We were planning to fly back to Montana at the next port and finish our honeymoon there. We were both so anxious to start our lives together there. Cyrus talked about building us a house on the ranch."

Flint had never known his brother to do anything this impulsive. Was it possible he had fallen head over heels for this woman and literally jumped into a marriage? Not the Cyrus he'd known. But no one had to tell him how falling in love changed a person. He thought of his wife, Maggie, and their baby daughter, Elizabeth. He'd kill for them and had.

"Where did you two meet?" he asked, hating his suspicious nature and yet unable not to question her.

"In Denver. I was staying at the same hotel as he was. It was love at first sight for both of us. The cruise was Cyrus's idea. He'd never been on one and thought it would be fun. Getting married on the ship… I don't even know how that happened. It was such a whirlwind romance, I felt as if I couldn't catch my breath. I just can't believe he's gone." She began to cry again. "I'm sorry. I didn't call to upset you more. I need to know when the funeral is going to be held."

"Funeral?" He saw AJ turn and disappear out the door. "AJ, wait!" He got to his feet, needing to cut this call short and go after her. "There isn't one planned yet. We just heard about his falling overboard. It seems a little…premature. Look, I have to get off the line."

"With the search being called off, I just thought… The captain said they are seeing about getting me his death certificate. After this many hours at sea…"

His brother's death certificate? Flint closed his eyes tight for a moment, pain making his chest constrict. The loss was almost more than he could bear. "I haven't heard anything about the search being called off," he said, his voice cracking. "I have to go. Give me your number. I'll call you back." He scribbled it down and went after AJ, catching her just outside the office.

She was crying hysterically and trying to walk away. He caught her arm, understanding her need to run away. He wanted to do the same thing himself.

"Come back in," Flint pleaded. "I don't like seeing you like this."

AJ swung around. Her tearstained flushed face was quickly set in both defiance and determination. "I'm going to find him. He's alive. I don't care what anyone says. Cyrus is alive." She put her fist over her heart, the tears coming again. "I feel it."

He couldn't imagine where she would even start. It was worse than a needle in a haystack. The Caribbean was over a million square miles of water. As he looked at her, he didn't know what to say. He could see that there was no talking her out of it. She was going to go look for Cyrus. It broke his heart.

But what worried him was what would happen when she didn't find his brother? When she'd have to finally face that Cyrus was gone?

CHAPTER FOUR

AJ? JULIETTE HAD heard Flint Cahill call out the name. Cyrus had mentioned an AJ but she now realized there must have been more to the story.

Just as she surmised that the woman must have been sitting in the sheriff's office when she'd called. Interesting. Especially how quickly the sheriff had gotten off the phone.

As she disconnected she tried to remember if Cyrus had told her the woman's last name. Juliette prided herself on her memory. She'd always been a good listener. Just as she was good at drawing a person out. Men especially tended to tell her their secrets.

Cyrus though had been a tough nut to crack. It had taken a lot to get him to open up. He was shy and reserved, definitely the kind of man she was attracted to.

The woman's name came to her as she waited at the rental car agency. Ashley Jo "AJ" Somerfield. Cyrus had especially been closemouthed about Miss Somerfield, now that she thought about it. Juliette hadn't been concerned. She'd never let some old girlfriend bother her. But she couldn't help being curious now.

She quickly pulled out her phone and thanks to the wonders of the internet, had the young woman's life history at her fingertips. What she found surprised her. A lawyer? She thought that Cyrus had told her AJ worked as a bartender at some place his brother and sister owned, the Stagecoach Saloon. So what was a lawyer doing serving drinks in some out-of-the-way place in Montana?

AJ wasn't just any lawyer, either. The firm where she'd worked was a big one. The girl must know her stuff. It made no sense, her bartending at the Stagecoach Saloon in Gilt Edge, Montana. Odd. It was those kinds of inconsistencies that bothered her. Who was this woman really? And what had she meant to Cyrus?

Thinking about AJ distracted her from thinking about Cyrus—or what awaited her at the ranch outside of Gilt Edge. From her phone call earlier with Flint Cahill, it was clear that she wouldn't be welcomed with open arms. He'd practically hung up on her.

She reminded herself that she wasn't just the woman who'd stolen Cyrus Cahill's heart but she had swept him away on a Caribbean cruise where he was lost at sea. And now she suspected she was also the other woman.

Just how close had AJ and Cyrus been? Close enough that he'd confided in the woman?

The thought shook her to her core. Juliette hadn't even considered that Cyrus would have shared anything with his family, not to mention his now-former girlfriend. He'd agreed not to say anything to any of them.

Not just that. She'd thought that all of his attention was on what was going on between them. Could she have been wrong?

It surprised her that she could still feel jealous, especially under the circumstances. It made her angry, angry with herself and even angrier with Cyrus who apparently had kept some things from her. She was going to have to find out just how tight he'd been with this AJ woman. AJ's very life depended on it.

BILLIE DEE WIPED her eyes as she heard the back door of the Stagecoach Saloon open. She thought it might be her fiancé, Henry Larson. He came by most mornings she worked for a cup of coffee, but he'd already been by earlier.

She was glad to see that it was AJ. She'd been worried about her. Now the young woman came in, stomping snow off her boots and looking as if she'd been crying.

"I thought you were still upstairs asleep," Billie Dee said, turning from the stove where she'd been cooking up a pot of chili. "It's snowing again?" A winter storm–warning alert had been issued, but she'd hoped it wasn't as serious as they were anticipating.

It was one of the reasons she'd made chili. Lillie and Darby had closed the bar temporarily so the family could meet here for updates. Billie Dee knew they'd be hungry. There was still chicken and dumplings left from yesterday, but they were Cyrus's favorite, so none of the family wanted them right now.

She wiped her hands on her apron and moved to the young woman. To see AJ so brokenhearted was tearing her up inside. She wanted to comfort her and yet knew there was nothing she could say. She'd seen the way AJ had looked at Cyrus when he came around the saloon. Had he really run off and gotten married knowing the way AJ felt about him?

Well, when he was found, Billie Dee planned to give him a piece of her mind. Dang fool.

"His wife called Flint," AJ said. "She wanted to know about Cyrus's *funeral*." Her voice broke. She wiped angrily at her tears.

Billie Dee could only stare for a moment. "His *funeral*?"

AJ choked out the words, "I overheard Flint say something

about the search possibly being called off," before she burst into tears.

Billie Dee took her in her arms. "Oh no." She thought of the handsome cowboy. Shy, adorable, sneaking glances at AJ. She'd wanted to prod him with a cattle iron at times. Didn't he see this beautiful young woman was in love with him? Hadn't he taken her horseback riding? How could he get married to some stranger he just met?

And now he was gone. Billie Dee fought her own tears as she tried to soothe AJ. There was nothing she could say.

AJ pulled out of her arms. "I have to pack."

"Wait. Where are you going?" She couldn't bear losing her too. "You aren't going back to Texas, are you?"

"I'm going to find Cyrus."

"Oh, sweetie." Billie Dee could see no good coming of this. "He's gone. If they called off the search—"

"He's not dead. If he was dead, I would know it." AJ shook her head adamantly. "He's still alive."

"If that were true, wouldn't we have heard something? Maybe if you give it a little more time…"

"All I know is that something is wrong, really wrong, and I have to find him." She started toward the stairs that led up to the apartment over the saloon.

Lillie Cahill had designed the upstairs apartment when she and her brother Darby bought the old stagecoach stop building to preserve it. Lillie had loved it but had moved out after her marriage to Trask Beaumont. Other family members had lived there before AJ. But AJ had made it her own and Billie Dee loved having the young woman up there since she spent so much time in the kitchen here. AJ had become like a daughter to her. Not to mention AJ was best friends with Billie Dee's birth daughter, Gigi. It had been AJ who'd brought them together.

"I'm scared for you," Billie Dee cried before AJ could disappear upstairs.

"Don't be," the young woman assured her, coming back down the steps to give her a quick hug. "I'll be back. With Cyrus." With that she was gone, leaving Billie Dee in fresh tears as she reached for her phone.

WHEN AJ CAME downstairs dragging her hastily packed suitcase, she found Flint waiting for her. He was dressed in his uniform coat, jeans and boots along with his Stetson, which he'd taken off and now held by the fingertips of his right hand. There was melted snow at his feet where he'd been waiting by the door. She shot a look at Billie Dee, who quickly avoided her gaze. Of course her friend had called him to try to stop her.

"You can't talk me out of this," she told the sheriff.

"The highway south is closed between Eddie's Corner and Harlowton. Also the road from Grass Range to Roundup," he said. "You're not going anywhere today."

She stared at him, feeling sobs of frustration rising in her chest. "Cyrus is out there. Alone. He needs me." As she began to cry, Flint pulled her into his arms.

His cell phone rang. He pulled it out to glance at the screen, and then at AJ. "I need to take this."

Billie Dee quickly moved to AJ, took the rolling suitcase from her and led her into the bar area of the establishment. "Would a drink help?" she asked, stepping behind the bar.

AJ shook her head. Nothing would help. She looked toward the front windows. It was snowing and blowing so hard that she couldn't see across the road out front. She pulled up a stool and plopped down as Billie Dee slid a glass of cola in front of her. She smiled at the older woman, knowing that she was just trying to help.

"I could put a shot of rum in it," the cook offered again.

"Don't tempt me." It was a temptation to lose herself in anything that would take her mind off Cyrus for even a few moments. The saloon wouldn't normally open for another hour. But AJ had seen the closed sign posted outside blowing in the storm when she'd returned from the sheriff's office. By now, the news about Cyrus would be racing like wildfire through the county.

"At least the water in the Caribbean is warm," she said and took a sip of the cola and shivered.

They both turned as Flint came back into the room. AJ looked at the sheriff expectantly as she tried to read his expression. Had the phone call been about Cyrus? Was there news?

"That was Juliette on the phone," he said as if he didn't want to call her Cyrus's wife any more than AJ wanted to hear it. But at Billie Dee's confused look, he said, "Juliette Cahill." He turned back to AJ. "Apparently she was just outside of Gilt Edge when she called me earlier. She's at the local hotel."

"She's in town?" AJ cried and looked around as if there was somewhere to run from all of this.

"I'm sorry," Flint said. "I know how hard this is for you. But she wants to meet the family."

AJ started to slide off her stool to leave, but he stopped her. "She said she especially wanted to meet you since Cyrus had talked so much about you."

She dropped back on the stool as if she'd been shot through the heart. Cyrus had told this woman all about her? This woman he'd run off and married?

Flint shook his head, looking just as surprised and upset as she felt. "You don't have to do this. But I thought you'd like to hear what she has to say."

For a moment, she'd just wanted to run. Meet Cyrus's wife? Meet the woman he'd fallen for in the snap of her fingers when he'd taken forever to ask AJ on a horseback ride and hadn't even kissed her? How could he *marry* someone he just met?

She took a deep breath and let it out. Both the sheriff and cook were staring at her, waiting for her answer. The lawyer in her, and her suspicious nature that'd made her good at her job before she'd quit to run off to Montana, wanted nothing more than to size up this woman and decide for herself exactly what had happened in Denver to make Cyrus Cahill do something so rash and so out of character.

"You're right. I want to meet her," AJ said.

"And pull out her bleached-blond hair a handful at a time," Billie Dee said.

Flint shot her a disapproving look. "I think we should try to keep this civil. We need to know what happened and this woman is probably the only one who knows."

"Except for whoever threw him overboard," AJ said.

Flint didn't bother trying to correct her. "Are you going to be all right?"

She nodded and listened as he got on the phone to the rest of the family. It wasn't until he hung up that Billie Dee said, "I should get back to my chili." None of them had questioned her cooking up a batch even though the saloon wasn't going to open. It was what the woman did. She fed people. It was the way she loved those she cared for.

"You're family," the sheriff said to Billie Dee. "And I know that you're going to want to meet her too. I also suspect that your chili won't go to waste, although don't expect me to have much of an appetite."

Billie Dee nodded, smiling and touching his shoulder as she passed on her way to the kitchen. "We all still need to eat. Especially now." She added, "You know we're going to hate her."

Flint gave her a sad smile. "I know."

JULIETTE CAHILL PARTED the curtains and stared out at the falling snow, feeling a chill that had nothing to do with the weather. It was her childhood all over again, she thought. Small rural western town in the middle of nowhere. Snow and cold. She'd buried the memory of the pain and hardship of her childhood deep, but not deep enough apparently. This place brought it all back.

As she'd driven through the town of Gilt Edge, she'd half expected to see her father coming out of the hardware store in his blue overalls, his dirty, worn canvas jacket pulled awkwardly around him, that permanent scowl on his cross face.

It had seemed so real and she'd been staring so hard at the door into the store that she'd almost run a red light. She'd hit the brakes, sliding on the icy, snow-packed road. The car had finally come to a stop in the middle of the intersection. Her heart had been pounding hard, all of it too familiar, all of it a nightmare she'd thought long behind her.

Fortunately, no one hit her rental car. Not that there was much traffic. All the way to this godforsaken town, she'd seen few cars. Anyone with a brain would be far from here.

Now, as she looked outside, she knew she had to pull herself together. But she couldn't help think of the way Cyrus had talked about this place. She supposed a town like this was easier to love when you had money.

Where did you grow up? he had asked her.

In the big city, she'd said, lying through her teeth. As a girl, that had been her dream. Anywhere but on a dusty dilapidated farm in the middle of Idaho where her father barely eked out a living enough to keep his large family fed. She thought of the threadbare dresses she'd worn to school, handed down from her sisters. She'd never had a new dress until she ran away.

Even now, she couldn't shake the image of her mother's red, chapped hands as she'd sewed the worn places in the rotting cloth to make the dresses last just a little bit longer. And always that same admonishment when she complained, *You should count your blessings that you have anything to wear at all.*

The taste of humiliation in her mouth, she let the curtain fall back into place. This rural town, this state, brought it all back. The nightmare of her childhood as well as her girlhood dreams of escaping that life. Her sisters hadn't, but she'd known that if she stayed past sixteen, she'd be married to some good ol' boy like her father and have a half-dozen hungry mouths to feed.

The night she ran away, she kept telling herself that she would never go hungry again. Never wear someone else's discarded clothing. Never again know the defeating, soul-stealing grip of poverty, no matter what she had to do.

When she'd left that dusty farm, the dilapidated paint-bare house, she'd left poor little Julie Barnes behind and never looked back.

Juliette fumbled out the keys to her rental car, dreading the drive. Sheriff Flint Cahill would be waiting with the rest of Cyrus's family, including his former girlfriend AJ. She wasn't looking forward to the drive out to the Stagecoach Saloon on the edge of town. For a woman who left little to chance, she hadn't counted on a winter storm. On the way up, she'd heard about the highway closures. Now she was snowed in here and had no idea how long before she would be able to leave.

All she could think was that this trip had better be productive. She was anxious to see the Cahill Ranch, but after what she'd seen of the tiny rural town of Gilt Edge, she feared Cyrus had been exaggerating about not just the place, but the size of the ranch.

She hadn't been interested in the town and hadn't really been listening when Cyrus had told her about it. What she'd wanted to know about was the ranch.

"I know it's rude to ask, but how many cattle do you run?" Juliette had asked anyway—once she had a few drinks into Cyrus. When he'd told her, she'd thought, not bad. "And land?" Also not bad. It had made her think of her family's pitiful little plot.

She'd told Flint that it had been love at first sight for both of them. That hadn't been exactly true. A cowboy wasn't her type under normal circumstances. Even one dressed as if he had money.

But that night in Denver hadn't been under normal circumstances, she reminded herself. Beggars can't be choosers, her mother used to say. It certainly fit in this case. If there had been anyone but the cowboy in the bar that night who looked like a more likely prospect, she would have steered clear of Cyrus, leaving him to his one drink on his way to bed. Clearly he hadn't wanted company. All he could talk about was getting back home and eating Billie Dee's chicken and dumplings—whoever Billie Dee was.

But the moment she heard from the man with him that Cyrus had bought himself a three-hundred-thousand-dollar bull, she'd gone for him straight as a bullet. If he could afford a bull that cost that much…

But Montana was all he talked about. It was clear that he couldn't wait to get back here. Even then she'd suspected there was a woman. No man was that antsy to return to his horse.

Which made Juliette all the more anxious to meet AJ and find out just how much this woman and Cyrus had shared.

She took another breath and let it out slowly. She was Mrs. Cyrus Cahill, the grieving widow. Still, she felt a shiver of apprehension. Too bad Cyrus hadn't mentioned that one of his brothers was the sheriff. But she'd dealt with small town law before. Why would this one be any different?

WHEN THE CAR pulled up in front of the Stagecoach Saloon, Darby hurried to the front door to open it. They had all gathered again in the saloon after Flint had given Juliette the directions to the establishment just outside of town.

"I already hate her," Lillie said, sounding near tears.

Her sister-in-law Mariah had taken her hand. "Let's not forget that Cyrus fell in love with her and married her."

How could any of them forget that? AJ thought. She stared at the door, trying to see through the falling snow as a figure emerged from the car and headed toward the entrance. Her heart felt as if it would beat from her chest. She kept saying the words in her head. Cyrus had married this woman. But no matter how many times she said it, her next thought was always the same. *Something is wrong. Something is very wrong.*

Now though, she was finally going to meet the woman and decide for herself if it was possible that Cyrus had really fallen for her, married her and then died after falling off a cruise ship in the Caribbean. It all felt surreal, like a nightmare she just wanted to end. She'd wanted Cyrus to drive up to the front door of the saloon—not his wife.

Darby opened the door for the woman and ushered her inside. She came in on a gust of wind and a flurry of snowflakes. She stopped just inside. She wore a long red wool coat, sleek black boots and a scarf that hid most of her blond hair and part of her face. Everything about her said privileged, AJ thought, having grown up the same way. But she wasn't quite believing it. That something-is-wrong feeling even stronger.

As Juliette Cahill took off her scarf, she raised her gaze to them gathered around the bar. Her blue eyes sparkled with unshed tears and for a moment, she looked as if she might faint. Darby grabbed her arm to steady her and Flint moved toward the two of them.

AJ stood frozen in place. Was it possible that all of it had been real? That the only thing that was wrong was that Cyrus had fallen in love? She could actually see how that might have happened. Juliette was a striking beauty, slim and graceful as she slipped out of her coat and let Darby take it.

Flint led her over to the family and began to introduce each one. By the time he got to her, AJ could barely speak. Juliette had been polite and gracious to each member of the family, even Lillie, who everyone could see took an instant dislike to her—just as she'd said.

But when Flint got to AJ, Juliette grasped her hand in both of hers and drew her closer.

"Cyrus told me so much about each of you, but especially you, AJ," the woman said. "I feel as if I already know you." She released her hand and pulled AJ into a quick hug. "I hope we can be friends."

She breathed in the woman's expensive perfume and felt the brush of the cashmere sweater as well as Juliette's strong grip. As she stumbled back a little from the unexpected embrace, she felt more than off balance. Was she really believing this? As she stared into Juliette's perfect face, she couldn't help but think of that determined strong grip, and how those hands might have been the last thing Cyrus felt before he went overboard.

FLINT SUGGESTED THEY all sit down at one of the tables. Darby offered Juliette a drink. She asked for water and as he poured her a glass, Flint led her over to a table. He was as shocked by the woman as the rest of them seemed to be. There was no doubt that she was a beauty, but she also seemed gracious and real. He hadn't expected that.

He'd thought Cyrus must have been tricked into marriage. Swept off his feet by a woman with a whole hell of a lot more experience than him. A gold digger who'd trapped him somehow.

Juliette came off as cultured and sophisticated, nothing like he'd expected. Also she didn't appear to need Cyrus's money.

Before she'd arrived, he'd warned everyone, "Let's not all mob her with questions right off the bat." He was hoping to get answers. While he might see what his brother had seen in this woman, it still didn't make any sense to him.

Cyrus was a *cowboy*. Even if it had been love at first sight. Even if he had agreed to a Caribbean cruise without telling his family he wasn't coming back for a while. But a quickie marriage on the ship? Flint wouldn't have expected that in a million years. Not even to this woman.

"Cyrus spoke of you all so often, I'm sorry, but I feel as if you're already family," Juliette was saying after everyone sat down. "The way he talked about Montana and the ranch..."

"We had no idea you were coming here," Lillie said. "I thought you'd want to be in the islands for when...if..." Her voice broke.

Juliette reached out and took Lillie's hand. "I couldn't bear to stay down there. It was bad enough being on the ship, looking out at the ocean, praying I would see him." She let go of Lillie's hand to wipe her eyes. "I realized I needed to be with his family to wait for news."

"What about your family?" Hawk asked.

She shook her head. "I'm afraid I don't have any. That's why when Cyrus talked so lovingly about all of you..." She sniffled into her tissue.

"You should have told us you were coming," Flint said. "We could have picked you up at the airport."

"I didn't want to be a bother. I rented a car since I have no idea how long I will be staying."

"Can you tell us how you and Cyrus met?" AJ asked.

Juliette nodded. Flint listened, her story almost verbatim from the report he'd received from the ship's captain of the initial missing persons report. She cried through some of the story but ended with, "Cyrus and I had never had anything like this happen to us before. It was so magical. We couldn't believe we'd found each other. We had such plans for the future." She cried into her tissue, the room falling silent.

"Had you been married before?" AJ asked.

Juliette looked up, a flash of annoyance in her gaze before she squelched it. "Yes. I lost my husband and now... Please let me help with the funeral."

"Funeral?" Lillie echoed.

"Like I told you on the phone, arranging a funeral seems a little premature," Flint said. "Cyrus might still be found."

"We can only hope," Juliette said. "It's just that..." She looked around the table as if unsure how to proceed. "The captain of the ship told me that Cyrus's death certificate will be faxed to me in the next few days. Apparently after this much time at sea..."

Flint saw the grief in AJ's eyes. It broke his already shattered heart. "Like I said, we haven't even thought about funeral services. We're still hoping there will be good news."

A phone buzzed. Juliette dug hers out of her bag, looked at the screen, and then up at Flint. Tears flooded her blue eyes. "That was the coast guard. The search has been called off."

Flint couldn't look at AJ, couldn't look at anyone. He stared at Juliette, a lump in this throat the size of Montana. He couldn't keep lying to himself. Cyrus was gone.

CHAPTER FIVE

JULIETTE DROVE THROUGH the blizzard, just wanting to be anywhere but here. Everything about this place brought back too many memories. She hadn't seen snow in years. That was because she'd purposely not lived in places where it got cold—let alone snowed. She needed sunshine and heat. She felt the cold as she had as a child, that deep ache that never went away, coupled with a hunger that she'd never been able to quench.

Back at her hotel, she turned up the heat and replayed the scene from the saloon. She thought it had gone well. Cyrus's sister despised her. She could live with that. The sheriff had been cordial enough. Same with the brothers and their wives.

The one who interested her—and worried her—was AJ, who had looked as if she'd been hit by a train. They'd all taken Cyrus's death hard, but nothing like AJ. It confirmed what Juliette had feared. AJ had been in love with the cowboy. She suspected Cyrus had felt the same way or damned close to it.

Her stomach roiled at the thought of the attorney-turned-barmaid. Maybe the best thing she could do was ignore the woman. After all, Juliette didn't plan on being in town that long. Once her business here was over, she would be off to some tropical island for the rest of the winter.

But she couldn't get AJ off her mind. After she'd hugged her, she'd looked into those wide blue eyes. The woman was cute. She could see how Cyrus could have been attracted to her. But AJ was also smart. Too smart for her own good.

What she'd seen in all that blue was suspicion. Which wasn't surprising. But that coupled with smarts and love? That woman wasn't going to let this go. She was the kind who would dig her heels in. She was going to be a problem.

Sighing, Juliette considered what—if anything—to do about it. She didn't want any trouble. She already had a dead husband. An accident. She couldn't risk another death. Anyway, what could AJ really do?

Cyrus was her legal husband, which meant that anything that was his was now hers. Let any of them try to stop her from taking it.

"WELL, WHAT DO you think?" Flint asked everyone after Juliette left.

They were all silent for a long moment as if they were as shaken and surprised as he was. Juliette was gorgeous, the kind of woman who would stop a man in his tracks. Just not Cyrus. Unless he hadn't known his brother as well as he'd thought he had.

"She's too perfect," Lillie said, shaking her head. "That's not the kind of woman Cyrus would have been attracted to. He liked women who were more down-to-earth."

Hawk spoke up to disagree. "Come on, sis, she was a knockout. If she turned that smile and those big blue eyes on Cyrus..."

Lillie made a rude disgusted sound. "Looks aren't everything."

"Said by one of the most beautiful women—inside and out—in Gilt Edge," her brother Darby stated, clearly trying to lighten the moment.

"She certainly played the part well," AJ said and stepped behind the bar to make herself a drink. "The tears, the sincerity. Just the right touch." They all looked at her, hearing the bitterness but no one said anything for a few moments.

"Of course she isn't going to be as inconsolable as all of us," Maggie said, taking Flint's hand. "She might have fallen in love with Cyrus at first sight, but she only knew him for a few days."

Flint had to agree with his wife. While seeming upset, Juliette wasn't as heartbroken as they were. She would get over this and move on. It wouldn't be that easy for all of them. His heart especially went out to AJ. She'd fallen for Cyrus. It was no wonder she didn't want to believe any of this was real.

"I was surprised that she plans to stay around for a while," Tucker said.

His wife, Kate, agreed. "I'd like to know more about this woman."

That had been Flint's thought.

Tucker pulled Kate to him and kissed her. "It's that investigative reporter in you coming out again." He shook his head, smiling at her. "I thought you didn't miss it?"

"I don't," she said. "Except when something like this happens and then I want to dig."

"Don't worry," Flint assured her and the rest. "I'm going to find out everything I can about her."

"She keeps asking about the funeral," Darby said. "What are we going—"

"It's too early for that," AJ said, stepping from behind the bar. Her eyes were bright with tears. "As soon as the storm lets up, I'm going down there."

"Down there?" Lillie asked. "To the Caribbean?"

"I know you all think it's foolish…" AJ's voice broke. "But I'm going. I have to go. Cyrus could have been picked up by a boat, unconscious. He could be lying in a hospital…"

"AJ—"

Flint cut off Lillie. "Maybe there will be news before the storm lets up." But he could see that once it did, AJ was going to be on the first plane out. He didn't blame her. He'd thought about doing the same thing himself. But he had a job, a family and, like the others, he thought it was a wild-goose chase.

AJ just didn't want to accept that Cyrus was gone. As the person who had always looked after the family, Flint had to help them not only accept it, but also figure out how to live with the loss. Had there been anyway to get word to their father in the mountains, he would have. But why worry Ely yet. He knew he was holding out, hoping that Cyrus wasn't dead, that there'd been a mistake.

There was also Juliette to deal with. He didn't want to rush into a funeral at this point, but soon. Once the funeral was over, he got the feeling that Juliette would leave, realizing there was nothing here for her. The truth was, he wanted her gone. She would always be a reminder of their loss.

JULIETTE FOUND HERSELF pacing as she waited the next afternoon for her lawyer to call. She knew these things took time, but she didn't have time. The sooner this was over, the sooner she would get to that warm villa waiting for her.

"What have you found out?" she demanded when he finally called. The two of them went way back as if from another life.

"Nice to hear your voice too, Julie."

"The ranch, what is it worth?" She had no patience with small talk and he knew it. "And it's Juliette."

"My mistake," he said with a sneer. "There could be a problem." This was not what she wanted to hear. "You're right about the ranch being signed over to Cyrus and Hawk by one Ely Cahill."

"So what is the problem?"

"While, they have been working the ranch, the proceeds have been divided between the two of them. The other siblings have been getting dividends. But should the ranch ever be sold, Ely divided it equally between his six children."

"But Cyrus and Hawk have *worked* the ranch. The others became bar owners or lawmen or married someone who doesn't care about the ranch."

"Doesn't matter. Cyrus and Hawk profited from running the ranch. After probate, you'll get what Cyrus had in his accounts, which is sizable and one-sixth of what the ranch sells for. Truthfully, selling it now in the middle of winter isn't your best option."

She agreed. Nor did she have time to wait for probate, let alone for the ranch to sell. "I'll get them to buy me out. How much are we talking?"

"One-sixth of the ranch."

Juliette groaned. "Money. How much money?"

"About a million and a half."

She perked right up. It wasn't as much as she'd hoped, but it would do nicely under the circumstances. "And his personal worth?"

"Another five hundred thousand, but like I said, it will have to go through probate and so would the ranch if you decide to—"

"I'm not waiting for the ranch to be sold," she snapped. "They'll buy me out. A cash settlement separate from any probate. I know they won't want to sell the ranch, so they'll pony it up."

"Legally—"

"Tell me about my lawsuit against the cruise line. I sent you the names of the people who saw Cyrus drunk the first night on board. They'll testify that the barmaid was flirting with him and plying him with free drinks."

"Your chances of a settlement aren't that good, but if that's what you're determined to do I'll proceed."

"Isn't that what I pay you for? Get what you can out of them." She disconnected. She thought of Cyrus. He'd been a good man. A fool, but a decent man. She'd met so few of them that she actually felt bad that he was dead. But she quickly got over it as she glanced around the hotel room and wished she could move faster on this.

But if she seemed too anxious the family might put up more of a fight. No, she would have to give this time, time she didn't have. She had to win over at least some of the family. It wouldn't be easy though, given what she'd seen earlier. The sister was definitely out. Maybe the sheriff's wife. She seemed sympathetic.

Her stomach growled, reminding her that she hadn't eaten though she'd smelled something cooking at the saloon. They hadn't offered her anything to eat, that should tell her everything she needed to know. She doubted they were suspicious, but then again, she couldn't count on that. It probably wouldn't be long before the sheriff tracked down her past.

She could feel the clock ticking. But time wasn't her only problem, she reminded herself. The more she'd thought about AJ, the more she had to know if Cyrus had talked to the woman in the hours before he'd gone overboard. If Cyrus had told AJ anything about the two of them…

Pulling out her phone, she opened her browser and searched for the number for the Stagecoach Saloon where AJ apparently lived upstairs. The woman she'd met named Billie Dee, apparently the cook, answered.

"I was calling for AJ," she said and planned to say more when the cook cut her off.

"She's right here. Can I say who's calling?"

"A friend." Just as she'd known would happen, Billie Dee turned over the phone.

"Hello?" AJ sounded as if she'd been crying. Juliette made a face at the phone, hating that AJ existed and worse that the family was all on her side.

"I need to talk to you about Cyrus," she said without preamble, putting just enough anguish into her voice. "Could we meet for a late lunch somewhere? I really need to talk to someone who knew him."

It worked like a charm.

When AJ spoke, there were no tears in her voice. She was all business. "You're staying at the hotel. There's a café just down the street. I can be there in fifteen minutes."

Juliette smiled. "Thank you so much. I'll see you then."

"YOU'RE GOING TO lunch with her?" Billie Dee demanded as AJ pulled on her coat and boots. "Why would you do that?"

"She was probably the last person to see Cyrus alive."

"I have a bad feeling about this."

AJ smiled at her. Billie Dee was like a second mother to her. Nothing like her own mother, who was a renowned heart surgeon and cool professional, the cook was the kind of mother AJ wished she had growing up.

A large woman with an open face and a wonderful hug, Billie Dee was warm and loving and always available to talk or just listen. She'd been so happy to bring her best friend together with her birth mother. Gigi didn't really know yet how lucky she was.

"It isn't like she can push me off a cruise ship. I'll be fine," she said and hugged the older woman. "I want to find out more about what happened in Denver—and on the cruise ship."

Billie Dee looked pained. "Are you sure, honey? I don't want to see you hurt any more than you have already been."

"I'm tougher than I look. Anyway, Juliette made the overture. For whatever reason, she said she feels the need to talk to me about Cyrus. But I suspect she wants something from me."

"Like I said—"

"Don't worry. I have a pretty good idea what's going on. Stop looking like that. I've said from the beginning that something is wrong about all of this. I'm sure Juliette is going to try to convince me that I'm wrong. We'll see. But she might give something away, something that can help Cyrus, once I can get out of here and go look for him."

Billie Dee looked as if she might cry.

"I'm not delusional, okay? I know he could be gone, but this is something I have to do, all right?"

Hesitantly, the older woman nodded. "I just worry about you."

"I know you do. But it's just lunch."

"But if you go down to the Caribbean—"

"I'll be back for your wedding. Gigi and I both will," AJ told her. "We wouldn't miss seeing you marry Henry for anything in the world. Your wedding is three months away. I'm sure I won't be gone that long."

Billie Dee had joked that she'd come to Montana from Texas looking for a cowboy. She'd met one in Henry Larson and fallen in love and was now engaged to be married. AJ couldn't be happier for her.

The only thing that had held up the wedding was that Billie Dee had wanted the daughter she'd given away at birth to be there. That was where AJ had come in, bringing the two women together. They'd thought that nothing could hold up the wedding after that, but then this had happened with Cyrus.

"Wish me luck," AJ said and headed for the door.

"Luck," Billie Dee said and crossed herself. "Watch your back."

CHAPTER SIX

JULIETTE WAS ALREADY waiting for AJ at the café when she walked in. She'd picked a back booth and, because it was between lunch and dinner, the place was nearly empty. She'd ordered an iced tea, wishing she had travel-size liquor to pour in it to relax her nerves.

But even as she thought it, she knew it was a bad idea. She needed her wits about her. AJ was sharp. She had to be careful, she warned herself as AJ came in the door on a gush of cold winter air. Their gazes met across the café and Juliette felt her survival instinct kick in as AJ made her way toward the booth.

Juliette gave her a weak smile after reminding herself that she was in mourning. She had a wadded-up tissue in her hand that she used to dab her eyes as AJ took the seat across from her. She couldn't help but notice that the other woman was dry-eyed, a hard, determined glint in those blue eyes that definitely could be cause for concern.

"I ordered an iced tea," she said in her let's-be-friend's tone. "I didn't know what you would like."

The waitress appeared next to their booth, put down two

menus and two waters. AJ ordered a cola. Juliette watched her cup her hands around the sweating ice water glass for a moment as if trying to cool down. Or was it calm down? It was clear that the attorney was worked up.

But when AJ spoke, her voice was deceivingly calm. "I'm glad you called. I have a lot of questions. I hope you don't mind me asking?"

Was this what the woman was like interrogating a witness on the stand? Then Juliette could understand why she'd done so well with her law degree.

But she could be just as sweet, just as calm, just as conciliatory. "Of course not, although it's so painful."

"I'm sure it is for you," AJ said as if she didn't believe it for a moment. "I heard you met at the hotel where Cyrus was staying in Denver."

Juliette had known she would have to tell this story again, but it still annoyed her. She wanted to question AJ, not the other way around. But she played along, talking like one female friend to another.

"As I told you yesterday—"

"But you failed to mention what you were doing at the hotel."

Juliette hadn't expected that. "I have a friend in Denver I visit from time to time."

"And this friend makes you stay at a hotel?"

She swallowed and tried not to let AJ get to her. "She lives with her mother who has Alzheimer's. She's a full-time caregiver and needs a break occasionally, so my room seems like a haven for her."

"You didn't mention her name."

The waitress returned and took their orders. Juliette ordered a burger and fries. AJ glanced at the menu and said she'd just stick with the cola.

As the waitress walked away, AJ said, "I see you haven't lost your appetite though."

Juliette bristled. "I eat when I'm upset."

"You must not get upset very often."

"You sound like you don't believe me. My friend's name is Dara." She wasn't stupid enough not to have someone available to back up her story—for a price. "As it was, I didn't get to visit her this trip. She was busy interviewing nursing homes for her mother whose condition has gotten worse."

AJ was looking at her as if she didn't believe anything that came out of her mouth.

"I don't go to Denver just to see Dara. I also go there to shop." AJ looked as if she might push for Dara's full name, but she didn't give her a chance. "Anyway, I was in the bar the night before I was set to fly out—"

"Back home. Where is that?"

"Miami. I winter there. And before you ask, no I don't have a home there. I usually do an Airbnb. I hadn't gotten one yet."

"So no home base?"

"No. I like being able to go anywhere I want."

"You apparently don't have a job," AJ said.

"No, I'm fortunate. I have an adequate trust fund, but from the looks of you, I would think you probably know how trust funds work."

"Actually, I've never touched mine. So you just happened to be in the bar."

Juliette felt as if she were in a sword fight. She was holding her own. Bleeding, but not badly. She'd been in worse. "He walked in, our eyes met. He bought me a drink, we talked. He was so charming and sweet. I got the feeling that he didn't get out much and the next thing you know we were in the elevator together heading up to his room."

"That surprises me. He's always been so shy and cautious."

She shrugged. "You know how it is when you meet someone and chemistry takes over. Is that how it was with you and Cyrus? Love at first sight?"

AJ's smile had teeth. "Cyrus and I were friends."

She cocked an eyebrow at her. "Oh, I think it was more than that—at least on your part. Tell me about you and Cyrus."

"We were friends."

"Close friends."

"Yes. Close."

"I thought maybe..."

"Thought what?" AJ asked.

"I thought as his close friend he might have called you and told you what had happened."

The attorney-turned-bartender said nothing.

"Cyrus and I promised each other that we wouldn't tell *anyone.* We were determined to surprise everyone when we got home. But I thought if he would have contacted anyone..."

"You're afraid that he called me."

Juliette swallowed. She considered denying it, as if that would have helped. "Did he?"

"And told me what was really going on?" AJ asked.

She felt her pulse jump. Was it possible Cyrus had broken his promise not to tell? "I'm not sure I know what you mean."

"Whose idea was it to take the cruise?" AJ asked, clearly ignoring the question.

Juliette wanted to reach across the table and choke the truth out of the woman, but she played along since she had little choice. Also, she figured if Cyrus had called her, then AJ would have already told the sheriff.

"I had already booked the cruise as a surprise for my friend."

"The one whose mother has Alzheimer's and is going into the home."

"Yes. I can give you her name if you don't believe me. Dara

had problems finding a nursing home that would take her mother. Her mother was violent. Such an insidious disease, you know. I mentioned the cruise to Cyrus. I said I was going to have to cancel. At first he said he had to get back to Montana, but…"

She shrugged and couldn't help smiling at how easy it had all been—at least for a while. "Cyrus said he'd never been on a cruise. He thought it would be fun."

"So it was your idea to get married on the ship," AJ said.

"Is that what you think?" She shook her head. "You think you knew Cyrus, but there was a side of him that had never cut loose. I helped him find that side. He was having a ball—"

"Until he fell overboard. Not twenty-four hours after the wedding, Cyrus was in the ocean alone at night." AJ tilted her head, studying her. "How did that happen?"

"If you're trying to make me feel guilty, don't bother," Juliette snapped, and then calmed herself. "I feel guilty enough. There was a storm that night. The ocean was rough. I was seasick. Cyrus wanted to take a walk around the ship. If I hadn't taken that medicine and I'd gone with him…"

"So you have the perfect alibi. Unless you turn up on the surveillance cameras on the ship that night. Sheriff Cahill is having them sent to him. He'll be studying those in the hopes of seeing what really happened on that ship—before and after his brother went overboard."

Juliette tried not to let on how hard her pulse was now pounding. Just her luck that Cyrus's brother was a sheriff. No way would a family member go through all the surveillance videos. Nor would they even know what to look for.

She met AJ's challenging gaze, holding it, daring her to disprove that everything had happened just as she'd said. At the same time, her heart raced with worry that she hadn't been careful enough.

"I was in the cabin the rest of the night. I ordered some chamomile tea. The porter brought it and turned down the bed. I showered, took the seasick medicine and went to bed."

"And Cyrus wasn't back. Didn't that seem strange?"

Juliette let out a laugh to ease her growing tension. This lunch wasn't going anything like she had planned. "Strange? Not when you're married to a cowboy. Him and his long legs. He felt cramped on the ship. It was one reason I'd agreed to get off at the next port and fly home with him. He missed his wide-open spaces. He was also excited to share his news with his family, who apparently thought he would never get married."

AJ said nothing.

"I was hoping you and I could be friends," she said after the waitress slid her burger and fries in front of her along with a huge bottle of ketchup. "Help yourself to a fry. They look delicious."

AJ gave her a disbelieving look. "You and I ever being friends is out of the question. Anyway, you aren't going to be around that long, are you." It wasn't a question.

"Cyrus's family and friends are strangers right now but once they accept that I'm family..." she said carefully. "Also it's clear to me that you all want to blame me somehow for this." AJ didn't deny it. "But I guess if they don't accept me, then there's nothing here for me without Cyrus."

AJ studied her openly, making Juliette more nervous than usual.

"I can see that something is on your mind," she finally said, tired of being examined like she was something AJ had stepped in. She picked up a french fry, dredged it through a pile of ketchup and put it into her mouth to chew slowly, all the time keeping her eyes on the other woman.

"I was just wondering what will happen when I find Cyrus and bring him back home," AJ said.

"Find him?" Juliette choked on her fry. Dropping the rest of it back into her plate, she said, "You aren't seriously going to go look for him."

"Why not?"

"Because he's gone. He fell overboard and drowned. Days ago. There is no chance that he could have survived."

"We don't know that," AJ argued.

"He couldn't have survived that long in the water—"

"He could have swum to shore."

"There was no shore in sight," Juliette said, wondering why she was arguing with this woman.

"How do you know that? You were in your cabin knocked out from a seasickness pill. Or did you see Cyrus go overboard because you were there?"

She picked up her napkin, stalling for time, as she dapped at her mouth and tried to gain control of her temper. "I told you what happened," she said in her most calm tone. "The captain said that we were miles from a string of islands at the time Cyrus went overboard. Believe me, I made this same argument to him. I wanted to believe that Cyrus could survive somehow, but I've accepted that he couldn't. He's dead. His death certificate is being sent to me as we speak."

AJ turned to look out the café window for a moment. "But what if he isn't dead?" She shifted her gaze back. Juliette saw a fire in those blue eyes as if fueled by a love stronger than any she herself had ever known. "What if he somehow survived because he's Cyrus Cahill? What if it is only a matter of time before he tells us what really happened from the moment he met you until he went overboard on that ship?"

Juliette stared at the woman. "You're delusional. I feel sorry for you."

"Don't," AJ said, getting to her feet and placing her hand over her heart. "Cyrus is alive. I feel it. He isn't gone or I would know it. And when I find him…" The woman smiled then. "You'll understand if I don't stay. Enjoy your…lunch."

Shaking with anger, Juliette watched her walk out. Cyrus must have called her, must have said something that had AJ suspicious. She tried to compose herself. She was letting the foolish woman get to her. If AJ knew anything, she would have said something. Or she would have told the sheriff. No, the woman was clutching at straws, driven mad by love and loss.

Let her go look for Cyrus. She wasn't going to find him. Juliette had done her research. Few people who'd gone overboard survived even for a few hours. It was going on days now. Cyrus was dead.

But the worst part was that AJ Somerfield had ruined her appetite. She pushed the burger away and signaled the waitress for her check. It was time to move things along. This town and these people were getting to her.

ONCE THE STORM moved east two days later, the snowplows opened the roads again. It had been almost a week since they'd gotten the call about Cyrus. Flint knew he couldn't go back on his word to AJ. Just as he knew she hadn't changed her mind about going to look for Cyrus.

They spoke little about his brother on the two-hour drive to Billings to catch her flight. But not everything had been said. He couldn't let her go without knowing everything. Not that it would change her mind. He understood that she had to do this. He figured it was her way of finding closure.

"There's something I need to tell you," he said as they neared the airport. She looked over at him as if expecting a blow. "The entire search was called off days ago. Juliette requested a death certificate."

"By now she already has it."

He shot her a look. "So you already know."

"It doesn't make any difference. She can get all the death certificates she wants. Cyrus is still alive and I'm going to find him."

"There's something else. Another passenger went overboard the same night as Cyrus, different cruise line, only a few miles from where he went in."

"You think they are somehow connected?" she asked.

He shook his head and then thought better of it. "I honestly don't know. I'm still shocked by Cyrus even being on that ship, let alone..." He glanced over at her and didn't bother to finish the sentence. No one in the family believed his brother would marry Juliette the way he had. "The missing man's name is Jordan Hughes. Like Cyrus, no one knew he was missing the entire night. They began to search for him when it was discovered that he was missing and that wasn't until the next port. He was apparently a businessman traveling alone. He also hasn't been found. These ships are so huge I doubt you see the same people twice, especially if you aren't on the same level."

"You said the captain was sending you copies of the surveillance videos taken on board Cyrus's ship," she said.

"Once I get them, I'll go through the footage." He could see that he was getting nowhere. She was going. Nothing could stop her.

"I'd be interested to know if Juliette was on those videos."

"I'll let you know if I find anything," Flint said as he turned into the airport. "We know she wasn't in the one right before or after Cyrus went overboard. Her alibi seems to be airtight." He pulled up in front of her airline. The terminal was small by most standards. He left the engine running and turned to AJ. "Here," he said, handing her a thick manila folder. "This is everything I've been able to get from the cruise line, the police commissioner, the coast guard."

She met his gaze as she took the envelope and smiled, tears

welling in her eyes. “Thank you. I know you think I’m wasting my time…”

He shook his head. “I’m worried about you, yes, but truthfully, I’m glad you’re going. I feel like someone should. Just be careful down there and good luck. If you need anything…”

AJ nodded. “I’ll keep in touch.” She opened her door.

He hopped out to help her with her suitcase. She traveled light, one small bag. “Seriously, if you need anything at all… And, AJ?” She looked up at him. “Just know when to come back, okay?”

She took the handle of her bag from him. “I’ll be back. With Cyrus. He’s still alive. I…still feel it.” With that, she turned and walked away.

He stood out in the cold for a few minutes, watching her disappear inside before he climbed back into his SUV and headed toward Gilt Edge. If there was a chance in hell that Cyrus was alive, he thought, AJ would find him.

Flint wished he believed there was any chance at all after all this time. He was more worried about AJ. There was no way she was coming back the same woman who’d left and that broke his heart.

CHAPTER SEVEN

AJ SAT ON the plane that would fly her to Minneapolis where she would catch a flight to Miami. From there she'd hired a private plane. As she buckled up, she was feeling anxious and yet she would be in St. Augusta by tonight. Had she been forced to fly commercial it would have taken her days and she didn't have days.

If Cyrus was out there… The thought of him floating somewhere in that ocean made her sick with worry. How long could he last? She'd read everything she could get her hands on about cruise ships and missing people who had gone overboard. One had made it over fifteen days.

She couldn't imagine the horror of going overboard, coming up and seeing the stern of the ship in the distance. Had he called for help? Had he been unconscious when he hit the water? Had he been pushed? Jumped? She shook her head, unable to think about it and yet unable to stop. Nothing felt right about any of this. Worse, she could feel the clock was ticking.

That feeling that Cyrus was alive was so strong days ago. She hated to even admit to herself, let alone voice it. But the feeling was weaker. If she didn't find Cyrus soon…

Her phone buzzed. When she saw that the call was from Lillie Cahill, she quickly took it, praying that it was good news.

"Can you believe he married that woman?" Lillie cried.

Not the news AJ had been praying for. "Juliette?"

"Her lawyer just contacted the family attorney." Lillie sounded mad enough to chew nails. She also sounded scared and close to tears. "She wants Cyrus's part of the ranch."

"What?" AJ thought of the woman she'd met at the café. A gold digger. She didn't believe for a moment that Juliette had fallen in love with Cyrus or vice versa. It must have come as a shock to her though when she realized the Cahills weren't rich. Far from it. They were what was known as land-poor. Everything was invested in the land. "But all the money is tied up in property."

"Trask said she could force the family to sell the ranch to buy her out," Lillie said. "And her name. Juliette. *Juliette*," Lillie repeated as if that explained anything. "She keeps pestering us about the funeral. She tried to get me to go to lunch with her." Lillie was crying now. "She says she needs to be with her husband's family. She told me that she had Cyrus's death certificate in her purse!"

It all felt suddenly too real. For a moment, AJ wondered what she was doing flying off to some island. Shouldn't she be there trying to help the family against this woman? But under Montana law, Juliette had a right to one-sixth of the ranch and all of his personal wealth.

There would be only one way to stop her. If Cyrus was alive… Was she merely in denial? Unlike the Cyrus she'd known, she'd always been impetuous. Why couldn't she accept that he was gone? Because of some crazy feeling like an extra heartbeat?

"I'm sorry," Lillie said. "I didn't call to upset you too. I heard you're on your way to the Caribbean to look for him. You have to find him."

"If he's alive, I'll find him." The flight attendant announced that all cell phones and computers should be shut down for take-off. "I'm glad you called. But right now I have to get off the phone. We're about to take off."

"Call me when you get there," Lillie said.

"I will." She disconnected and put her phone on airplane mode before settling back in her seat. Closing her eyes, she thought of Cyrus—the one she'd known, not the one Juliette had told her about. That feeling deep inside her that he was alive—and in trouble—felt so sharp for a moment, it took away her breath. She opened her eyes. She was doing this.

FLINT HUNG UP from talking to the family lawyer again and swore. Earlier Lillie had been in his office. She already knew what was going on. He realized he couldn't keep it from the rest of the family any longer—that's if Lillie hadn't already called them. Picking up the phone again, he called Maggie and asked her if she would mind setting up another family meeting.

"Have they found Cyrus?" she asked.

"No, sorry. It's about Juliette."

Maggie made a dismissive sound. "Maybe we should have the funeral so she'll leave town."

"I'm afraid it wouldn't do any good. How about four tomorrow afternoon at the saloon? Make sure everyone comes." He hung up and stared for a moment at nothing. Just when he thought things couldn't get worse.

His phone rang. He hesitated, no longer hoping for good news. Now when his phone rang he expected more bad news. He picked up on the second ring. "Sheriff Cahill."

"We've got an altercation down here at the bar," Deputy Harper Cole said.

He sighed. "I'm sure you can handle it, Harp."

"It's your father. I've never seen him like this."

Flint swore under his breath. He knew what must have happened. His father had come out of the mountains and no doubt heard about Cyrus. Maybe they should have gone up in the mountains and tried to find him and tell him. Flint hated that their father had found out this way.

When their mother had died, Ely had turned the ranch over to his sons and daughter and headed for the hills. He spent most of his time up there panning for gold, trapping, living like a mountain man.

But every few months, he would show up in town and get rip-roaring drunk and cause trouble. Today wouldn't be the first time Flint had to lock his father up in jail. "I'll be right there," he told Harp. "Let me handle him."

AJ SAT IN the uncomfortable chair in the St. Augusta Island Police Commissioner's office. A small overhead fan turned noisily and so slowly that it barely moved the hot evening air. When the commissioner returned with the papers she'd asked for, she quickly rose, anxious to read them alone in an air-conditioned hotel. After Montana's winter weather, this heat felt unbearable.

"I hope this answers all of your questions," the commissioner said as he handed her the latest report. "If not..."

AJ stared at the updated report in her hands. The word *blood* had leaped off the page. Her hand began to shake, making it hard to read the typewritten statement. She knew blood had been found on a lower railing where the surveillance camera had witnessed Cyrus falling. The FBI had taken a sample to compare with Cyrus's DNA. Her heart dropped like an anchor into the well of grief she'd been fighting since hearing the news. The DNA report had come back.

The blood had been his. Cyrus had definitely been hurt before he'd gone into the water. Bleeding in an ocean full of predators?

She closed her eyes, squeezing them shut to hold back the tears.

"I'm so sorry," the police commissioner said not for the first time.

AJ forced her eyes open and brushed angrily at her tears. She'd been hoping the blood wouldn't be his. Every turn, common sense demanded she give up this quest. Cyrus was gone. And yet even now, she couldn't. Wouldn't.

"I understand a toxicology screen was also done on the blood found?" she asked.

He looked surprised and at a loss for words for a moment. "I haven't seen the results for that. Nor was I aware one had been done. I'm sorry. You have reason to believe he was on drugs?"

She shook her head. "Just covering all the bases."

The commissioner sat back in his chair as if he only then remembered that she was a lawyer. He leaned forward, picked up his phone and began to dial.

AJ concentrated on breathing as she surreptitiously wiped at her eyes. It was Cyrus's blood. She thought about what Flint had told her about Cyrus probably being unconscious by the time he hit the water. He would have drowned. Right now that seemed the most humane way he could have gone. If he was gone. She was clutching at straws. But if he'd been pushed...

"You're right," the commissioner said, sounding relieved. "A toxicology screen was done. Drugs were found in his system. That report has been sent to Sheriff Flint Cahill in Gilt Edge, Montana."

He'd been drugged. She knew it had to be something like that. She rose to her feet. "Thank you for your help."

The police commissioner nodded as he too rose to see her out. There had been only one thing in the report that could help her find Cyrus—the location of the ship at the stamped time on the surveillance video of Cyrus falling off the ship.

Unfortunately, the camera, on one of the lower decks, had caught only him falling past it. No camera had caught him on the deck from where he'd fallen. So there was no video of him sitting on the railing, climbing over it or possibly being pushed.

The police commissioner handed her his card. He'd already provided her with the number for the ship's captain—and lawyer. "Again, my condolences."

She'd had to tell a white lie to get the information she needed, saying she was the attorney for the Cahill family. Now she took the paperwork and once outside where the air was even hotter and more humid, she walked the few blocks to the hotel rather than brave another wild taxi ride. The one from the airport had been bad enough.

Once in her room, she stripped down, showered and sat to read what the commissioner had given her.

But there was little else new. She already had learned that the only thing harder than falling off a cruise ship was surviving the fall. It had happened in a few cases. Very few. She kept telling herself that if anyone could survive, it would be Cyrus.

FLINT HAD HIS father changed into clean clothes by the time he drove a somber Ely out to the Stagecoach Saloon where everyone was already waiting the next afternoon.

"Dad," Lillie cried when she saw him. She ran to him to throw her arms around him.

Darby poured his father a tonic water and put it in front of him. Most everyone else had opted for a real drink. They all hugged and cried and said they still couldn't believe it. Ely looked pale and shaky from the shock.

"You have news?" Hawk said. "About Cyrus?"

Flint shook his head as he took a chair. Darby asked him if

he wanted a drink but he declined. "Juliette's lawyer contacted our lawyer concerning Cyrus's portion of the ranch."

"What?" Hawk barked as the others put up a similar uproar. All except Lillie. She sat dry-eyed and furious, having already heard. "We haven't even buried him yet."

Flint didn't have to tell him or the others that they would be burying an empty casket at best. The chances of Cyrus's body being found had dropped after the first forty-eight hours. Now it had been over a week. But he knew what Hawk meant. They hadn't had time to even accept that Cyrus was gone.

"She wants the ranch?" Ely said, looking up a little blurry-eyed. "I would imagine that was what she was after all along."

The room fell silent. By now, they'd all figured that had been the case. Juliette had somehow seduced Cyrus thinking he had money. Hell, he'd just purchased a three-hundred-thousand-dollar bull.

"Her lawyer has suggested that we buy her out," Flint continued. "She wants a million and a half."

This time the room erupted. He waited until they all calmed down before he said the obvious. "There is no way we can raise that kind of money." The ranch was in debt, like most ranches. Also Lillie and Darby had borrowed against their share of the ranch to start the Stagecoach Saloon. The bull that Cyrus had gone to Denver to buy was on its way to the ranch, the deal done. Eventually, the bull would pay for itself and more. But everything about ranching took time and since none of the family had demanded their share, they'd put money back into the ranch by buying up more land.

"She'll force you to sell it," Ely said into the heavy silence. "You'll have no choice."

Hawk shook his head. He and Cyrus had been running the ranch while the others had chosen different occupations. "I can't believe this is happening. There has to be a way to stop her."

"Let her sue us," Lillie said, "and see how far that gets her."

"She would win," Flint said. "She's Cyrus's legal wife. The marriage on the ship… She's also suing the cruise line. I doubt she's a novice at this, given how little time it took to send her lawyer after us."

"AJ is going to find Cyrus and bring him home," Lillie said emphatically.

No one said anything. Like Flint, they held little hope of that happening.

"Let's at least hold Juliette off as long as we can," Ely said. He looked even more pale and sick. Flint had hated to tell him this news on top of Cyrus being gone.

"You all right, Dad?" he asked his father.

Ely nodded and took a sip of his tonic water. He'd had a minor heart attack not that long ago. They all worried he'd have another one up in the mountains. But it was when he came to town that he seemed to have the medical problems.

"I hate her," Lillie said, crying. "Can't we…"

"Kill her?" Darby suggested and laughed. "Let's not, sis."

Ely said something that Flint didn't catch only a few moments before he keeled over onto the table.

CHAPTER EIGHT

AJ COULDN'T BELIEVE the news when Lillie called. Her father had suffered another heart attack, this one serious. He was in the hospital, stable for the moment but still unconscious. There was even more bad news.

"Juliette wants a million and a half dollars," Lillie blurted. "There is no way we can raise that kind of money except to sell the ranch. Even then..."

AJ's first thought was to come up with the money herself, but while she was what most people would consider rich, her money was tied up in the trust fund. Her grandmother had made sure that large sums of the trust couldn't be taken out or borrowed against—just in case AJ fell in love with some lowlife who would try to bilk her.

"Don't worry," she told Lillie. "I'm going to find Cyrus. Let Juliette try to get the ranch then."

Lillie hadn't sounded all that relieved. "I hope you're right about him being alive."

"I am," she said with more conviction than she felt. She hated getting Lillie's hopes up when all of this was probably a wild-goose chase. "Try to hold Juliette off as long as you can. And please keep me updated on Ely's condition."

AJ disconnected and spread the map of the Caribbean out before her. When she called, the cruise ship captain hadn't wanted to talk to her on the advice of his lawyers. Of course Juliette was suing the cruise line. Nothing the woman did should have been a surprise. She'd told the captain that she was Cyrus's girlfriend from back home and that she believed he was still alive and was trying to find him. It was eerily close to the truth.

"I'm looking at the information you gave the police commissioner in St. Augusta. At the time Cyrus fell off the ship, you were miles from the nearest islands. But there was a storm that night, right? I just need to know about drift. Had he survived, where might he have ended up? Captain, if he is still alive, then his so-called wife won't have as much ammunition to sue you. Help me. Please."

She could tell that the captain felt sorry for her. He probably thought she was delusional. There were moments when she questioned it herself.

He explained about drift and how to estimate it. "Yes, there was a storm that night. The seas were rough. If he'd found something he could hang on to he might have been able to make landfall. That is a huge *if*."

What he hadn't said was that if Cyrus had been unconscious, he wouldn't have been able to hang on to to anything. He would have drowned. And if he'd made it to shore, wouldn't someone have found him, gotten him medical attention, called the authorities? She pushed those thoughts away since she didn't need him to tell her any of that. She'd told herself enough times.

She thanked him, disconnected and studied the map. There seemed nothing else to do but check each island. She would start with the hospitals, morgues, police stations. If a man had been found, maybe unconscious, who'd washed up on a beach, wouldn't one of them know about him She could do that by phone, but she knew she wouldn't be satisfied until she went to each of the islands and showed his photo around. She had all the time in the world.

What she feared was that Cyrus and the Cahill family didn't.

JULIETTE SWORE AS she paced the hotel room, her phone pressed to her ear.

"You can't get blood out of a turnip," her attorney said.

Was she ready to settle for less? Not yet.

"When I spoke with the family's lawyer, he indicated that they aren't convinced that Cyrus is dead."

"I have the death certificate!"

"I understand someone in the family is in the Caribbean looking for him," the lawyer said.

AJ. Juliette groaned. Cyrus's sister, Lillie, had called to tell her that AJ had flown down there to find him. What a waste of time and money, but apparently AJ Somerfield had both.

"There is no chance for that to happen," she assured the lawyer. She knew the statistics. Out of eighty man-overboard incidents, only sixteen were rescued. And those had been within hours. The longest anyone had trod water was eighteen hours. It had been days now since Cyrus had gone overboard. He was dead. Probably eaten by sharks. If the Cahills were hoping for a body to bury, they were out of luck. He would never be found. Not after all this time.

But how long could she wait here? "Push for a payoff," she said.

"There's something else," her lawyer said. "Blood was found on one of the lower decks. A sample was taken at the time it was found and sent to a lab. A DNA test has been requested on it."

"So?"

"If they determined the blood alcohol content at the lab, it could help with your lawsuit against the cruise line."

"Would they have done that?" she asked, her heart in her throat.

"Depends on the lab and what law enforcement would have ordered," he said.

"Would they have checked for drugs?"

"Probably, why?"

"Just curious."

"Juliette, if he had taken drugs, that will kill any chance of reimbursement from the cruise line. The FBI has jurisdiction over any incidents on the high seas. If they suspect foul play—"

"Just find out what tests were run," she demanded and disconnected, angry with herself. Nothing seemed to be going the way she'd planned it. She'd miscalculated on how much money the cowboy would be able to come up with should he meet a fate such as death. She could feel time running out.

Meanwhile, that foolish young woman was searching for Cyrus. Good, it would keep AJ out of her hair, she told herself. But at the back of her mind, worry nagged at her. What if the cowboy had somehow survived?

She told herself that it wasn't possible. He'd hit the railing before he'd gone into the water. He'd gone right under and hadn't come up. He'd probably been half-dead even before he hit the water. Once in the water, he would have drowned. Unless…

At the window, she moved the curtain aside to look out. There were piles of fresh snow everywhere and the weatherman was calling for more. She hated winter, hated this place, hated the reminders of her childhood. She had to get out of here.

Her phone rang. She let the curtain drop back as she turned to look at the dingy hotel room. She picked up her phone, saw who was calling. "You aren't supposed to call me."

"It looks bad in Florida. If they decide to press charges…"

She didn't need him telling her what that would mean. She wouldn't be able to get out of the country in time. "I'm hurrying as fast as I can," she said and hung up.

How much more could she take? Last night she'd had the nightmare again.

As if her waking fears weren't enough.

THE NEXT MORNING AJ flew to Grenada. According to the captain, the island would be the farthest point that Cyrus might have floated. Of course, there was always the chance that a boat had picked him up. But if that had happened, they would have heard by now.

She went to the hospital first, showing anyone who would look the photo she'd brought of Cyrus. She got the same reaction, a shake of the head, a look of sympathy. She went to the morgue and then the police station. Nothing.

As one day slipped into another she went from Grenada to St. Vincent and the Grenadines. Each hospital was the same. Each morgue. Each police station. No one had seen the man in the photo she showed them. Each day was the same. The recent hurricane had hammered many of the islands. Everywhere she went, she saw construction—and destruction. Some of the residences and businesses would be rebuilt. Others would turn into ruins.

She even stopped people on the streets. No one had seen anyone who looked like Cyrus.

More days went by, each more discouraging than the last. She continued up the crescent-shaped line of islands, refusing to give up.

She flew to Barbados and then St. Lucia. She went through the same thing she had been doing for days. She went to the hospital, the morgues and the police departments, showing Cyrus's photo with the same results.

No one had seen him.

She was about to get on a flight to Martinique when she got a call from Flint. He asked where she was and where she was headed.

"I've got what could be very bad news," he said without preamble.

She braced herself for the worst.

"What is left of a body has washed up on the beach in Martinique."

"I already have a flight there," she said. "But it's not him." She hung up close to tears. Her heart ached. She tried to feel Cyrus and that heart assurance that he was still with her. For a moment, she felt nothing but exhaustion.

What if this body that had washed up was Cyrus?

ELY CAHILL OPENED his eyes. This time, he was certain that he'd died. He remembered the pain in his chest. Like a shotgun blast to his heart. It was the big one.

Now he blinked, uncertain. He felt weak and seemed to be connected to every medical device there was. So he was in a hospital but how was that possible? Hadn't the doctor and his family said that the next one could be The One and that it would kill him? They'd all been convinced he would be up in the mountains when it happened and no one would find his body until spring—if they ever found it.

More than likely some animal would drag his body off and bury it. Or birds and other critters would chew it down to nothing but bones. He'd always been fine with that. When his Mary had died, he'd taken to the mountains, leaving the ranch to his kids, though only a couple of them had taken to ranching.

Now he wished he'd stayed up in the mountains. Up there, he would have died—died not knowing that he'd lost a son. He couldn't bear to think of Cyrus and what had happened to him.

He moved his head and saw out of the corner of his eye that

his son Flint was beside his bed. Flint, the sheriff. The son who took care of everyone else. He had to smile to himself. From the time the kid was in short pants, he'd looked after the others even though Tucker was the oldest. It would be Flint who would hold this family together when he was gone, he thought, and cleared his throat.

The sheriff's eyes blinked open and he sat up. "Dad."

"Still here." His voice came out hoarse. "How long?"

"You've been unconscious for a while."

"The ticker?"

Flint nodded. "Another heart attack."

"I figured..." He didn't finish the thought. "I need you to get something for me. Out at my cabin—"

"Dad, whatever it is, it can wait," his son said, getting to his feet.

"No, it can't. I need you to get my journal."

Flint stared at him. "Your *journal*?"

"It's leather. It's hidden in the wall behind my bed. It's all in there. Everything. If the government has heard about my heart attack..."

His son groaned. No one had ever believed what happened to him back in 1967 and he doubted they ever would—without the journal.

"Dad—"

He wasn't up to arguing about aliens or spaceships or what the government was up to at the missile silo on their land. "Just get it." He began coughing and motioned to the water by his bed.

Flint poured him a cupful and held the straw so Ely could get a sip.

"It's more important than you know," he said, his voice sounding even weaker and more hoarse. "The government will try to cover up what they're doing out there at the site. But it's all in the journal. Get it to someone you trust. If I'm right—"

The monitors began to go off. A nurse came running in, followed by a doctor. He could barely breathe, barely get the words out. "You have to get it. Promise me you'll go now?"

"Okay, I promise." Flint stepped back as the doctor rushed to the monitor.

"You have to calm down, Mr. Cahill."

"I promise," Flint said as he was pushed toward the door. "I'll get it and bring it right back here. Do what the doctor says."

Ely leaned back into the pillow, his chest on fire. He motioned for his son to step closer. "I suspect it's chemical warfare," he whispered, even though he could no longer see Flint with the nurse and doctor fiddling over him. "Tell someone. Before it's too late."

But even as he said it, his voice barely a whisper, he feared it was already too late to get the journal.

FLINT DROVE AWAY from the hospital headed toward his father's cabin at the foot of the mountain. He'd lived with the whole county believing Ely was a crackpot, but sometimes it was all he could do not to tell the old man to just knock it the hell off.

Chemical warfare? Was he suggesting what Flint thought he was. His father had said that there was more activity around the site. What if it wasn't just the missile site on their property? What if his father was right?

He shook his head. His father had always been suspicious of the government. He reminded himself that Ely believed he'd been abducted by aliens. No one believed that back in 1967 even though there had been an UFO sighting in the area.

Government documents that had been declassified since then confirmed the sighting. According to the report, whatever the flying object had been, it had shut down eight of the missiles in the silos around the area.

That night, Ely swore he was near the silo on their ranch

when he was grabbed and taken aboard a spaceship where experiments were done on him. Since then, he'd been spying on the missile silo and had seen…things. Things he'd apparently written down in his…journal.

As Flint neared his father's cabin, he frowned. There was a light on inside and two government cars parked outside. His heart began to pound.

The moment he drove up, two armed men stepped from the cabin.

"What the hell's going on?" he demanded as he climbed out of his patrol SUV.

"I'm sorry, but I can't let you beyond this point," one of the armed soldiers informed him.

"This is my father's cabin on private property, so why the hell not?"

A figure darkened the doorway. He recognized Bruce Smith, the air force commander in charge. He and Bruce had fly-fished together on the spring creek and butted heads a few times when Ely had gotten too close to the missile silo on their property even though his father had never entered the chain-link fence that surrounded it.

"What's going on, Bruce?" Flint sounded winded from the shock. He'd never believed his father's nonsense about aliens or government secrets involving the silo on their property. "My father had a bad feeling that you would be here. Now I'm wondering which of us is delusional."

The commander told the two men to stand down and walked out to where Flint was waiting. "I'm afraid this is a matter of national security."

He looked past the uniformed man to the small cabin where his father had lived since losing his wife—when Ely wasn't in the mountains.

"What in that cabin could have something to do with national security?" he asked, even though he suspected he now knew.

"I'm afraid that is also classified."

"Are you trying to tell me that some old man's belongings are a matter of national security?" Flint met Bruce's eyes in the glow of light spilling out of the cabin.

"I'm afraid I can't tell you anything."

He swore. "All this time, my father was right." The commander said nothing. "Not about the aliens but about the government being up to something."

"All clear," a soldier said from the cabin doorway.

Even from where Flint stood, he could see that the man had a leather-bound journal in his hand. He watched him put it in a high security pouch and wanted to laugh—and cry.

"I do wonder how you heard about the journal," the sheriff said. "I didn't hear about it until a short while ago at the hospital. My father has said that the government put some kind of tracking device in his head. That would explain how you knew he was in the hospital. It just wouldn't explain how you knew about the journal."

The soldiers began to load up. He could tell that Bruce was anxious to leave, as well. "What if what's in that journal is just the ramblings of an old man who never came back from the Vietnam War the same?" Flint asked. "Otherwise, I hope to hell my father wasn't right, whatever he wrote in that journal." He felt a chill and knew he would never look at the fenced missile silo on his ranch the same way again.

"Have a good night," the commander said and walked to his waiting car.

The sheriff watched them drive away before going to his father's cabin. The place would have to be cleaned up from the mess the government had made inside it.

His phone rang. He stood for a moment just listening to it ring before he finally answered, already knowing. It was the hospital. He thanked the doctor for letting him know and closed the cabin door. Ely Cahill wouldn't be returning here.

THE MOMENT AJ landed in Martinique she went straight to the morgue. The taxi let her off in front of the building as a woman and two men came out. The last man began to lock the door.

"I need to see someone about the body that was found on the beach," she said, quickly paying the taxi as she delayed those leaving the morgue.

"Come tomorrow morning," one of the men said.

"No, please, it can't wait until morning. The body that was found, was it Caucasian?"

The men exchanged a look.

"Please, it will only take a moment. I have to see the body."

"It has deteriorated badly," the woman said. "If it is a loved one, you don't want to see it."

"Not a loved one," AJ lied. "I'm a lawyer from the States. I've just come to identify the body. Please."

The man with the key sighed, and then told the others to go on without him, and he'd meet them at the bar. He opened the door, all the time telling her she'd better not throw up or faint. He didn't have time for either.

She promised that she would be fine when all the time she had no idea how she would react if the body were Cyrus's.

Opening a door into a cold room, the man stepped in and she followed. She shivered as she watched him move to one of the refrigerated drawers. She hadn't been cold since she'd landed in Miami, let alone the islands. Now she couldn't keep her teeth from chattering.

The man rolled out the drawer. The first thing that hit her was how small the body was beneath the sheet.

"I warned you that there wasn't much left," the man said, eyeing her as if he expected her to possibly throw up *and* faint.

Her heart beat so hard against her rib cage that it hurt to breathe as he pulled back the sheet. The body had been chewed on. Both arms were nothing more than nubs. One leg was completely gone. The other was chewed to the bone. But most of the chest was intact.

AJ braced herself and looked to where the head should be. The skull was open on one side and empty. For a moment she felt her stomach rise in her throat. Her legs wobbled under her as she looked at what was left of the face and felt all the blood drain from her head and rush to her feet.

The nose was mostly gone but there was enough of the face left and the top of the skull to see that the man was blond with at least one brown eye, though it was now mostly milky. Her gaze dropped to what was left of his shoulder. There was an old tattoo on the man's shoulder with the name Cherie. It appeared the man had tried to have it removed at some point.

Jordan Hughes? The other man who'd gone overboard from another cruise ship? She stumbled back a step. "It's not him. You should let everyone know about the tattoo along with at least a little description. He was blond with brown eyes."

The man grunted and threw the sheet back over the body as she turned toward the door. Behind her she heard the sound of the drawer sliding back into the wall and the clang of metal. She hurried, bursting through the door outside into the heat and dust. She made it as far as the curb before she threw up.

CHAPTER NINE

AJ HAD BEEN so exhausted after visiting the morgue that by the time she'd checked into a hotel and called Flint with the news, she'd fallen onto the bed, still dressed without even brushing her teeth, and passed out.

While her news about the body that had washed up on the beach was good news, Flint had given her a heartbreaking update on his father. Ely Cahill had died of a massive heart attack. She'd given him her condolences and, shocked and saddened, had succumbed to fatigue.

Cyrus came to her in the middle of the night. She felt his breath on her ear, warm and tempting. She sighed as the bed shifted and she felt him spoon her, his body warm against her backside. He kissed her earlobe and then dropped his lips to behind her ear before his lips trailed down her neck to her bare shoulder.

She kept her eyes closed, afraid to open them. When he stopped kissing her shoulder, she wanted to cry out. But then she felt him behind her. He lifted her nightgown and pulled down her panties. She heard the sound he made when he pressed closer, his arms coming around as he pulled her against his now naked body.

She felt her nipples pucker and harden even before the tips of his fingers brushed over one or the other. She snuggled against him, wanting more, desperately needing more. His fingers touched her between her legs, a brief promise of what was to come and then he pulled her onto her back as if, like her, he could no longer stand just touching her.

Her eyes opened and she looked into his handsome face as he smiled down at her. Cyrus. He was so handsome with his dark hair and gray eyes. That gray gaze shifted from her eyes to her lips as he slowly dropped his mouth to hers.

She closed her eyes, anticipating the kiss she'd waited for so long.

Her lips trembled. But his never touched hers.

"No!" Her eyes flew open. She was lying on the hotel bed, her sundress she'd worn yesterday tangled around her, her heart beating fiercely. She felt the side of the bed where Cyrus had been only a moment ago—in her dream.

A sob broke free of her throat. It had only been a dream. She closed her eyes tightly, the pain and frustration and grief bringing her to her breaking point. She'd wanted that kiss so badly, had yearned for it for so long. And now he was gone.

She rolled over onto her side, drew her legs up into a fetal position and, burying her face in her pillow, she sobbed as if the dam inside her had finally broken.

Spent, she must have fallen asleep because when she opened her eyes sunlight was pouring into the room. For a moment, she didn't move. Couldn't. The memory of last night had taken all her hope from her. Cyrus was gone. She had to accept that.

And now Cyrus's father had died. She thought of Ely and felt tears burn her eyes. She'd liked the mountain man. He was sweet and caring and she loved hearing his stories about his life with his wife, Mary, before her death. She told herself that they were together now, Ely and Mary.

But it was just another loss for the Cahill family.

She had to force herself to climb out of bed, shower and dress for another day. She'd been down here for over a week. She should give up and fly home. But where was home now? Could she go back to Montana with Cyrus gone? She thought about calling her father and telling him she would take the job with the family business.

But as she pulled out her ticket for her flight to the next island, she knew she had to finish what she'd started. If she didn't find him today… Well, she would decide what to do then.

Empty inside, she headed for the airport and a late flight to the island of Dominica.

THE DESTRUCTION IN Dominica from last year's hurricane was worse than even the other island. It was so bad that she'd asked taxi drivers at the airport about places to stay and had gotten, "All full. No place to stay in the city."

Weary from traveling and feeling despondent, she hadn't known what she was going to do. There were a couple of chairs in the tiny airport that maybe she could sleep on tonight and resume her search tomorrow.

She pulled out the photo of Cyrus and felt tears burn her eyes. There were only a few more islands and they were all long shots at best. Maybe she should spend the night here and fly back tomorrow.

A man in uniform was walking past. "Excuse me," she said. "Have you seen this man?"

The policeman shook his head and kept going. She was about to put the photo away when one of the taxi drivers came over to her.

"May I see?"

She handed him the photo. He looked at it for a long moment before handing it back.

"A friend of yours?" he asked.

She nodded too tired to speak.

"I heard you say you were looking for a place to stay. I might be able to help you, if you don't mind leaving the city."

AJ knew she should be suspect. "What is your name?"

"Hermon. My aunt has a place. Very pretty. Not really open for the season, but there is one cottage you could stay in."

She wanted to believe him. What's the worst that could happen? He would take her into the jungle, rob her, rape her, kill her. She was so tired, so discouraged, so heartsick that she knew she wasn't thinking straight. "Thank you. I appreciate your help."

On the drive over the mountains, she realized that even if her taxi driver didn't end up killing her, she could no longer do this. She was physically, emotionally and mentally exhausted. Worse, she was out of islands where it was reasonable that Cyrus might have drifted—if he'd been alive, if he'd found a way to keep afloat, if he had been rescued. From what she'd read, she knew that exhaustion was what finally got to those who had been at sea for hours. The person finally gave up and drowned.

That's if he hadn't been dead after hitting the ship's railing and drowned within minutes of going overboard. She finally admitted that he could have been dead all this time. Which meant she'd only imagined the connection she'd felt between them.

She'd never given up on anything. But as the taxi turned down a narrow road that dropped down to the sea, AJ felt herself giving in to her own exhaustion. She was drowning in grief. Cyrus was gone. She had no choice but to accept it.

She'd looked everywhere she could think. Every island she asked around, walked the beach and stared out at the vast ocean, wishing and hoping and praying. With each island she'd felt that tenuous thread to Cyrus slipping away.

Now she had to question if it had even existed. She had run out of places to look for him. She didn't know what else she could do. It had been more than two weeks since he'd gone overboard. The news back in Montana was even darker. Juliette's attorney was pushing for a settlement. Lillie and Darby were talking about selling the Stagecoach Saloon to come up with at least some of the money to save the ranch. AJ couldn't bear the thought. But Juliette was in Montana demanding her share of the ranch and AJ couldn't stop that any more than she could bring Cyrus back from the dead. She felt defeated, something new for her. She'd never felt so helpless.

Despondent, she stared out at the sea through the palms, hating it even as it turned silver in the moonlight. Her only hope had been to find Cyrus.

That hope was gone, she thought, as the taxi driver dropped down the mountain on a narrow dirt road that ended in a small secluded cove. Through the taxi's headlights she could see a row of cottages facing the beach that had been rebuilt after the hurricane.

She'd been so lost in her thoughts that she hadn't realized how far from town the driver had brought her. "Where are we?"

"Don't worry," he said seeing her concern. "Crystal Cove. I told you. It belongs to my aunt. You will be comfortable here, I promise. When you are ready to leave, you call me and I'll take you back to the airport." He pressed his card into her hand and then got out to open her door.

She could hear waves crashing on the beach beyond the cottages and the sound of music coming from somewhere close by. Her driver tooted his horn once and an older woman appeared. She waved for AJ to come up to where she was waiting on the larger building's portico.

Taking her suitcase, she paid her driver and started up the hill, when a man came from around the corner of the newly rebuilt cottage nearest the beach. In the taxi's headlights she could see that he was tanned, his dark hair looking lighter as if bleached by the sun. He had a beard and a scar on his right cheek, but AJ could never have forgotten that handsome face.

"Let me take that," he said and, stepping closer, reached for her suitcase.

AJ couldn't move. Couldn't breathe. Couldn't speak.

"Joe… Take her luggage to cottage one," the older woman called down.

AJ released her grip on the suitcase as he took it from her. Their gazes met for an instant. In those familiar gray eyes she saw no recognition at all.

CHAPTER TEN

AJ BLINKED, HER mind racing. Cyrus. But the woman had called him Joe. Were her eyes playing tricks on her? He'd stopped a few yards away from the first cottage and was staring back at her.

The taxi driver who called himself Hermon stepped up behind her and touched her shoulder, making her jump. "Be very careful what you do next," he whispered. "This is not the man you're looking for. That man drowned before he washed up on our beach. My aunt is very partial to Joe so I wouldn't tell her you think you know him. Maybe in time..."

"Come up here!" the older woman called from the portico again, drawing her attention.

When she looked again, Cyrus was gone. She swallowed the lump in her throat. Hermon had recognized Cyrus in the photo she'd shown him. He'd known when he'd brought her here. She thought about his warning. What was he trying to tell her? That there was a reason he went by Joe instead of Cyrus?

None of that mattered, she told herself. Her heart felt as if it was going to burst from her chest. It was him! It was Cyrus. He looked different, but there was no doubt, was there?

There was a scar on his right cheek that hadn't been there. Nor had the one on his forearm. His hair was long, curling at his neck. His skin was bronzed and he had a beard. He wore a faded short-sleeved shirt and a pair of baggy shorts that sagged from his tall, slim body.

It was Cyrus. There was no doubt about it, but he'd looked right at her as if he hadn't known her. Worse, there'd been a wariness about him…

She shook herself and headed up the hillside to where the woman was waiting for her. Stepping inside, AJ followed her to a registration desk. The woman introduced herself as Marissa and began telling her that they only had a few cottages open because of the hurricane damage.

All AJ could think of was that Cyrus had been so close she could have reached out and touched him.

"That man, the one you have working for you? Joe, is that what you called him?"

The woman looked up. "Yes?" Suspicion tinged her voice. She heard the protectiveness. "He's been working on restoring the cottages."

"Is he from around here?" she asked.

"American." The older woman's eyes settled on her with too much interest.

AJ could see that Marissa didn't like her asking about Joe. Hermon had warned her. But she had to know what was going on. She shrugged as if it didn't matter. "He reminds me of someone from back home."

"He's been here for a while, a good worker. Keeps to himself and likes it that way." The woman was giving her notice to leave him alone. "How long will you be staying?"

"At least a few days. I need a vacation. Don't worry, I won't bother your worker," she said with a laugh. "Just broke up with my boyfriend."

That seemed to relax the woman. "Meals here," Marissa said, pointing toward a small dining room. "There's the beach, hiking trails, a hot spring not far from here. If you need a map or need to go back into town, let me know. My nephew Hermon will take you anywhere you need to go."

"Great," AJ said, still shaken. She felt as if the blood was finally rushing back to her head. All the color must have drained from her face when she saw Cyrus. She'd wanted to throw her arms around him, but something in his eyes—

As she signed the registration form, her fingers shook as she realized what it had been that she'd seen in his gaze. Fear. Of her. "I'm so tired," she said, seeing that the woman had noticed her trembling. "I'm not a good traveler, that's why I'm looking forward to a rest."

"It is very restful here," the woman said after running her credit card. "Your room will be open. Joe will have left your key and luggage."

Joe. As she followed the moonlit trail to cottage number one, she looked for Cyrus, but she didn't see him. Her key was on the table inside the cottage, her suitcase in the bedroom where he'd left it. She closed the door and leaned against it, suddenly weak with emotion. *Cyrus.* He was alive!

Tears burned her eyes. Her heart had assured that it was true. Cyrus was alive, but something was terribly wrong. Even the older woman who ran the place was protective of him. He'd looked right at her and hadn't known her. Amnesia? She thought of the scar on his cheek and forearm. There was no doubt that he'd experienced some kind of trauma, physical as well as mental, possibly. Was that why he had no memory of her? What if he had no memory at all? Otherwise, why was he going by Joe?

She had so many questions and no answers. She'd dreamed about finding Cyrus—but never had she imagined it would be like this. And yet she didn't care. Cyrus was alive. That's all that mattered. She pulled out her phone but only stared at it. She couldn't call just yet. Flint would want to fly down. The whole family might want to. Whatever was wrong with Cyrus… She thought of the wary way he had looked at her. The fear she'd glimpsed in his eyes when he'd reached for her suitcase. Her instincts told her that if she moved too fast he might vanish again.

And yet it seemed impossible to be this close to him and not go to him. Taking a breath, she let it out slowly, reminding herself that she'd found him. Whatever was wrong with him… Both Hermon and Marissa knew, whatever it was. Given time she would be able to reach him. She thought again of his reaction to her. Why would he be afraid of her?

HE WOKE, HEART pounding and sweating from the nightmare. It was always the same. Confusion, terror, alone in the dark heaving water. Alone fighting for his life as waves washed over him, dragging him under.

He sat up gasping for breath as he fought his way out of the nightmare—just as he'd fought his way to the surface as the sea pulled him down again and again.

He'd had no idea where he was or what had happened. But he quickly became aware that his clothing was pulling him under. He kicked off his shoes, slipping under the water as he wriggled out of his dinner jacket. Something hit him on his right. He spun on it, ready to fight, knowing it wasn't the first time tonight that he'd fought for his life.

An untethered buoy had bobbed beside him. He grabbed hold of it, wrapping his arms around it as he tried to still his panic. He was stranded in a huge body of water. He could see nothing but darkness and the immense sea all around him. He hugged the buoy and told himself that however he'd gotten here, whatever had happened, he was going to make it. He felt a surge of determination. Someone did this to him. Someone wanted him dead. That alone should have added to the terror. Instead, he was even more determined not to let that person win, promising himself that he would survive in spite of everything. That became his mantra. He would survive. He would survive.

Hours passed. He clung to the buoy that must have come untied in the storm and was now adrift, his life depending on it even as exhaustion made his arms weak. His determination to survive stayed strong.

With daylight came his first land sighting. He knew he was too weak to swim to shore. So he floated, feeling himself being swept along in the waves and tide. That land disappeared and for hours without more land in sight, he'd felt as if he would never set foot on solid ground again.

His arms were numb from clinging to the buoy. He began to question how much longer he could hang on. He'd seen a ship in the distance, but he couldn't let go of the buoy to try to wave his arms for help. Anyway, the ship was way too far away. After a while, he thought he'd only imagined it.

Just as he thought he'd only imagined the island that came into view. At first it had only been a dark line on the horizon. But then he saw the color green. Trees. Palm trees.

Until that moment, he had no idea where he was in the entire world. But the water was warm. Had he gone into colder water, he knew he wouldn't have survived more than a few hours at best.

He hung onto the buoy until he was only yards from shore, afraid that he couldn't trust gauging the distance. To drown so close to shore would be too cruel.

Finally letting go of the buoy that had saved his life, he swam only a few yards when his feet touched bottom. He stumbled and fell, swallowed salt water, coughed and regained his footing. His legs felt boneless. He fell again and ended up crawling up on the beach on his hands and knees.

He sprawled on the sand, completely spent. The sun beat down on him. He closed his eyes and must have passed out, because when he woke, the sun was low in the sky and there was an old woman standing over him. She offered him water. His lips were cracked and dry, his body sunburned.

With her help, he was taken to a small hut where she cleaned his wounds and found him some clothing to wear that was too large for him but soft and clean. He lay down on a woven mat and slept until he woke starving. Following the smell of food, he found the woman working in the larger of the buildings of what had once been a small resort.

"Hurricane damage," she said when she saw him eyeing the destruction around them.

"Where am I?" It was the first words he'd spoken. They came out raspy through his cracked lips.

She put a plate of food in front of him. "You are at what is left of Crystal Cove, my resort."

"An island?" he asked between bites as he shoveled in the food.

She nodded. "Dominica."

When he frowned, she said, "In the Caribbean."

He stared at her for a moment before going back to eating. The Caribbean? He had no idea how he'd gotten here, all he knew was that he was alive—for the moment. The knowledge that someone wanted him dead seemed deep within him but no less real.

"Are you in some kind of trouble?" she asked.

He didn't answer right away, just scraped the last of the food into his mouth before he looked at the row of badly damaged cottages in the small cove. Some were missing walls, others roofs. Most of the debris had been piled up away from the main building as if she planned to eventually burn it.

"I don't know," he finally told her.

She studied him for a long time. He'd never felt more vulnerable. He had no idea what he was doing in the Caribbean, let alone how he'd ended up in the dark ocean. Nor did he know what he was going to do now. He was weak and afraid. If whomever it was he had to fear found him before he could regain his strength...

"I could work for room and board," he said.

She looked past him to the cottages. "Help is hard to find. So many places destroyed by the hurricane last year."

"I can fix the cottages and get them ready for guests," he said. "I would start with the ones that need the least amount of work. If you get me the supplies, I can help you while I get my strength back."

"I have a phone you could use to call..." She motioned to the gold band on his left ring finger.

He stared at what appeared to be a wedding ring. "There's no one," he said shaking his head.

"Do you have a name?"

That was the most frightening and unsettling part, he realized. He had no idea who he was. "Joe," he said.

She nodded, as if suspecting that was as good as she was going to get. "Joe, I'm Marissa. You don't give me any trouble and you can stay in the hut up in the trees where you slept. You work, I'll feed you and give you enough money to buy some clothes and anything else you might need."

He reached out his hand, shook hers and then rose to take his plate and fork to the kitchen—even though the effort was almost more than he could manage. The walk back to his hut took far longer than it should have. He had to stop several times to catch his breath. Once there, he found part of a broken mirror.

Before then, he hadn't seen his own face. Holding up the shard of glass, he'd stared at the man he saw there. It was frightening to look into his gray eyes and see a complete stranger who appeared to have seen better days.

Gently, he touched the healing scar on his cheek. He'd found another one on his forearm and another on his side. There was also a lump on the back of his head that was tender to the touch. He had no idea how he'd gotten the wounds. But they were healing, he was healing.

Each day after that, he worked as long as he could. He was still weak from his ordeal. He ate, he slept, he worked. He avoided the ocean, finding a small creek where he could bathe.

The days passed in a blur. Each morning he woke, hoping today would be the day that he remembered who he was and how he had gotten here. With each new day, he also hoped he would remember whom and what he had to fear.

Most days Marissa was the only person he saw. The first time her nephew Hermon came by, he'd hidden and watched the two conversing on the portico of the main cottage. A few days later when he was working, the nephew came down to meet him. Hermon had asked if the law was looking for him. Joe had no idea but said he didn't think so. That seemed to satisfy the young islander.

Once the first cottage was inhabitable again, he went to work on the second one and then the third. He had no idea what day it was or even what month. His life before ending up in the ocean was a black hole—except for the fear that someone had tried to kill him and would again.

Lately he'd fallen into a routine and had begun to feel safe. He answered to the name Joe and had begun to embrace island life. Hermon had offered to take him into town anytime he wanted to go, but he'd declined, saying he was happy in this little cove. He wore the hand-me-down clothing Marissa had found for him and was thankful just to have clothing. Hermon offered to buy him anything he needed in town, but he didn't need anything more than the construction tools and wood the man delivered every few days.

"I will have guests coming soon," Marissa had said when he'd thanked her for a new shirt, a pair of shorts and a pair of sneakers she'd had Hermon buy for him. "I need you to look respectable or you'll scare away my guests." She'd said it half-jokingly, but one look in the mirror and he could understand her fears. The scar on his cheek was healing, but he still looked rough.

Marissa gave him a pair of scissors and a razor to clean up, but he hadn't used either more than to trim his beard a little. When he looked in the mirror, he felt as if he'd never had a beard or let his hair get this long before and for some reason, it made him feel safe, as if it was his old image he was running from and had to fear.

CHAPTER ELEVEN

When the woman arrived at the reopened cottages that evening, Joe had been working late in one of the structures. He'd heard the vehicle coming but hadn't worried because he'd recognized the sound of the engine as being Hermon's taxi. Marissa's nephew came to visit a few times a week. No one else had come—until last night.

The headlights of Hermon's taxi blinded him at first when he'd stepped out of the shadows of the cottage. Marissa had asked if he would mind helping with the guests' luggage until all the cottages were ready and she could hire staff. He'd been happy to accommodate her since she had been so kind to him. She'd fed him, nursed him back to health, given him a place to stay and paid him. She'd also trusted him.

But he hadn't expected guests so soon. Only one of the cottages was finished. He'd thought Marissa would wait until he had more repairs completed before she allowed guests to stay at the resort.

So as the taxi had pulled in, he'd stepped out to say hello to Hermon. He'd taken a liking to the big islander. With a start, he'd realized that the man wasn't alone. He'd quickly stepped back into the dark shadows along the side of the cottage, that deep-rooted fear suddenly alive inside him.

As the woman stepped out, he'd seen her silhouetted against the night, that slender body, and his heart began to pound. She'd triggered something in him. He'd stood against the building, fighting to breathe through the panic that filled him. For an instant, he'd almost turned and run.

His memory had been a blank slate for weeks and nothing had sparked even an inkling of concern. Until he'd seen her. He told himself that he didn't know her and that it seemed impossible that she'd come here to harm him. And yet his initial response to seeing her had been surprise and alarm.

When Marissa had asked him to take her suitcase to the first cabin, he'd almost not responded. But he'd felt oddly drawn to the woman. Stepping forward from the shadowy darkness, he'd watched the young woman's eyes widen when she'd noticed him, as if she too was surprised to see him.

Looking into her face, he hadn't recognized her. He hadn't been able to put a name to her or a place or even one single memory. But she'd made his heart pound and he'd felt vulnerable and afraid.

This morning, he remembered both of their reactions. Was it possible she hadn't come looking for him? Hadn't known he was here? He'd tried to convince himself that she'd been startled by him, especially given the way he looked. But the woman had appeared shocked to see him, as if…as if she knew him. He'd searched her eyes for a moment, but then quickly dropped his gaze to take her suitcase to cottage one. Once there, he'd quickly checked the luggage tag.

Ashley Jo Somerfield, Houston, Texas.

Ashley Jo. He repeated the name and felt something stir inside him, but quickly slip away. He'd left her cottage to rush to his own hut in the trees. He'd thought again about running, but where would he go, what would he do? He had no money except for the little Marissa had paid him on top of room and board. He wasn't even sure where he was in relation to the rest of the world. Worse, as long as he didn't know who he was, he had no way off the island—at least not legally. And there was that feeling that someone had tried to harm him and would again. Someone he wouldn't even recognize.

Although still feeling off balance, he told himself that if there was any place he was safe, it was here. Well, as safe as he could be anywhere under the circumstances. He knew the area well. The small cove was sheltered on three sides by a mountain covered with dense vegetation. There was only one road in—he could hear a vehicle coming long before it came into sight. The only other way to get to the small resort was by sea but there was no place to land other than the beach. Not that it would stop anyone with a boat. If they knew he was here.

So he'd decided to stay and keep his distance from the woman and yet watch her and wait. He couldn't understand her reaction to him. Or his to her. But if anyone knew who he was and what he was doing here, he thought it might be her.

And if she'd come here to kill him?

Well, then, she'd found him and the next move was hers. He wasn't sure he could trust his instincts when it came to her. He was attracted to her at the same time he feared her. If she knew him and had answers, he desperately wanted them and yet he was terrified of what she might tell him.

And could he believe her?

Trust was something he was in very short supply of right now.

After a restless, sleepless night, AJ rose, showered and headed up to the main cottage for breakfast. She was disappointed to find out that she was the only one eating. On the walk up to the dining room, she'd looked for the man she'd seen last night, but he didn't seem to be around.

She took a seat by the open French doors with a view of the ocean and the beach—and one of the cottages being repaired. She worried that he might have taken off and that she would never find him again. If he'd even been Cyrus.

AJ had almost convinced herself that she'd imagined seeing him last night. In the light of day, she expected the man she'd seen to look nothing like Cyrus. She was thankful she hadn't called Flint. It would be worse to give him false hope after everything he and the family had been through.

Marissa told her about the breakfast menu. "We're still not completely back up to our usual fare."

"That's not a problem," she assured the woman and said she would take coffee and whatever else Marissa had. The way she felt, she wasn't sure she could get a bite down anyway. The woman returned a few minutes later with her coffee.

AJ had just picked up her cup and taken a sip when the man came into view. She slowly put down the cup with trembling fingers as she stared at him. His chest was bare and sun-browned, his strong shoulders looked even stronger as he carried a stack of two-by-fours from the parking area to the cottage he was working on. He wore a pair of shorts that were too large for him and hung low on his slim hips. On his feet were a pair of worn sneakers.

She stared, realizing that she'd never seen Cyrus in anything but jeans, boots and a Western shirt. As she sat there, she kept getting glimpses of his tanned sweat-glistening upper body as he worked. She couldn't take her eyes off him.

"Nice view, isn't it," Marissa said as she put a plate in front of her.

"Beautiful." She dragged her gaze away to see a plate of fresh fruit, a smoked fish spread and homemade bread with a slice of cheese. "You said there's a map of the area?"

The woman nodded. "I could call my nephew to show you the way to the hot spring. You would like that. Very relaxing."

"I can find it. Today though, I think I'll go for a swim and spend some time on the beach."

"Anytime you want to go up to the hot spring, let me know. I'll make you a picnic lunch today and leave it in the refrigerator," Marissa said. "I have to go into town. Is there anything I can get you before I leave?"

"I think I have everything I need," she said and watched Cyrus out of the corner of her eye. She took a bite of her breakfast. "This is delicious."

It wasn't until Marissa went back into the kitchen that she turned her attention from the food on her plate. She knew she had to eat. But her gaze kept going to the man working down at the beach cottage.

SHE'D NEVER BEEN INDECISIVE. But she had no idea what to do next. Had she only imagined the fear in Cyrus's eyes last night? She didn't think so. She finished breakfast, eating what she could. The sun hung over the sea to the east, a huge ball of fire lighting up an already hot day. She walked back to her cottage. Cyrus was at work on cottage number three, two doors down. For a few moments, she stood on the portico of her cottage, letting the salty breeze lift her long hair.

Down the beach, a shirtless Cyrus swung a hammer, his muscled torso flexing with each blow. She watched him, aching with a need to go to him. Whatever had happened, it had changed him so much that she hardly recognized him. Physically, he looked as if he'd been wounded but had survived. But mentally... When she looked into those beautiful gray eyes, she didn't see the Cyrus she knew. The warmth and humor had been replaced with suspicion and a wariness. He was like an animal that had been beaten, she thought with a sob rising in her throat. She yearned to take him in her arms and assure him that everything was going to be all right.

But was it?

He stopped hammering as if feeling her gaze on him and lifted his head to look in her direction. Their eyes locked for a moment before he quickly turned back to his work. What she'd seen in that instant broke her heart. He didn't know her. Worse, he didn't trust her.

But she knew she couldn't put off the call any longer. Going inside her cottage, she rang the sheriff.

Flint answered on the second ring, "AJ? Are you all right?"

"I'm sorry I haven't called sooner," she said. When she'd first arrived in the Caribbean, she'd called him, giving him updates as she went to one island after another. But it was always the same news. No sign of Cyrus. She hadn't wanted to keep giving him that depressing news any more than she could keep saying it herself.

"What is it?" He must have heard something in her voice.

She swallowed. "I found Cyrus."

He made a choked sound. "Is he…?"

"He's alive, but—"

"But?"

She told him about seeing him come out of the dark and again this morning. "He looked right at me and didn't recognize me. He's going by the name Joe. He doesn't appear to either know who he is or he's hiding out here."

"But you talked to him."

"Not really. He seems…scared. When he saw me, his reaction was more wary and suspicious than anything else. I'm afraid if I move too fast he might run."

"I'm coming down there."

"I don't think that's a good idea," she said quickly. "He's working here at a very small and secluded resort on the island. I think he needs time."

Flint swore. "But he's alive."

"He is. He looks good, different. Whatever happened to him, going overboard, somehow surviving in the ocean against all odds…it did something to him. Let me try to gain his confidence."

"But if he knew he had a family back in Montana—"

"I'm not sure he could handle that right now. He's skittish. I'm afraid he'll bolt. Flint, right now, he's like an animal that's been beaten."

The sheriff cursed, sounding close to tears. She knew the feeling.

"All right. But I'm going to have to tell the others."

"It's best that you don't know where I am. I know Lillie. Nothing could keep her from coming down here."

"I know you're right, but I want nothing more than to be on the next plane down there. What if he is more spooked than you think and takes off?"

She'd worried about that after his initial reaction to seeing her. A part of her had worried that he'd be gone this morning when she got up. "He's broke, has no identification, he can't go far."

"I'm going to trust your judgment. All your instincts told you that he was alive. You're the one who went looking for him and found him. It should have been me."

"You have a wife and new baby, a job," AJ said. "I had to do this, so even if you had come down here, I would have been here, as well."

"Thank God, AJ, that you did. Otherwise, we would have gone on believing he was dead. Now I have to trust that you know what is best for Cyrus."

Did she? She wasn't a doctor—not even close. She had no

idea how to deal with this kind of possible traumatic brain injury. But she had to try.

"Take care of yourself," Flint said to her.

"I'm going to bring him home. I promise," she said, her voice breaking. "He's going to need a passport."

"Could you send a photo? I believe you that it's him, but—"

"I'll try. I know you need to see him to believe it. I understand."

AFTER FLINT DISCONNECTED, he took a moment to pull himself together. He was overwhelmed with relief and choked up with worry. *Cyrus was alive.* But the man AJ described was hurt and confused with no memory. What had happened to him from the last time he'd seen him? Something. He had to agree with AJ, something was definitely wrong with all of this. The man he'd known wouldn't have married Juliette—not even drunk. Which meant, whatever had happened to Cyrus had started in Denver when he met Juliette.

He picked up the phone and called his sister. Lillie answered on the third ring sounding harried. He worried about her because Maggie had told him that she was pregnant again. Having a toddler who kept her on her toes was enough without everything else that had been happening.

"What's happened now?" she said as if hearing something in his voice.

"AJ just called." He swallowed the lump in his throat. "She found Cyrus."

Lillie screamed. "He's alive?"

Tears filled his eyes. He made a swipe at them. "He is. He needs to recuperate a little before he can come home."

"Recuperate?"

"He apparently got pretty beat up before ending up on a beach down there."

"Beat up?"

"He's going to be his old self but it could be a week or two before he comes home."

"Is there something you aren't telling me?"

He'd made the decision not to tell Lillie everything because he knew his sister. If he didn't want everyone knowing about Cyrus's mental state, then he had to keep it from her.

"Have you told Juliette?" she asked. "Oh, please let me."

"I'm about to call her."

His sister pretended to pout. "This means she can't demand part of the ranch, right?"

"Not as Cyrus's widow." But as his wife, if she were to divorce him… No reason to bring that up now.

"I thought you could let the rest of the family know." He got off the line, knowing that his phone would be ringing off the hook soon with more questions. He'd gotten off easy with Lillie but only because she hadn't had time to think about it.

He placed the call to Juliette.

WHEN JULIETTE SAW that the sheriff was calling she smiled to herself. Maybe he was going to finally make her an offer. She was at the point that she would take any reasonable amount.

"Hello?"

"Juliette, it's Flint."

As if she couldn't see that. "Yes, Flint?" All she could think about was getting out of this town. It had snowed every day until she thought she would lose her mind.

"I just got a call. Cyrus is alive."

She couldn't help but laugh. "That's not funny."

"I'm serious. He apparently survived. AJ found him."

AJ? She cursed under her breath. Hadn't she known the bitch was going to be trouble? "How is that possible? They said he couldn't have survived after the first twenty-four hours."

"Clearly, you didn't know my brother very well."

This wasn't happening. He couldn't have survived. Flint was lying. She stood stock-still, heart racing. But what would be the point of lying? It had to be true. Cyrus was alive? She glanced toward the door, expecting the police to bust it down any moment.

If it was true… Cyrus would have talked. He would have confided in his brother the sheriff. He would have yelled bloody murder.

So why hadn't he? Was he waiting until he got back to Montana?

Her gaze swept the room, lighting on her suitcase. Run! It wouldn't be the first time she'd had to. Still she hesitated, unable to shake the feeling that Cyrus's brother the sheriff wasn't telling her everything.

"Juliette? You still there?"

"If true, why haven't we heard from him?" she demanded.

"He's been recuperating."

"All these weeks? He must not be in very good shape."

"AJ said he's in great shape. Apparently, there's a reason he hasn't contacted you."

She felt as if she'd been slapped. "Or contacted you."

"I thought you'd want to know."

"Where is he?" she asked quickly before he could hang up. "I want to talk to my husband."

"He doesn't want to talk to you."

"You can't keep him from me. He's my *husband*."

"I'm not. It's my brother's choice." He disconnected.

Juliette screamed and threw her phone across the room. She balled her hands into fists. It was some kind of trick. A way to get her to take less money…or confess.

No, she thought with a curse. The sheriff was too smart to try something like that. Somehow Cyrus had survived. And if he really didn't want to see her…

She rushed across the room to pick up her phone and hurriedly tapped in the number. "You messed up big-time," she spat into the phone when he answered. "He's alive."

"Who's alive?"

"Who do you think? Cyrus Cahill."

"That's impossible."

"That's what I said, but I just got a call from the sheriff. He swears that Cyrus survived."

"Where has he been all this time?"

"I have no idea. The sheriff said Cyrus didn't want to talk to me, that he's recuperating somewhere down there in the Caribbean. I don't think I have to tell you what this means. You have to find him."

"How would I do that?"

"The same way his girlfriend did. You're the one with the connections. All you have to do is track a woman named AJ Somerfield. Blonde, blue-eyed, sweet-looking rich girl. She's been down there asking questions. Just follow the trail she's left and you'll find Cyrus before he gets back to the States and goes to the authorities and takes us both down."

"Wouldn't we be better to cut our losses and end this now?"

"No. It changes things, yes. But I think I can get the family to pony up just to get rid of me. We need this money."

He sighed. "I warned you against this one."

"This isn't the time for that."

"He's going to blow the whistle on us."

Juliette shook her head, eyes narrowing as she thought it through. "No, if he was going to do that, he would have done it by now. I suspect he isn't in as good of shape as the family wants me to believe. Find him. You'll have to take care of both of them."

He swore. "This going to cost you."

She sighed. "It always does."

CHAPTER TWELVE

Ely was buried in the plot next to his wife, Mary, on a cold day in late February. The whole county turned out. Toward the end, before the first shovel of dirt was thrown onto the casket, the sun came out of the clouds and shone down on them.

Flint had been holding it together until then. He'd turned to his wife, Maggie, and she'd hugged him tightly. They were a family, raw with grief and worry. They'd lost so much. They couldn't lose any more. Cyrus had to get well and come home.

The day of the funeral he realized the mistake he'd made. He'd been so filled with grief over his father's death and grief and worry over Cyrus, that he hadn't been doing his job. With the cold keeping most people inside, there'd been little to require his attention as sheriff. His deputies had been able to handle the occasional bar fight or domestic dispute.

Flint realized he hadn't been thinking clearly. Juliette. Hadn't he planned to find everything he could about her? They needed to know who they were dealing with. He had a pretty good idea, given her demands for Cyrus's part of the ranch, but as a sheriff he should have had that information by now.

He got on his computer and after a few minutes let out a curse. He'd thought the woman was a gold digger and that she'd somehow trapped Cyrus into marrying her, but he'd had no idea just who Juliette really was until he saw her track record.

Cyrus wasn't her first husband—far from it. The woman had been married five other times. While her first husband was still alive, four out of the other five husbands had died.

Letting out a curse, he began to investigate further. When he made a call to the detective in charge of her last husband's death, he couldn't believe what he was being told. Juliette was under investigation and not just in that state but in Florida, as well.

"We believe she's a black widow," the detective told him. "She marries them and then they die under suspicious circumstances. I suspect you wouldn't be calling unless she's struck again."

"As a matter of fact, she married my brother on a Caribbean cruise. He went overboard but fortunately survived."

"He's damned lucky. A Caribbean cruise, huh? That's a new one. Nothing is going to stop this woman unless we can get her behind bars and even then…"

"How close are you to an arrest?"

"Soon, but maybe not soon enough for your brother. One of the husbands we believed she killed lived for a few hours until someone pulled the plug on him at the hospital at the same time there was a power failure. By the time the auxiliary power came on, he was dead and she was a wealthy widow."

"So it's about the money."

"The way she goes through it, yes, and no. I think she likes the game. But I can tell you right now, she is going to need a lot of money for an attorney and soon.

"That's if she doesn't skip the country before we can get all our ducks in a row. Florida is investigating and possibly close to filing charges, as well. She could be more desperate than usual."

Flint had hung up in shock. He picked up his phone and called the detective in charge of her husband's death in Florida, hoping they would be putting her behind bars even sooner.

"I'm calling about Juliette Carrington," he told the detective after telling him who he was and why he was calling.

"What'd she do now?"

"I understand she is being investigated in the possible murder of her husband?"

"Not just here but in the death of her previous husband, as well," the detective said. "Her MO is to marry men with money, become a widow and move on to the next one. She's gotten away with it so far. If your brother can testify, we might be able to put this woman away where she belongs."

"Unfortunately, my brother had a head injury after he went overboard on a Caribbean cruise during their short marriage. At this point, he has no memory of what happened."

"Too bad. If he should remember..."

"You will definitely be hearing from me. And if you do file charges against her, I can tell you where to find her."

His brother Deputy Tucker Cahill stuck his head in the door.

Flint motioned him on into the office. "I'll get back to you." He hung up and said to Tucker, "Close the door. You aren't going to believe this."

"More news about Cyrus?" Tuck asked, sounding worried as he closed the door and took a seat.

He shook his head. "News about his *wife*. I should have done some research on her to begin with so we'd know what we're dealing with long before this. Cyrus married a black widow."

"A what?"

"Juliette has been married six times and all of her husbands but her first one and our brother have died. It's a miracle that Cyrus survived. Anyway, she's being investigated in two states."

"What are you saying? That she killed her other husbands?"

Flint just looked at his brother. "Cyrus would have been

number five to make her a widow." He let out an oath. "Only this time, the husband didn't die. Unfortunately unless he gets his memory back..."

"So what will she do now?" Tucker asked.

He looked at his brother, worried. "If Cyrus can remember what happened, she'll be going to prison."

"And if he can't?"

"The thing is, she doesn't know he can't remember at this point but I'm betting she's suspicious. If Cyrus remembered what happened and told authorities, she would be on her way to jail," Flint said, growing more anxious.

"So she thinks she's safe."

"Unless he remembers. Which means his life is in danger still. If she isn't working alone..."

He picked up his cell phone and called AJ. She answered on the second ring. "Can you talk?"

"I'm on the beach, what's wrong?"

He told her what he'd found out.

"I told you something was wrong," AJ said when he'd finished. "Five other marriages?"

"Two under investigation in two states. They're hoping Cyrus remembers so he can help them put her away."

"So you think she targeted him."

"Don't you?" Flint asked.

"But that still doesn't explain why Cyrus married her."

"No, I guess we won't know that until he remembers."

"*If* he remembers," she said.

"I'm not trying to rush you, but if Juliette didn't act alone, whoever tried to kill Cyrus might try again before he reaches the States. That means you're in danger, as well."

AJ WALKED THE BEACH, swam, sat in the shade and pretended to read as each day passed since Flint's phone call. As anxious as she was after getting the news from Flint, she hadn't approached Cyrus. Like her, he'd kept to himself. But with each day, she saw him getting stronger. He also seemed less anxious when she was around. He would nod and she would nod back. She left him to his work.

A German couple arrived one evening and moved into the cottage next door. Cyrus had finished cottage number three and moved on down the beach to the fourth one.

She'd wondered where he stayed until one morning she saw him coming out of a small hut back up the mountainside in the dense vegetation. He'd started when he'd seen her. She'd nodded and kept walking, but she'd felt his gaze on her. It warmed her, making her want to smile and cry at the same time.

That night she'd called Flint. He and the rest of the family were anxious about Cyrus. She pleaded with him to have patience, knowing that he could find out where she was staying—and find his brother.

"He's starting to trust me."

"You've talked to him?"

"Flint—"

"AJ, I appreciate what you've done more than you can ever know. But I'm worried about you both. Juliette's freedom is riding on Cyrus never being able to testify against her. Maybe if you told him who he was..."

"It's not that simple. He's scared. If we're right, then someone threw him off that ship and if all he remembers is the fear and not who tried to kill him..."

"Of course he's scared. Who wouldn't be terrified to find themselves floating alone in the ocean, injured. Let alone, as you said, if he remembers being thrown overboard. But even if that is the case, it isn't enough to put Juliette away."

"How could Juliette do that to him?" AJ thought that if she

were still in Montana knowing what she did now, she would rip every strand of hair out of the blonde's head.

"She thought Cyrus had money. Apparently she needs cash. Her lawyer wants to settle. She's offering an annulment as long as she gets a large settlement."

AJ couldn't believe the gall of the woman. "She really thinks she can get away with this."

"She has numerous times before," the sheriff said. "But what bothers me is how she was able to talk him into marrying her."

That bothered her, as well. She refused to believe he'd done it willingly. "I have more questions than you do, believe me. It's unbearable being this close to him and not being able to… help him. I'm making progress though. Just give me a little more time."

"Juliette is beside herself. She wants proof that he's alive."

"I'm sure she does. Hold her off a little longer, please. I'll try to get a photo. I just can't let him catch me doing it."

FLINT FINALLY RECEIVED copies of the surveillance videos from the ship after getting a warrant through a local judge he knew. He called Tucker in. "I'm going to need help going through these." He told him what he was looking for. "If Juliette is true to form, then she planned to marry Cyrus and then get rid of him. She would have needed help. If we can find her on any of these videos with another man…"

They began the long process and hadn't gotten far when the rest of the family showed up wanting to help.

"If there are more of us looking, it won't take as much time," Lillie said.

Flint agreed. He felt the clock ticking. If Juliette had orchestrated Cyrus's death, then they needed proof. But not just that. Now that she knew her so-called husband was still alive, would she make another attempt on his life? She had nearly succeeded before. Flint didn't doubt that she would try again.

He couldn't shake the feeling that Cyrus might not make it out of the islands. If Juliette could get rid of him, then they would never be able to prove that he'd survived from going overboard. Because he was just as sure that AJ wouldn't make it back alive, either, and she was the only one who'd seen Cyrus and could prove that he'd survived.

Flint worried about them both. Too much was riding on this. He'd seen the greed in Juliette's eyes and the emptiness that came from lack of a soul. He'd met few killers, but those he had definitely had that same look.

The family brought laptops and they settled in to the Cahill ranch house to begin going through the videos. It was painstaking work. There was always the chance that Juliette had met her coconspirator or coconspirators behind closed doors and they wouldn't find any proof. It was a large ship. Maybe there wasn't even a chance of catching them in passing—let alone with their heads together. But Flint knew they had to try.

If they could find out who Juliette was working with, then maybe they could stop whatever the woman had planned now. Flint had no doubt that Juliette hadn't given up. If anything, the last time he saw her, she was more anxious than ever to profit from this marriage at sea.

As she walked down the beach, AJ saw Cyrus come out of the cottage he'd been working on. He stopped on the small portico and leaned against the railing in the afternoon sun.

She smiled at him and for the first time, he smiled back. Tears welled in her eyes. She had to look away and keep walking, her heart in her throat. All the way down the beach, her pulse pounded. She tried to breathe. That smile—it had been the old Cyrus.

Continuing to walk, she thought about what Flint had told her. She could feel time running out. Was someone coming to finish the job? She knew she had to make more progress with Cyrus and soon.

On the way back she heard hammering inside the cottage and looked around. The German couple was further down the beach sunning by the water's edge. She slowed, warning herself to be careful as she climbed the steps, the hammering growing louder.

Cyrus was bent over nailing in a two-by-four to a stud. As if sensing her, he suddenly stopped and turned, clearly startled.

"Sorry, I was just curious," she said quickly and looked from those gray eyes to the wall he'd replaced. "Looks like it's coming along. I noticed that this cottage is larger than the others. More work, huh."

She let her gaze go back to him and smiled. "I don't mean to stop you." She started to turn away, when he said, "How was your walk, Ashley Jo?"

"Long." So he'd made a point of learning her name. "My friends call me AJ."

"Is that what we are now? Friends?"

She laughed and saw his expression change. Had he recognized her laugh? "Would that be so awful?"

His gaze never left her face. He seemed to be waiting for her to say more. She chose her words carefully. "The German couple is having a good time. I suppose it's odd, me being here alone, huh." She glanced out at the Germans. Their laughter reached them, sounding so sweet, so poignant.

"I did wonder," he said.

She turned back to meet his gaze and didn't want to lie to him. "I had hoped my friend would show up but..." She shrugged.

"His loss."

She smiled, titling her head. "What makes you think it was a man?"

He laughed and picked up his hammer again.

"It was nice visiting with you," she said and turned to leave.

He watched her go, trying to understand why the woman made him feel the way he did. When she'd laughed...and the way she'd smiled and tilted her head... It was almost as if... He shook his head frustrated at his inability to remember. He was haunted day and night, but what was it he had to fear? That was just it, he couldn't remember and yet all his instincts told him he wasn't safe. That fear had grown when the woman had arrived.

But as the days slid languidly by, he'd worked and waited, becoming more convinced he wasn't in any danger from the woman. And yet, he felt connected to her in some strange way. It wasn't that he remembered her, at least not consciously. But there was something there he couldn't put his finger on and it was driving him crazy.

What was also worrisome was that she seemed just as interested in him. What if Ashley Jo's interest in him had nothing to do with his fear of being in danger? Or was that just wishful thinking?

AJ. She'd told him to call her AJ. He pounded a nail into the wall he was reconstructing. He liked her smile. When she'd stopped by the cottage he was working on, he'd picked up no threat—just the opposite. Maybe Marissa was right and the woman was lonely. She'd come here alone, saying she'd thought her friend might show up. He'd assumed her friend would be male. He'd noticed that, unlike him, she wasn't wearing a wedding ring.

Still, he planned to keep his distance. He felt as if he was waiting for the other shoe to drop. He'd found a fishing knife in the shack where he lived. He kept it by his bed, unable to shake the feeling that someone would be coming for him. It was just a matter of time until they found him. If they hadn't already.

He stepped to the doorway to get a breath of air and felt the young woman's gaze on him. She'd stopped a few yards from the cottage and had turned to look back.

"I forgot to ask you," he called to her. "How did you like the waterfall?"

"It was beautiful. The water was so warm. Have you been there?"

He shook his head. He and water didn't exactly mix anymore, other than a quick bath in the creek.

She turned her face up to the sun, as if enjoying its heat. As if pretending that a few moments before she hadn't been staring at him.

He studied her, trying to understand what it was about her that pulled him to her like gravity. She was pretty, no doubt about that, but not a raving beauty. Instead, her beauty seemed to come from within and radiate outward.

It made him wonder why he still worried he might have something to fear from her. He realized that the only way that could be true was if he'd seen her before. Maybe even knew her. Why else would her laugh and the way she tilted her head seem…familiar?

He thought about her initial reaction to him the night she'd arrived. His head hurt thinking about it because unless he confronted her… Maybe it was just his imagination—or his paranoia. She was probably just a pretty young woman alone on a beautiful island and lonely just as Marissa thought.

And yet, as he turned from the doorway and went back to work, he couldn't stop himself from trying to remember. Not just the past, but her. If she was in his past, he needed to know how and why. He turned the gold band on his ring finger. Was he married? It appeared so. But to whom? To her?

But as hard as he tried to remember, there was nothing before he'd found himself in the middle of the ocean. His past was a deep, dark hole filled with frightening images and confusing thoughts. That had been the worst part, realizing he had no memory. He didn't even know how old he was.

He looked down at the gold band on the ring finger of his left hand again. When he'd landed on the island there hadn't been any difference between the skin color under the ring and his finger. Now when he pulled it off, there was a pale strip of skin under his tanned finger. Did that mean the ring hadn't been there very long before he'd ended up in the sea?

And if he was married, why did he have no memory of a wife or a marriage. That haunted him. How could he forget someone he'd loved so much that he'd married them?

Cursing at himself for letting his thoughts circle again, he tried to bury himself in his work. But he couldn't forget Ashley Jo Somerfield. If she had indeed come here to harm him, then she was certainly taking her time. Or maybe she was waiting for someone. He kept thinking about her startled expression the night they'd first seen each other. She'd looked shocked but then...relieved?

It struck him that if AJ knew him, then she had probably been looking for him. Why hadn't he thought of that before?

When Hermon stopped by to take the German tourists into town, Joe asked him for a favor.

"Could you see if anyone has been asking around about me in town?"

Hermon looked worried. "The woman who is staying here now? She asked about a man who was missing from a cruise ship."

"Ashley Jo did?"

Hermon nodded, looking as if he wanted to say more. "I can see if anyone else has been asking around town, okay?" He said he would be back soon if he had any news.

A man who was missing from a cruise ship? If she thought

it was him, then why hadn't she said anything? There was no doubt that Ashley Jo Somerfield had been watching him. He'd caught her numerous times. She always quickly looked away, but it seemed she was as curious about him as he was about her. Marissa had mentioned that AJ had asked about him.

"What did she ask?" He'd tried to sound nonchalant but knew he'd failed.

"She wanted to know your name. I told her Joe." She'd shrugged.

"That was it?"

"I got the impression that she's interested in you. I told her to leave you alone because you had work to do." The old woman had smiled then. "But I've seen her watching you. Just don't let it interfere with your work. I get calls every day from anxious guests so I need those cottages finished."

Marissa thought the woman had a crush on him.

"I won't," he'd promised and smiled even as his heart pounded against his ribs. Was that all it was? Simple attraction?

He might have believed that if he hadn't seen her take his photo.

CHAPTER THIRTEEN

AJ MANAGED TO get a photo of Cyrus, but feared he might have seen her do it. She'd been so careful, knowing that she couldn't get caught taking the photo on her phone and yet having no other choice but to take a quick shot. Which meant it was from a distance and not a full-on view. But as she checked what she'd captured, she knew that Flint wouldn't have any trouble recognizing his brother.

She stared at the photo, feeling sad to think what Cyrus must have gone through—would still have to go through to get back to the life he'd left. If that's what he wanted.

What haunted her was what had happened in Denver. How had Juliette gotten Cyrus to fall for her? AJ groaned at the thought of the woman. Yes, she was beautiful and no doubt seductive given the number of husbands she'd had. But would Cyrus have fallen for that? An impulsive, heat-of-the-moment decision to not only take a Caribbean cruise, but also get married.

She'd heard Juliette's version. Unfortunately, they might never know Cyrus's. Maybe when he saw his wife, his memory would return. And then what? Even if Cyrus had fallen for her head over heels at first sight, he couldn't stay with a black widow.

AJ shook herself mentally. No way would Cyrus stay with the woman who they all believed was responsible for him going overboard and almost dying. Unless he had somehow fallen off the ship accidentally. She thought of the wedding photo. Cyrus had looked drunk. Or drugged, she thought remembering that the toxicology screen had shown drugs in his system the night he'd gone overboard.

He wouldn't have taken any drugs, she was sure. But she wouldn't put it past Juliette to drug her husband and push him overboard.

Unless Cyrus remembered though it might always remain a mystery. She suspected that only Juliette knew what had happened on the ship that night.

The knock at the door startled her. She quickly put her phone away and answered the door, surprised to find Cyrus standing there. He wore a short-sleeved unbuttoned shirt and too-large shorts that hung from his hips. His skin was so beautifully browned and covered with a fine mist of sweat.

"Just wanted you to know that I'll be working right next door today to change out some fixtures," he said. "It might get pretty noisy."

"It's fine. I'm going down to the beach."

He nodded. "Nice day for it." Those gray eyes locked with hers for a few breathless moments. She fought the urge to cup his strong jaw with her hand, wanting to touch that bristled beard. Wanting to run her thumb pad over his lips, lips she'd longed to kiss.

"Well, you have a good day," he said and started to turn away.

"Thank you, Cy—Joe."

He paused for a moment, studying her and then with a nod, left.

She stood in the doorway watching him go, feeling her heart break. Closing the door, she realized she'd been holding her phone all this time. Cyrus hadn't seen her take the photo, had he? She hurriedly sent the photo to Flint, telling herself there was nothing she could do if Cyrus had. But would he be scared enough that he might run?

"I THINK I have something." Lillie's voice sounded tired, but when she looked up, her eyes shone.

The family had all been on their laptop computers. Now they moved to hers where she'd been reviewing the surveillance videos from the ship. On the screen, standing back out of the way of people moving along one of the upper decks, were a man and a woman.

"It's definitely Juliette," Flint said as Lillie got up to stretch and let him have her computer. He sat down and enlarged the shot.

"She's handing him something," Tucker said from behind him.

"Possibly," the sheriff agreed. "But they do seem to know each other even though they are avoiding eye contact."

"Maybe they don't know where Cyrus is and are being careful," Lillie suggested.

"More than likely they're trying to avoid the surveillance camera," Hawk said. "From what I can see, the cameras are all over the ship. Especially in the hallways, so that would keep them from meeting in one of the rooms. They would be forced to meet on deck."

"Whether she is handing him something or not, I want to know who that man is," Flint said. He printed out the photo of the two of them after cropping it. Then enlarged the man's photo as much as he could and printed that along with sending it out over the wire. "If he's a known criminal, we might get a hit. I'll also send it to the cruise ship line to see if any crew recognizes him and can match him with the name of a guest. It's a long shot."

"Maybe we'll get lucky," Tucker said.

Flint said nothing as they went back to work. It was late and he knew they couldn't all keep going. But if they could find another instance of the two of them in the same shot…

The response to his inquiry was so fast that they all looked at each other for a moment before he clicked on the email.

"Did you get an ID on him?" Darby asked.

Flint rubbed a hand over his neck and let out the breath he'd been holding. "He's an ex-cop. Otis Claremont out of Arizona."

"Didn't Juliette have a husband in Arizona?" Tucker asked.

"She did," the sheriff said. "I'm betting Otis Claremont was one of the former cops investigating the death of her husband."

"Blackmail?" Lillie asked.

"Or kindred souls," Flint said. "It looks more like the cop was onto her and decided to join forces. Clearly it's been more lucrative than law enforcement. Juliette has made money on every marriage except her first. But she's also spent it like it was water through her fingers."

HERMON FOUND HIM working in the last cottage several days later. The moment he saw the islander's face, he knew the news wouldn't be good. He waited, bracing himself, worrying that he might have to leave here not knowing where he would go or what he would do. He'd come to feel safe here, even though he had no idea what he had to fear.

But also, his work here was almost done. He thought Marissa would keep him on to maintain the cottages and grounds, but he hadn't talked to her about it. In the back of his mind, he'd always known that he couldn't stay here forever.

"So far the only person who was asking around was the same

woman who was asking on other islands," Hermon said, pulling him aside and keeping his voice down. "Ashley Jo Somerfield."

So no one else. Yet. "Did she mention the name of the man she was looking for? She told me there was a man who was supposed to meet her here on the island, but he didn't show up."

Hermon studied him for a moment before shaking his head. "No name. She was showing around a photo of you."

He felt his heart bump against his ribs. She had a photo of him. So she definitely knew him. Or someone had paid her to find him.

"Well, she's found me."

"That's what I was thinking," Hermon said. "You have no idea why she was looking for you?"

He patted his new friend on the shoulder and smiled. "Not to worry. I can take care of myself." He was reminded of the shock of finding himself in the dark sea, injured, drowning. He remembered the waves, the darkness, the feeling of being in terrible trouble and completely alone. Perhaps he couldn't take care of himself, after all.

"Women can be dangerous," Hermon said. "The more beautiful, the more dangerous. But this one? I think not."

He laughed, not sure about that. He'd thought about nothing else but AJ since he'd first seen her and felt something. Something he couldn't put his finger on nor explain. And there was always her reaction to him when she'd first seen him. If she had been looking for him, then it was no wonder she'd looked shocked and then relieved. She'd found him. So what was she waiting for?

FLINT HEARD THE text ping on his phone. He was having trouble focusing. They'd been at this for hours. His eyes hurt along with the rest of his body. He wasn't sure how many more surveillance videos he could look at, plus it was almost dawn. They all needed rest. He'd insisted Trask take Lillie home. He worried with his sister pregnant. Mariah had caught a ride with them earlier since she too was pregnant again, insisting Darby stay and help.

Maggie was home with the baby, even though she'd dropped by last night to bring the food Billie Dee had sent over. Leave it to Billie Dee not to let them starve.

Flint pulled out his phone, glad for the diversion for a moment. A photo came up on his screen. He let out a cry and couldn't hold back the tears.

It was Cyrus—just as AJ had said. He hadn't doubted her, but seeing him with his own eyes, he was swamped with relief. He'd been so sure that Cyrus was lost to them.

His brothers circled around him to see what was wrong and immediately a cheer went up.

"It's him!" Hawk cried. "It's really him!"

Darby started laughing and soon they were all crying though trying hard to hold back the tears.

"I have to send it to Lillie," Flint said and shared it, knowing what it would mean to her.

After that, they all went back to work on their laptops, even more energized and determined to get to the truth. But soon, Flint had to shower and get ready for work. He'd taken off a few days to go through the surveillance videos. But now he had to get back to his job. His brothers were going to keep looking through the videos, but he feared that the one frame of Juliette with the former cop might be the best shot they got.

But at work at the sheriff's department, Flint looked again at the photo of his brother on his phone and reminded himself that Cyrus hadn't recognized AJ or seemed to have any memory of his life before going overboard. AJ thought his memory might return in time. But what if it never did?

Flint couldn't let himself think that. Before tackling the paperwork on his desk that had stacked up in his absence, he got a call from his sister.

"It's really him?"

"It is. He looks pretty scruffy. Seems he's become a beach bum," he joked. "It's going to be all right," he said, his voice cracking. "I hope it wasn't too much of a shock seeing him."

"Are you kidding? I sent the photo to Juliette."

He winced. He wasn't sure that had been a good idea. But he knew his sister. She thought just because Cyrus was alive they might be able to get rid of Juliette. He could hear a child crying in the background. "I have to go. I've missed enough work lately. I'll talk to you later." He disconnected and looked up to find Juliette standing in his doorway. From the expression on her face, she wasn't happy. How long had she been just outside his office? Had she overheard his conversation with Lillie? Had she already gotten the photo?

He motioned her in. She closed the door behind her but didn't take the seat he offered her. Instead, she stood over his desk, anger making her Botox-perfect features masklike.

"I want to know where my husband is," she demanded.

"I'm sorry," he said. "Didn't you already file his death certificate?"

She let out a snort. "So all this has just been a stall tactic? He really isn't alive." She sounded relieved. "You were just being overly cruel."

"No, he's alive."

She scoffed. "I need to know that for myself. If it's true, then I demand that you tell me where he is so I can talk to him." Just then, her phone emitted a few musical notes no doubt to let her know a text was coming in.

She looked from him to her purse, and then slowly reached into her bag. She stared down at her purse for a moment in confusion before pulling out her phone.

He watched her face. The blue eyes widened as she stared down at the photo of Cyrus that Lillie had sent her. She took a breath and let it out slowly before she swallowed and finally glanced up at him.

"I'm sure you already know about this photo your sister sent me. It's not a very good photo." She looked at her phone again. "Why was it taken so far away? That's the best AJ could do?" There was suspicion in her tone. "What is it you aren't telling me, Sheriff?"

"It's my brother and once he's back here, we'll sort this whole thing out."

"Sort this whole thing out? Cyrus and I are married. I'm his wife and…"

She looked as if she wanted to stomp her foot in anger and frustration. "You can't keep him from me." That wasn't true and they both knew it. At least he hoped it wasn't true. She looked again at the photo on her phone. "I don't believe this man is my husband."

"Guess we'll see when he gets back to Montana."

"And when will that be?"

"Well, it's a bit difficult for him to come home since you were so quick to file his death certificate. He doesn't have his wallet or passport."

She licked her lips, seeming deep in thought before she said, "I have his passport. He didn't have it on him when he…" She reached into her purse and brought it out, but then merely held it as if having second thoughts. "I'll be happy to get this to Cyrus when you tell me where he is. If I have to, I will get my attorney to—"

"You would be wasting your money since I don't know where he is."

Juliette stared at him. "So the only person who knows is AJ

and you're all right with that?" When he said nothing, she added angrily, "I'm his wife."

"So it seems, but AJ spent her money and her time to look for your…husband because she believed he was the kind of man who could survive just about anything. I guess we're going to have to do this her way, don't you think?"

The woman appeared to be trying to contain her fury. She rose to her full height, fire in those blue eyes. "Well, she can't get him back without this," she snapped, holding up the passport. "When I know where he is, I'll be happy to send his passport so he can come home."

"That is thoughtful of you," Flint said. "But I've already filed for a new one for him and put a rush on it. One of the joys of being in law enforcement. So he doesn't really need his old passport anymore. The new papers are on their way to the police commissioner in St. Augusta. AJ and Cyrus will be picking them up there." It was a bluff, but Cyrus wasn't coming home soon anyway. "I'll let you know when he gets here since the FBI will be wanting to talk to you both. They're as anxious for him to get back here as you are."

She threw the passport down on his desk and stormed out. He waited until he was sure she was gone before he picked it up and called AJ. Cyrus would be able to come home without waiting for the new paperwork Flint had applied for. Even he couldn't make bureaucracy move fast.

But first AJ had to tell Cyrus that he had a home—and family—waiting for him. The fear was that he wouldn't care because all of that had been stripped from his memory forever.

CHAPTER FOURTEEN

"Enjoy your swim?"

AJ jumped. She hadn't seen Cyrus standing in the shadows of cottage number four and the one closest to the beach as she returned from her walk.

"Sorry, didn't mean to scare you," he said as he stepped out of a shadow. He'd changed clothes from earlier and now wore a short-sleeved white shirt and khakis. If it was possible, he looked more handsome, more sexy, even more male. His dark hair was still damp from his bath and she caught the sweet scent of soap as he closed the distance between them.

Her heart took off at a gallop. She felt sixteen and tongue-tied, so she merely smiled and nodded as she slowed her pace. He fell in beside her as the moon rimmed the horizon over the ocean. A breeze stirred the palm fronds and ruffled her hair.

She stopped to brush it from her eyes. Before she could, he reached over, his work-roughened fingertips grazing her cheek. A shiver ran the full length of her. She slowly raised her gaze to meet his gray eyes, remembering the dream she'd had. Heat rushed to her center, her legs weak under her.

What she saw in his eyes though confused her, which was why she never saw the kiss coming. One minute he was looking at her, searching her gaze as if he thought if he looked deep enough in her eyes he could see her soul.

The next he'd slid his hand around the back of her hairline and drew her into the kiss.

For months, she'd been waiting for him to kiss her. To make that first move past just friends to something more. And now, out of the blue, he was kissing her. It came as such a surprise, she didn't react at first.

It ended as quickly as it had begun.

She felt dazed, off balance, disoriented. She hadn't realized that she'd leaned into him, into the kiss, until he pulled back and she had to get her feet under her. But before she could, he grabbed the front of her beach cover and pulled her over to the side of the dark cottage, pinning her against the wall in the ebony shadows.

"Who are you?" he demanded, his voice sounding hoarse as if filled with emotion. She stared at him, breathless and wide-eyed. He still had a handful of her beach cover in his big fist. He gave it and her a little shake. "Why were you asking around town about me?" She opened her mouth, but nothing came out. "And don't lie to me."

Her voice sounded strained and small when she finally found the words. "It's true. I have been looking for you."

"Why?" he demanded, keeping her pressed against the wall, his body blocking her escape.

"I'm a friend of your family."

He blinked and loosened his hold on her a little. *"My family?"*

She nodded. "Your family in Montana." She could see the suspicion, the fear. "I know you're having trouble with your memory. I'm not sure how much you remember about falling overboard from the cruise ship."

Shaking his head, he said, "Nothing before I woke up in the water near drowning." She listened as he told her about hanging on to a buoy until he washed up on this shore with no memory of how he'd gotten there.

She felt like crying. "I thought that might be the case when you didn't seem to recognize me. But maybe I can help you."

He let go of her but stayed where he was, his body so close that she would have to push him aside to leave. "What makes you think I need help?"

She swallowed, uncertain how to proceed. "Don't you want to know what happened to you?" She saw barriers come up but just as quickly fall. All the anger and fight seemed to go out of him, draining away like water into sand. "Come to my cottage and we can talk. I'll tell you everything I know. Maybe it will help you remember."

He studied her as if still uncertain. "We've never kissed before."

"No, we haven't," she said. Tears filled her eyes. After all that time of dreaming about their first kiss, she'd never imagined it would be like this. "We were friends."

"Friends? So you aren't my wife?"

The question took her by surprise. "No." She swallowed and looked away, afraid he could see how much his question had hurt her.

"But we were close."

She shifted her gaze to him again. His intent gaze made her squirm. "I thought we were getting that way before you left."

"Then how do you explain this wedding band on my finger?"

"I can't explain why you would do something so impulsive as marry a woman you just met. It wasn't like you. It shocked us all because it was so out of character."

"Especially you."

Her eyes filled. She hastily wiped at them. "Yes."

"I can see that I hurt you. And yet, you're the one who came looking for me."

She swallowed. "I had a strong feeling that you were still alive."

"And my wife? Why isn't she here?"

How did she tell him that Juliette had gotten his death certificate as quickly as she could and was now pressuring his family to pay her off by selling the ranch? Worse, that there was a good chance she was the reason he'd ended up going overboard at sea? "She refused to believe you could have survived."

He said nothing for a long moment. His gray gaze bored into her. "But not you. You thought you knew me better."

She raised her chin in defiance. "Yes."

Cyrus chuckled before looking out at the ocean for a moment, but he didn't move. She held her breath, unsure what would happen now. "Why didn't you say something right away when you saw me?"

"I could tell you'd been hurt and I was afraid you might run away thinking I'd come here to harm you." His gaze came back to her. "I just want you to be...well."

"My memory may never come back."

"Or something might trigger it. Perhaps...your wife."

"Is she coming down here?"

"Do you want her to?"

"I'm not sure what I want." He glanced over his shoulder again. "This family you say I have, why haven't they come down here?" He quickly answered his own question. "You haven't told them where I am."

"No."

He cocked his head as if curious about her motives. "Why is that?"

"Because I felt you needed time. I was afraid even hearing this might overwhelm you. Was I wrong?"

"No. Tell me about you and me."

AJ took a moment to gather herself. "The last time I saw you we went horseback riding together."

"When was that?"

"Weeks ago now, before you went to Denver to buy a bull for your family ranch. You're a rancher back in Montana."

He looked disbelieving. She couldn't blame him. He had no memory of that life apparently. Also he had to be wondering how he'd ended up here after what he'd been through. She'd spent sleepless nights, wondering the same thing.

"A rancher? Shouldn't I remember that?" Before she could answer, he said, "Come with me." He reached for her hand. "We can talk in my hut."

She nodded and, taking a steady breath, walked with him across the moonlit-drenched beach and up into the trees and dense vegetation. It was cooler up here. The sea breeze stirred the palm fronds, the night shimmering in moon glow and deep shadows. It seemed to her a symphony of soft sounds, the waves washing onto the beach, the palms sighing, the nightly insects chirping in.

When he let go of her hand at the doorway into where he'd been staying, AJ hugged herself, afraid of what was going to happen, afraid of what wouldn't. He drew back the netting at the door and stepped back to let her enter. His "hut" was a basic lean-to with a hammock and a couple of chairs that he might have found in the hurricane debris and repaired.

"Understand, after you left Montana, there's a lot I don't know," she said as she took the chair he offered her. He stood silhouetted against the night. The view through his netted doorway was spectacular. She wondered how many nights he'd lain in the hammock looking at the sea that had spit him out on this beach, wondering how he'd gotten here and why. "Could you please sit down?"

He hesitated, but only for a moment. As he took a chair he said nothing, waiting, studying her with both suspicion and fear, and maybe hope?

"The last time I saw you, you promised to come back after a few days. Billie Dee was making her Texas chicken and dumplings, your favorite." He frowned. "She's the cook at the Stagecoach Saloon that your brother and sister own."

"I thought my family ranched since I'd gone to Denver to buy a bull?"

"Your brother Flint is the sheriff, Tucker is a deputy, Darby owns a saloon with your sister, Lillie, and Hawk ranches with you."

He shook his head. "Wouldn't you think that if any of this were true I'd remember?"

"You've been through a lot. You were injured when you fell off a cruise ship…or were pushed."

His eyes widened. "Why would you say that?" He was nervously turning the wedding ring on his finger.

"You were married on the cruise ship to a woman you'd just met only days before."

He raised an eyebrow.

"I don't know what happened on the ship, but I've met your wife."

He looked down at the ring on his left hand and quit fiddling with it. "But I was with you before I left?"

She nodded. "I thought you and I were getting…close. We liked each other and I thought…" She cleared her throat. "Then we got a call that you'd fallen off a cruise ship. At first we didn't believe it. We thought you were on your way back from Denver. You'd purchased the bull and should have been home by the time we got the call. Then we found out that you'd gotten married on the ship. It was so out of character…"

"But you say you've met my wife and that's why you suspect I was pushed overboard?"

"Juliette."

She could see that the name meant nothing to him.

"She said it was love at first sight."

"You don't trust her."

She let out a bark of a laugh. "She is in Montana right now trying to force your family to sell the ranch and buy her out. She showed up with your death certificate as quickly as she could get it."

AJ hadn't meant to blurt that out. "I'm sorry."

He sat back and rubbed his neck. "If this is true, then you must think me a fool."

"That's just it," she said leaning toward him. "The Cyrus Cahill I know would never have done something so impetuous and I think I know you pretty well."

"Cyrus Cahill." He tried out the name on his tongue and cursed under his breath. Nothing felt familiar—except this woman. He'd wanted to kiss her again, as worried as he was that she might be the danger he had to fear. According to her, he'd already been fooled by one woman—his apparent wife.

He was so close to AJ in the confines of his hut that he ached to kiss her. She touched the tip of her tongue to her lower lip. It was his undoing. He reached over, cupped the back of her neck and pulled her to him. This time, he kissed her the way he'd been wanting to from the beginning.

Her hands went to his chest. She pressed her palms into his flesh. And for a moment, he was lost in her wonderful mouth, lips, the surprise flick of her tongue, before she pushed him back, shaking her head.

"Maybe I'm more impetuous than you thought," he said.

"What you are apparently is married."

He looked down at the ring again. "So it seems. But it doesn't sound like much of a marriage since you believe she's the one who tried to kill me."

They sat within inches of each other, their knees almost touching, both breathing hard. His body ached for her, but she was right. He had enough problems without falling for this woman. Because if he made love to her, that's exactly what would happen, he feared.

He got to his feet. "What do we do now?"

"Your brother Flint—"

"The sheriff."

"Is sending your passport. He got it from—"

"Juliette. My wife."

"Once it arrives, we should be able to leave. If that's what you want."

"And you have purposely not told her where I am." He lifted a brow in question. "Are you protecting me? Or hiding me?"

"Maybe both. I have good reason to believe she was behind you going overboard on that cruise ship. You aren't her first husband to die under suspicious circumstances. In fact, you're the fifth. Your wife is being investigated in two states for the deaths of her husbands."

He let out a humorous laugh. "And here I was thinking you were just jealous."

She lifted her chin, her eyes sparking. "Who says I'm not? But if you really did fall in love with her at first sight… Well, then, I plan to get you back to her—and your family in Montana, and wish you luck."

"And if I don't go back?"

"Is that what you want?"

He moved to the doorway, his back to her as he looked out. "How could I know what I want? Remember? I have no memory before I woke up in the ocean, alone in the dark, confused, afraid, injured and drowning." When he turned, she was beside him, so close he could smell the sunscreen and sea salt on her skin.

She placed a hand on his arm and he felt a ripple move through him. "It's why I didn't tell you right away. I could tell that you were…scared."

Because of the feeling that he had something to fear. *Someone* to fear. "You really believe my wife pushed me from the cruise ship."

"Or someone she got to help her, yes, based on what we know about her. I'm told it's hard to fall off a cruise ship unless you were drunk and climbing on the railing."

He thought about that. "Maybe that's what I did."

"You've never been much of a drinker."

"Right. But apparently I never did half of the things I did before I ended up in the ocean."

She pulled her hand back. "Maybe you're right. Maybe when you see your wife, your memory will come back, all of it including what happened after you met her."

He studied her for a full minute. "What does she look like?"

"Blonde, blue-eyed."

"Like you," he said. "She sounds as if she married me for my money. Do I have money?"

"You're comfortable but your brother said you're what is called 'land-poor.' Your wife might have gotten the wrong idea because you were buying a three-hundred-thousand-dollar bull."

"Is that a lot for a bull?"

She laughed. "I have no idea. You were cautious about buying it but Hawk—"

"The brother I ranch with."

"Yes, he thought it was a good investment."

He considered all of this. She made him sound like a cautious man who wasn't impulsive or rash. But standing here with her, he also knew what powerful feelings for a woman could do to a man. "I have a lot of things to think about. Do you have photos of my family?"

She pulled out her phone and moved closer to him. He could smell the sweet scent of her.

"This is your brother Flint and this is your sister, Lillie, and her husband, Trask. This is your brother Darby and you at the Stagecoach Saloon."

He stared at the photo of himself. He looked so different, he wasn't even sure he would have recognized himself. So clean-cut, so confident in who he was, so…cowboy.

"This is Hawk."

"The brother I ranch with. We all have the same dark hair and gray eyes."

"Yes, and this is Tucker and his wife, Kate. Tucker is the oldest of you boys."

"You don't have a photo of you and me together?"

She seemed to blush. "No, we never…" She hesitated and then said, "On that horseback ride we went on?"

"Yes?"

"We almost kissed for the first time but your horse got jealous and tried to nudge you off the mountain we were on."

He laughed, feeling his heart beat a little faster. "That could explain why I've wanted to kiss you for days now." But it explained little else, he thought. "I'm sorry, but I'm afraid none of those people—"

"Maybe this one will make you remember." He looked at her phone screen and saw himself sitting on a horse. "I thought you might recognize your *horse*."

He chuckled. "My jealous horse." For a moment, they stood together listening to the island sounds around them as if they were the only two people in the world.

As he breathed in the warm sea air, he felt the weight of the wedding band on his finger. A chill moved over his skin like a premonition of what was to come. If AJ was right, then his wife had tried to kill him. Would she try again? He still couldn't shake the feeling that he was in danger, but maybe now he knew where it could be coming from.

He looked out at the waves breaking on the beach. "Thank you. But I think I need to be alone now. I'll walk you back to your cottage."

"That isn't necessary. I can—"

"Oh, I'm perfectly aware of how independent you are and capable as well, since apparently you have gone from island to island looking for me," he said, smiling over at her. "I want to walk you back."

"I HOPE I HAVEN'T messed up," AJ told Flint when she called him after Cyrus walked her to her cottage. "He confronted me. I told him everything."

"How did he take it?"

"I'm not sure he believed me at first. He doesn't remember any of it."

"He doesn't remember us."

"No." She felt sad for his family, sad for herself. "He's scared. What is Juliette up to?"

"Still pushing for money along with demanding to know where her husband is. She was going to have to wait until after probate. But now with him alive… She's offered to have the marriage annulled—for a price."

"He's wearing a wedding band. Maybe he did marry her in the heat of the moment."

"Come on, none of us believe it's a real marriage," Flint said. "Juliette's past, along with her actions, prove that."

"Then, knowing your brother, how did they end up in front of the captain on the ship?"

"Cyrus, do something that impulsive? You know my brother."

"I thought I did."

"What happens now?" Flint asked.

"I guess that's up to Cyrus. He's going to need papers to get home—if that's what he decides to do."

"Tell me where to send his passport I got from Juliette. Don't worry, I'm not about to come down there—or tell the others where you are. With his passport, he should be able to get back to Montana with your help," the sheriff said. "After that..."

"What if she tries to kill him again before we get out of here?"

"If that happens, you're in just as much danger as he is. Juliette doesn't know he can't remember. She also won't know how much he's told you."

CHAPTER FIFTEEN

EACH DAY HE STRUGGLED. Not just with what AJ had told him, but everything about the woman. The kisses. The look in her blue eyes. The way he had to fight his urge to go to her. Worse, he had to fight that gnawing fear inside him that he still wasn't safe. That he wouldn't be safe until…

That was just it. Until he returned home and faced this wife of his? If she really had killed her other husbands, then even his family might not be safe around her. It was still so hard to imagine a wife, a family, life in Montana. But he had no reason not to believe AJ. He'd seen a photo of himself.

Still, without any memory… All he knew was that he wanted AJ like he'd never wanted anything in his life. Apparently he'd dragged his feet back in Montana, putting off kissing her… Maybe he was that shy, cautious rancher she'd told him about. Cyrus Cahill.

But the man he was now feared putting anything off and at the same time couldn't bear the thought of leaving the one place he'd come to feel safe.

At the sound of a vehicle, he looked up, suddenly worried.

But as Hermon's taxi roared up, he saw that the big islander was alone. He kept working even as Hermon made his way to him.

"I thought you should know," the man said keeping his voice down. "There has been someone else asking around about you on the island to the south."

"Someone else?" His family, his wife? AJ hadn't told them where he was but that didn't mean they weren't looking for him.

"A man." He described a large blond man. "He had a badge and was American. I thought you should know."

All Cyrus could do was nod. Hermon patted his shoulder. "Maybe you should think about leaving before he finds you."

After another sleepless night, AJ woke not sure if Cyrus would even still be at the small resort. The morning after they'd talked, she'd expected to find him gone. But instead she had awakened to the sound of hammering and saw him working on the last cottage as if it was just another day for him.

Since then, they'd been cordial to each other, nothing more. She could see that he was working through some things. She didn't think he would run. But in truth, she had no idea what he would do. She wasn't even sure he did.

As she left her cottage, she spotted him hard at work. Marissa had made her lunch and with map in hand, AJ headed for the walk up to the natural hot spring. She'd been meaning to go up there since she'd arrived, but had never made it. She'd wanted to stay near Cyrus. Most days she lost herself in long walks on the endless beach.

Today she knew she couldn't hang around the cove all day wondering what was going on in Cyrus's head. She'd done enough of that. That he hadn't said anything but went back to work said enough. She'd done what she could. The next move was Cyrus's.

His passport had come in the mail. She'd thought about telling him, but he'd seen Marissa bring it to her, so he probably already knew since she'd mentioned to him that it was on the way.

She speculated that he needed time, and yet if she gave him too much, what would he do? What would Juliette do, now that she knew he was alive? AJ felt the clock ticking. Flint was right. If Juliette was the black widow they now knew her to be, then she wouldn't let Cyrus get off this island alive.

But along with worry for his life, she was fighting her feelings for him. It was hell being this close to him and not even feel she could talk to him, let alone touch him. She second-guessed herself, worrying that maybe she'd told him too much. Maybe she shouldn't have told him about Juliette. If he really had fallen in love with her…

AJ shook her head. What was she thinking? The woman was a black widow. She had six marriages from which only two husbands had survived. At least two states were investigating the deaths of her two last husbands and trying to prove that she was a murderer, Flint had told her. AJ knew she wasn't wrong about Juliette. But that still might not save Cyrus from the woman.

As she climbed up to the path toward the hot spring, she tried to clear her mind. She'd worried enough about all of this and it wasn't helping. Cyrus knew the truth—well, as much of the truth as she could provide. What he did now was up to him, she told herself as she trailed through towering palms and thick vegetation along a rocky steep trail to the hot spring.

Once she topped out, she stopped, startled by the beauty around her and surprised how little she had enjoyed this amazing place. The turquoise water, the white sand, the palms and now this array of flat rocks, small waterfalls and little hidden coves set against the tall palms. It took her breath away just looking at how picturesque it was and how much she would have loved to share this with someone. But that someone was Cyrus. She wasn't even sure he'd ever been up here or that he could appreciate the island's beauty under his circumstances.

She spread out her towel on the warm ground of one of the tiny coves and drank a bottled water before rising and taking off her beach cover. Stepping along the warm flat rocks, she found a spot where there was a natural stairway down into the water. She inched in until the hot water was chest deep before she lay back, floating, staring up at the endless blue sky overhead and praying that Cyrus would find some kind of peace in what she'd told him.

AJ didn't know how long she lay like that in the luxurious water. Eyes closed she drifted as she tried to relax. So much was riding on her handling things well with Cyrus—

She sensed him an instant before she felt the lap of the water warning her that she was no longer alone in the shimmering pool. Her eyes flew open as he reached her side. She tried to stand but he stopped her.

"Don't move," he whispered. "I want to remember you just like this."

The words startled her, their meaning uncertain. She felt his hand in the small of her back as she met his eyes, not sure what she could see.

But his expression was calm, his gaze almost loving. Her heart hammered even harder. Water rippled over his strong, bronzed chest. His gray eyes intent on her, steam rose around them as he slowly pulled her into him.

"I know it's not our first kiss but..." He lowered his mouth to hers. This time, she melted into him. Her hand went to his shoulders. He drew her closer, the water lapping around them. She leaned into him, into the kiss, savoring it because her pounding pulse feared it was a goodbye kiss.

As he drew back, she looked into his eyes. "Cyrus—"

He pressed a finger to her lips. "This is our last day here. Marissa said a package came for you. My passport right?" She nodded. "I have no idea what will happen tomorrow, but Hermon will take us to the airport whenever we're ready."

"You're sure?"

"No, but I have to trust you." His gaze locked with hers. "AJ, you were the one who came looking for me. When I saw you, I felt…something. You tell me that the Cyrus Cahill you knew was a cautious man. I just know that as hard as I've tried to keep my distance from you, I can't resist you. I want this time with you. If you don't…" He started to pull back, but she caught his shoulders and drew him to her. She looked into his eyes and leaned forward to kiss him.

He dragged her to him, their naked bodies slick and warm from the caress of the silken water. He encircled her in his arms and deepened the kiss, lifting her off her feet, their bodies melded together.

HE GROANED, TELLING himself that he'd never felt like this before. He couldn't have fallen in love with that woman she'd called Juliette. Not with the way he felt about AJ. He'd felt it the moment he'd seen her that first night. He'd ached for her each day, fighting himself to stay away. He was through fighting. He couldn't bear the thought that he might die today and not have her.

AJ pressed her full breasts against his chest, her nipples hard as seashells. He stroked her long, wet hair, her slim back, the saddle before the rounded rise of her buttock. He lifted her up. She fit so perfectly against him. He cupped her behind and pushed her onto his hard shaft.

She groaned against him as the warm water lapped against their bodies. He lost himself in her. In her mouth, her breasts, the sweet cries that came from her lips as he took her with abandon and she clung to him and urged him on. Desire was like blazing sun overhead. It roared inside him with a familiarity that he remembered. It had always been this woman. Only this woman.

He cupped her head in his hands and looked into those blue eyes. "Whoever I am, whatever has happened, this is where I belong," he said as he plunged inside her. They rode each other like the strong waves of the sea, clinging to each other the way he'd clung to that buoy. He'd never felt more alive or safe than in this woman's arms.

SPENT, HE CARRIED her to the sandy cove where he'd spread his towel next to hers. He lowered her slowly, lovingly to her towel, and then he joined her. Lying on his back staring up at the never-ending blue sky, he reached over and took her hand. She squeezed his gently and he closed his eyes.

Why had he not kissed this woman sooner? Maybe he wouldn't have gone to Denver at all. Maybe they would have been lovers before he left. Either way, they would be together and this other woman… Juliette…his marriage and everything else would have never happened.

Like her, he couldn't fathom how he would have married someone else when these feelings for AJ were so strong. Almost drowning hadn't dampened his need for her. His yearning for her. He would have hurried home to be with her unless…

Unless what? This woman Juliette had done something to alter his thinking? It must have been some spell that he would walk blindly into a marriage with a woman he'd only known for a few days?

AJ COULDN'T BELIEVE that here they were in paradise together. She and Cyrus made love again, swam and then they'd shared the lunch Marissa had prepared. He asked no more about his family or his wife. Instead, they took a hike higher up the mountain to see the view. They held hands, they kissed, they looked into each other's eyes as if memorizing the moment.

AJ suspected he wanted to hold on to this day as much as she did because the future was too unpredictable. It was what she was doing, as well. They had this moment in this incredible place. Tomorrow they would leave. Suddenly she didn't want to go. Going back to Montana would mean Cyrus facing Juliette, remembering why he'd taken off with her on a cruise and married her. Worse, she wouldn't put it past the woman to try to kill him again.

She pushed the thought away, telling herself they had this time together. She didn't want to spoil it by thinking the worst. The day passed, the sun disappearing behind the mountain, the moon coming out.

They made love again, this time slower. In all her dreams AJ couldn't have imagined their lovemaking would be like this. The sound of the water, the cool breeze caressing their skin, Cyrus's hands on her, searching and finding her most sensitive spots, his mouth everywhere, lifting her up to suckle her breasts and lifting her even higher to probe her center until she cried out.

He'd gathered her up, her fingers buried in his hair, as he rolled her over on the towels spread out in the sand and entered her. She arched against him in the moonlight, her body aglow with the night sky and the flush of pleasure.

He took her higher and higher until she shuddered, a cry of gratification escaping her lips. He wrapped her in his arms, her arms around his neck, their faces bright from their lovemaking. He held her as their breathing returned to normal along with the frantic pounding of their hearts.

She lay there in his arms, him holding her as if he never wanted to let her go, protectively, lovingly. She wasn't surprised when he whispered, "I wish we could stay here forever." She met his gaze in the silver light, but before she could tell him she'd been thinking the same thing, he shook his head and said, "I know we can't, but right now there is nowhere I want to be but here with you."

Her throat closed with emotion, she could only nod and bury her face in his neck.

AJ's stomach suddenly growled loudly, making Cyrus laugh. She loved his laugh, but mostly she loved that he was capable of laughing again. They lay side by side, facing each other, their naked bodies cast in moonlight.

He traced a finger along the hollow from her rib cage to the rise of her hip. "We'd better get dressed and see if Marissa saved us dinner." His voice was soft, seductive. "If we keep lying here like this…" Her stomach growled again.

"Hunger wins out." Leaning into her, he kissed her and then got to his feet.

She lay on her back for a moment staring up at the starry sky. Montana had bowled her over with its incredible big sky. Being from Houston she'd never seen so many stars. But here on this island, so far away from any lights other than natural ones, she couldn't believe the night sky with all its galaxies.

Cyrus tossed her beach cover to her. Earlier she'd seen him lift his head as if he'd heard something. "Keep lying there like that and I'll tell you what is going to happen."

She smiled at him, tempted, but knowing he was right. She rose and dressed, feeling his caressing gaze on her as she did. "It is so hard to leave here."

He nodded and, stepping to her, cupped her face in his weathered hands and kissed her sweetly. "AJ." He said it on a whisper, the weight of it making her feel it at heart level. He seemed to breathe her in for a moment, before he stepped back and began to stuff their towels into her beach bag.

"The trail down is a bit tricky. Why don't you follow me." He took her hand as they worked their way through the rocks along the side of the spring. Once into the thick vegetation and trees, only a little moonlight fingered its way through to the path, forcing them to a slower pace.

They hadn't gone far when AJ heard a sound like an animal moving through the vegetation ahead of them. Cyrus stopped, turned toward her and motioned for her to remain silent. Ahead she could hear something headed their way.

She looked at him, trying to imagine what type of creature it could be. In Montana, it would have been anything from a bear to a mountain lion to a moose or elk or deer. But on this island…

One look at Cyrus's expression and she knew that here it had to be human.

CHAPTER SIXTEEN

"It could be Hermon," AJ whispered, wishing with all her heart that it was true. "Marissa could have sent him to check on us."

Cyrus shook his head. "It's not Hermon. I thought I heard a boat earlier. Listen. If something happens, I want you to run back down to the cottages and not look back. Marissa keeps a shotgun at the main cottage."

"I don't know how to—"

"Marissa knows how to use it and will. Go there," he whispered next to her ear.

She started to argue, but he pressed his finger to her lips. Her throat went dry at the look in his eyes. That danger he hadn't been able to shake had caught up with him? No!

They started down the trail again, moving faster, him keeping her as close behind him as he could. She strained to listen for the sound of someone in the darkness of the mountainside, but all she could hear was the frantic beating of her heart. In her head was only one thought.

She'd found Cyrus. They'd found each other. She couldn't lose him. Not now.

AJ screamed as the man came barreling out of the darkness of the junglelike vegetation. He tackled Cyrus, the two of them falling to the rocky path and tumbling downward into the darkness. She stood frozen for a moment before she charged after them, frantically looking around for something she could use as a weapon.

Cyrus had told her to run down to the cottage. But they were still a long way from there and she feared what would happen in the time it would take her to find Marissa and return with a gun.

In a shaft of moonlight, she saw the flash of a knife as the two men crashed into the base of a palm and came to a bone-crunching stop. She heard a groan, but neither seemed to be injured enough to stop fighting.

Panicked, she didn't know what to do. There were no limbs like on pine trees that she could use as a weapon—only dense vegetation and a few fallen palm fronds. She knew better than to try to get between the men, but she had to do something and fast. She could see they were struggling over the knife in the atttacker's hand.

Spying a rock the size of a small bowling ball, she hurriedly scooped it up and rushed toward them. She could see that Cyrus had hold of the man's wrist and was fighting to keep the man from stabbing him. The man, large and clearly outweighing Cyrus, shifted, throwing a leg over him and changing his position so he was directly above him. The knife blade gleamed as the man fought to thrust the blade into Cyrus's chest.

AJ didn't think. She only acted. Hefting the rock high, she brought it down on the attacker's head. A loud crack filled the air and for a moment she feared the man would drop on Cyrus, the knife blade burying into his chest.

She hadn't realized that she was holding her breath, until

Cyrus shoved the man away and stumbled to his feet. He was bleeding from a gash on his head as he moved to her.

"Are you all right?" he asked as he reached her.

"*Me?* Did he…?" Cyrus was covered with blood.

"I'm all right." He was breathing hard. There was blood on his hands and his face and the shirt he was wearing was splattered with it.

She threw herself into his arms. He held her close for a moment. She could see that his head wound was bleeding badly. She pulled off a strip of fabric from her beach cover and pressed it to his temple.

His gaze went to the man on the ground. "Do you recognize him?"

AJ didn't want to look, but forced herself to. The man lay on his back, eyes closed. Had she killed him? "I've never seen him before. Have you?" She pulled back to look into his eyes.

He shook his head. "We're going to need help," he said. "Assuming he was alone."

That thought sent a sliver of ice down her spine. "You don't think…"

"We need to get down to the cottage," he said taking her shoulders in his hands. "Give me your phone. You have Hermon's number on here?"

She nodded, realizing what he had already figured out. Hermon would know what to do. He made the call telling the islander where he was and that he needed help. Hermon apparently didn't ask any questions and the call ended.

"Let's go," Cyrus said.

Terrified, her legs like water, but she stumbled down the rest of the trail behind him feeling as if she was in shock. It wasn't until they reached her cottage that she got a good look at Cyrus.

"You're bleeding."

"I'll take care of it. You get cleaned up and then go to Marissa's. She'll feed you and make sure you're safe until I'm through here."

Get cleaned up? Until that moment, she hadn't realized that there were also splatters of the dead man's blood on her arms and legs. She began to shake.

"You saved my life. Keep telling yourself that." His gaze met hers and held it, holding her at arm's length as he forced her to look into his eyes. "You are a strong woman. Remember that."

HERMON LOST NO TIME. He arrived thirty minutes later. By then Cyrus had bound his head to staunch the bleeding. The islander asked no questions as the two of them walked up the path. Only faint moonlight pierced the dense vegetation. Neither spoke until the spot where the body had been lying. There was blood on the ground, but the man was gone.

"How badly was he wounded?" Hermon asked.

"Not as badly as I thought." He saw tracks in the dust. "He wasn't alone. Someone helped him." He looked back down the trail. But where were they now?

At the sound of a boat motor, he and Hermon glanced at each other, then headed back down the dark trail. They reached the edge of the trees in time to see a small boat leaving a small cove to the north. One man was at the stern steering the motor, the other was lying in the hull, one hand dragging in the water as the boat rocked over the waves.

"Any idea who they were?" Hermon asked.

Cyrus shook his head. "He attacked me as we were coming down from the hot spring."

"We?"

"AJ and me."

Hermon didn't seem surprised by his being with the blonde American woman or that there could have been a dead man just off the path.

"Do you recognize the boat?"

The islander nodded. "He's from one of the large families on the island."

Cyrus swore. "They'll go to the authorities."

Hermon shook his head. "No, they won't. But they will try again."

"If they're local, why would they come after me?" Cyrus asked.

"They would have no reason," Hermon said. "Unless they were hired to do so. I will come in the morning with the taxi. You must go."

Cyrus nodded. He listened to the steady putt of the engine, watching the boat take the ocean swells, until it disappeared. He had no choice now but to leave. The last cottage was nearly done. "AJ will be going with me."

"Of course," Hermon said as they walked back toward the row of cottages. "You will be all right."

He wished he believed that. As the islander headed for his taxi, Cyrus stood for a moment looking out at the sea before he walked to AJ's cottage.

AJ HAD BEEN horrified when she'd seen herself in the mirror. She quickly stripped down and stepped into the hot shower, letting the water wash away the dead man's blood. She'd killed a man. That thought made her shake even harder as she began to soap herself. As if she could scrub away the memory.

By the time the water started to turn cold, she'd scrubbed herself almost raw. She stepped out, and then ran a brush through her freshly washed hair and toweled dry enough to dress in a T-shirt and jeans. She doubted she could eat a bite even though her stomach continued to growl.

But she knew that if she didn't show up at the main cottage, Marissa would worry and maybe come looking for her—and

Cyrus. In his condition, she didn't want the woman seeing him and asking questions. She wondered how much Hermon shared with his aunt. She didn't want to take any chances.

Cyrus was right. If some strange man showed up to harm her or Cyrus, she had no doubt Marissa would take care of him. So she hurried up the hillside to find Marissa had left a note. She'd gotten a ride into town from a friend. She'd left food for her and Cyrus in the refrigerator.

With relief that she wouldn't have to face anyone right now, AJ opened the refrigerator and took out the plates the woman had left for them. She found a bag to carry them, and then looked for the shotgun. She found it leaning against the wall of Marissa's bedroom with a box of shells nearby. Taking it and the food and ammunition, she headed back toward her cottage, trying not to worry about Cyrus.

But how could she not? The last time she'd seen him, he'd been bleeding.

She pushed open her cottage door and stopped cold at the sound of running water. It took her a moment to realize that her shower was on again. She stepped in and closed and locked the door. After putting down the food, ammo and shotgun, she moved cautiously to the bathroom.

Behind the warbled glass of the shower door, she saw his body, a body she now knew intimately.

"I'm sorry I didn't leave you any hot water," she said through the glass.

"I haven't had a real shower in… I have no idea how long," he said with a laugh as he shut off the water and opened the door. "Cold or not, it was wonderful."

He was so beautiful naked, his body glistening with beads of water, that she could only stare for a moment. "Your head is still bleeding a little. There's a first aid kit in the other room. Let me see what I can do."

But he grabbed her wrist, and pulled her closer. "Marissa?"

"She'd gotten a ride into town from a friend. She left us food. I brought her shotgun and some shells."

"Did you lock the door?" he asked, his voice husky.

She smiled. "I did."

Later, as she bandaged his head properly, neither of them spoke for a bit. They'd made love in her cottage, holding each other as if they'd both needed the human connection to assure them that they'd lived through what had happened tonight.

Someone had tried to kill Cyrus. Again. That was never far from AJ's mind except in the throws of lovemaking.

"I didn't see Hermon?" she said after she was through bandaging his head. He was lucky, the cut on his head was superficial and should heal quickly. But that didn't keep her from worrying.

"When we reached the spot the man was gone."

She tried to breathe, but her chest hurt. "How—"

"He was still alive. He hadn't come alone. Hermon said both men are local and must have been hired for the job."

Her startled gaze met his. "Hired by whom?"

He shrugged. "From what you've told me, my first guess would be my dear wife."

AJ groaned. "Not that I don't believe Juliette is behind it, but how could she know who to hire even if she knew which island you were on?" At his expression, she asked, "What?"

"That photo you took of me on your phone."

She felt herself heat with guilt. "Your family needed to see for themselves."

"I understand, but unless you turned off the geotagging on your phone…"

"The what?" she asked as she pulled back.

He took the first aid kit from her and put it aside. "Unless you turn off the photo geotagging on your phone it is extremely easy to place the exact location of where the photo was taken on a map. It even provides the precise GPS coordinates to the spot where the photo was taken."

She was shaking her head. "How do you know this?"

"Good question. I have no idea. Had I thought of it sooner I could have stopped you from sending the photo. But it just came to me that someone might have passed the photo on to my wife..."

AJ groaned. "I didn't, but someone in the family could have. Juliette was demanding proof that you were alive."

"Then she knows exactly where we are," Cyrus said as he rose to his feet. "Hermon will be coming for us in the morning to take us to the airport." He stopped at the small table and picked up his passport. Opening it, he said, "I took my passport when I went to Denver? Doesn't that seem strange?"

"You'd recently misplaced your Montana driver's license and hadn't gone down to the DMV because you were convinced it would turn up. You would have needed ID to get on the plane in Billings."

He shrugged and dropped his passport back on the table before turning to look at her. "I'm not going to leave you alone tonight." He stepped up to her, drawing her to her feet and kissing her. "But I think we should try to get some sleep. We have a big day ahead of us tomorrow."

She nodded, wondering if she would get any sleep with him lying next to her, let alone reliving what had happened on the trail.

"You saved my life," Cyrus said. "Again."

"And jeopardized it by sending that photo."

He pulled her to him. "We're headed for Montana tomorrow."

"Montana and your family." She felt her expression sour. "And your wife."

"Yes, my wife." He pulled back to look down at the ring on his finger. Taking it off, he tossed it over his shoulder. It hit in a far corner, tinkling and going still. But even with the ring gone, the pale line was still on his finger. He was still married.

"Maybe with luck she won't try to kill me again." He smiled when he said it, but AJ saw no humor in it. She had a bad feeling that they'd be lucky to get off this island alive.

She thought she wouldn't be able to sleep, but the moment she lay down in Cyrus's arms, she dropped into a deep exhausted sleep filled with dark images.

FROM THE LIVING room at Cahill Ranch, Hawk let out a cry. "It's her. Juliette, but she's with a different man."

The family had gathered after he'd gotten off work to keep going through the videos. Now they all huddled around his computer screen.

"That's her, all right," Flint said from behind him. "But who is that with her? It *isn't* the same man." He knew Juliette talking to a man on the ship wasn't evidence that she'd known the man before the cruise. But it did look suspicious.

Hawk let the video recording continue as they all watched. "They seem to be arguing."

Flint agreed. "Let's see if we can identify him." Hawk got up to let him have the computer and watched as his brother enlarged the photo, copied a shot of the man's face and sent it to a federal facial identifying site.

They waited, with Flint telling himself that this one could be a bust. But it didn't take long for a matching photo to come up—along with a name.

"Bingo," he said as he recognized the name. "Arthur Davis. He's Juliette's first husband and the only one besides Cyrus not to die while married to her. I need to call AJ," he said after making a copy of Arthur's photo.

"Should we keep looking?" Hawk asked. "You don't think there are more, do you?"

"No, but keep looking. Maybe we can find something more incriminating. So far all we can prove was that she knew the two men on board the ship. That's not a crime."

"Having your ex-husband on the same cruise as your newly-wed husband isn't a crime?" Lillie demanded.

"Suspicious, definitely," Flint said, "but not criminal. Unless the two men threw Cyrus overboard. Unfortunately, he still hasn't remembered any of it."

He stepped away to make the call and was disappointed when it went to voice mail. "Call me. We found two men who were on the ship the night Cyrus went overboard—both are connected to Juliette."

CHAPTER SEVENTEEN

AJ TRIED TO remain calm as they waited for Hermon to arrive with his taxi early the next morning. What if he wasn't coming? What if the police—

"He'll come," Cyrus said next to her and took her hand. Earlier he'd gone up to tell Marissa goodbye and thank her. They'd hugged. Marissa, AJ noticed, looked worried. They'd returned her shotgun and shells. She hadn't bothered to ask why they had taken them. Did she know what had happened on the trail? Would Hermon have told her?

"You're shaking," Cyrus said and put an arm around her. "We'll be off the island soon."

She nodded, praying that was true. She'd had all the paradise she could stand. "Unfortunately, there is no easy way to get back to Montana and I won't feel safe until I'm back there." But even as she said it, she wondered if she would ever feel safe again. Or if Cyrus would.

He looked as anxious as she felt. He was just hiding it better.

She explained the flights she'd booked. "It will take a series of flights even with me setting up a private plane to take us from San Juan to Miami where we'll catch commercial flights to Minneapolis and finally Billings," she said, needing to talk about something that she felt she had control over. "It's the fastest I can get us back there."

"You think I'm in a hurry?" he asked with humor in his voice.

"Are you sure you're ready to leave here?"

He smiled at her. "My worst memories and my best are here, right? But we can't stay. We couldn't even before last night. I have to find out who I am and how I got here."

"You're Cyrus Cahill."

"Yes," he said. "But I don't know him."

She looked away for a moment, the pain in his eyes breaking her heart. Flint had wanted to meet them in Billings but she'd said she thought a rental car would be better. Cyrus's pickup had been left at the airport for his trip to Denver but Flint had seen that it was brought home weeks ago.

He hasn't remembered anything? the sheriff had said. *Not even you?*

I don't know if it's because of a head injury or from the trauma, but he has no memory of his life before going into the sea. Once he's back and can see a specialist... She hadn't told him that she and Cyrus had connected. That he remembered geotagging. And that he seemed to have remembered the feelings he'd had for her.

At the sound of a vehicle approaching, she looked to the road, fearing that it might be the police or someone else they had to fear. When she saw Hermon's taxi, she let out the breath she'd been holding.

He drove down the path through the thick vegetation that they called a road. All of the roads on this island looked much the same because of the hurricane and probably a lack of money for infrastructure.

Hermon roared up and jumped out to take their luggage. "We have plenty of time before your flight," he said to Cyrus. "You're going home."

"Home," Cyrus repeated.

The islander nodded, but looked worried. "So you remember?"

"I remember this woman," Cyrus said and pulled AJ closer. "She's my saving angel."

"We'll miss you," Hermon said. "My aunt says you are the best worker she has ever had."

Cyrus smiled at that. "Glad I could help since this place..." He turned to look out over the handful of cottages. "It was exactly what I needed." He frowned then as he turned back to Hermon and lowered his voice. "You haven't seen that man we talked about again?" A man with a badge had been looking for him. Not a local.

Hermon shook his head. "Probably long gone." The men shook hands and she and Cyrus climbed in the back of the taxi for the trip to the airport.

AJ whispered to Cyrus as Hermon climbed behind the wheel, "There was some man you asked him about?"

"Someone asking questions possibly about me." She felt her eyes widen in alarm. "Don't worry. We're leaving. But he is probably the man who hired my attacker last night."

Still, that didn't relieve her mind. "On someone else's orders."

"Hermon said the man was an American with a badge."

"A cop? Or FBI or—"

"Not someone with any authority or the local police would have been involved," he quickly assured her.

She sat back feeling sick to her stomach. "Wait, Flint told me that they have Juliette talking to a man on the ship on one of the surveillance videos. He's an ex-cop from Arizona where one of Juliette's husbands died and she's being investigated for the man's murder."

"Mystery solved," Cyrus said.

"He is probably the man who threw you off the ship that

night," she whispered back. It was all making sense. Except for why Cyrus would have married Juliette. "Why are you taking this so well?"

"Because worrying won't help," Cyrus whispered. "I'm with you. Right now, that's all I can ask for. So stop worrying."

It would have been easier to stop breathing. AJ tried to concentrate on the road ahead. She couldn't wait to get off this island. The road up the mountain twisted and turned, the taxi bumping along as Hermon tried to avoid the deepest holes and not always missing.

Cyrus reached over and took her hand, squeezing it as they took one turn on the edge of the mountain, the back wheel keeling over a little before Hermon got control again. She would have buckled her seat belt—if Hermon's taxi had one. The old car was lucky to have seats.

Cyrus gave her what he must have thought was a reassuring smile. She tried closing her eyes, willing the taxi to reach the airport, imagining herself sitting on the plane on the way to Miami. On the way home.

She opened her eyes as they hit a huge pothole that jarred her teeth. Cyrus tightened his hold on her hand. They'd reached the main road. Not that it was paved but in a few places. The road rose and fell as it wound across the mountains toward the largest city on the island and the only airport.

"Your family is going to be so glad to see you," she said, squeezing Cyrus's hand back. He nodded, his gaze straight ahead as if he was trying to see into the future.

AJ tried not to think about Cyrus's reaction to his family and them to him—once they realized he didn't know any of them. She especially didn't want to think about Juliette who was to blame for all of this, AJ was convinced. Still, she couldn't help but wonder how the woman had fooled him into marrying her. It couldn't have been love at first sight. It couldn't have.

She noticed that Cyrus wasn't looking ahead as she'd thought. He was staring into the rearview mirror—and so was Hermon. Both of them looked concerned. Turning, she saw another vehicle taking the curves behind them at what seemed like a dangerous speed—as if the driver was trying to catch up to them.

"Is there a problem?" she asked, glancing back again before turning her gaze on Hermon.

The taxi driver shook his head. "No problem." But he sped up, which didn't relieve AJ's tension in the least. On one side of the narrow road was a wall of dirt and thick vegetation that went up the mountain. On the other was a vertical drop down the mountainside at an alarming angle toward the sea. Hermon seemed to be fighting to keep the car on the road.

"Who is that following us?" she asked, but the islander didn't answer. He was busy trying to keep the car on the road. The rusted-out American car would have been in some wrecking yard in the States years ago. With every bump and turn she thought it might now fall apart.

Cyrus put his arm around her and pulled her close. He looked as anxious as she felt. He'd told her that all he'd known when he'd come to in the water was that he was in danger. That feeling had never subsided and last night proved that he hadn't been wrong. If, as she suspected, he'd been thrown off the ship, then he had good reason to feel he was in danger and still was. The ship had kept going along with whoever had tossed him into the sea in the middle of the night.

But now somehow, someone else had apparently been sent to keep them from leaving the island alive.

And they'd found her and Cyrus all because of geotagging that photo she'd taken of him. Now, someone else seemed determine that he would never leave this island. She knew who was behind it and swore that if she ever reached Montana, she would find Juliette and—

The vehicle that had been chasing them caught up and bumped into the back of them, making the taxi wobble dangerously on the narrow road. She would have screamed but her heart was lodged in her throat. Cyrus pulled her closer as she looked back to see that the other vehicle was directly behind them riding their bumper.

She shot a look at Hermon. Both of his hands gripped the wheel tightly, his knuckles white, his eyes on the road ahead, his expression no longer on island time as he floored the old car.

CHAPTER EIGHTEEN

"Hang on," Hermon said as they took several curves on what felt like two wheels. As they came to what appeared to be a short straight stretch, the islander hit the brakes.

AJ would have flown forward, either into the seat or over it headed for the windshield. But Cyrus had hold of her, his arm encircling her, his other arm wrapped about the seat to keep them both from taking flight.

The instant Hermon hit his brakes, he cranked the wheel hard to the right. With only steep rising mountainside on their right, the taxi's right front fender crashed into dirt and rocks and vegetation, all of it flying up over the hood.

At almost the same exact moment, the vehicle that had been following them, struck the corner of the taxi. AJ heard the sound of glass breaking and metal screeching. Out of the corner of her eye, she saw the other vehicle seem to ping off the taxi and disappear over the edge of the other side of the road and down the mountainside.

In the silence that followed, Hermon opened his door and

stepped out. Cyrus tried to get out as well, but his door was jammed.

A few moments later, Hermon climbed behind the wheel, glanced back at them as if to see if they were all right, and then, the engine still running, he reversed.

There was a loud scraping sound as the smashed front right bumper rubbed against the tire. He backed into the road, stopped, jumped out and pulled the rusted bumper away from the tire, before hopping behind the wheel.

As he went forward, the noise wasn't quite as loud and after a few minutes on the road again, part of the bumper fell off, cartwheeling down the road behind them. The noise, AJ noted, stopped altogether, making Hermon smile broadly at them in the rearview mirror.

"Shouldn't be any more trouble on the way to the airport," the islander said and began to hum.

AJ looked back. There was no sign of the vehicle that had been chasing them or the man who'd been driving it.

She looked at Cyrus. His face was grim but determined. He held her tightly. She laid her head on his shoulder and closed her eyes. She just wanted off this island. Once they were home…

As if she thought for a minute that Cyrus would be safe once in Montana. Juliette would be there waiting. But it was Cyrus's reaction to Juliette that had her worried.

AJ DIDN'T GET a chance to check her phone until they landed in Miami. They had twenty minutes before their next flight. They'd cut it close. They hurried to their plane and once aboard seated in first class, she called Flint back.

"Cyrus and I are on the plane."

"You're headed home?" He sounded overjoyed.

"We had no choice."

"What does that mean?"

"I can't get into it. We're about to take off."

"When do you get here?"

"It won't be until tonight. I can't really talk now."

"Then just listen as long as you can. We now know of two men Juliette spoke to on the ship. One is Otis Claremont, a former Arizona cop who quit after one of her husbands died. Arizona is one of the places investigating the man's death. The other man she spoke to on the ship was Arthur Davis, her first husband. He and Cyrus are the only ones to have lived through a marriage with Juliette."

"Let me guess, Arthur didn't have money."

Flint chuckled. "I'm putting a BOLO out on both men to find out where they are. Obviously, I have some questions for them."

"We're about to take off," she told the sheriff.

"How is Cyrus?"

"As well as can be expected under the circumstances. I'll tell you everything when we see you. Have to go." She put her phone on airplane mode as the flight attendant headed in her direction. Once they were in the air and leveled off, she told Cyrus what his brother had found out.

FLINT DISCONNECTED AND felt a rush of excitement. Cyrus was coming home. He knew he would never believe his brother was really alive until he saw him. Until he put his arms around him. AJ had said they would be home by tonight.

He'd come out to the ranch for lunch when Maggie had called to say that the family was gathered again going through the ship surveillance videos.

"I brought them all lunch," Maggie said. "I thought you might want some. I'm keeping the family hydrated and fed. Your daughter is napping, but you'll still get to see her."

Flint hadn't been there but a few minutes when he'd gotten

the call from AJ. Now he turned to his family and told them the good news.

"We should throw him a party!" Lillie said, and then sobered. "Or not."

"We will when he's back to his old self," Flint said. "The good news is that he's alive and coming home!" They all hugged, tears in their eyes. He'd worried that this day might never come. Even with updates from AJ, he'd worried that the brother they'd known was gone. He still worried about that but kept his fears to himself. Once home, Cyrus could get the medical attention he might need.

For a moment he'd forgotten about Juliette. He pulled out his phone and called her. Her phone went straight to voice mail. He left her the message, wishing that he could see her face when she got it. "Cyrus is headed home. Just thought you'd like to know." Was he hoping that she would leave town? Disappear? She'd lost. But after he'd done it, he started second-guessing himself. The last thing he wanted to do was put his brother in more danger.

He returned to his computer and the surveillance videos, more determined than ever to protect his brother from Juliette by exposing her and seeing that she spent a very long time behind bars.

"Got something," Darby said a half hour later.

"Not another man," Hawk said with a groan.

"Nope. It's with the two men we already saw her with."

Flint rushed to his brother's computer. There was no doubt about it. Juliette was having a heated discussion with the two men. She kept looking over her shoulder as if afraid Cyrus might be onto them.

"Let's make a copy. I've marked the spots on the videos," the sheriff said. "I'll be sending them to the police who are investigating Juliette. Maybe they will help."

"Maybe Cyrus will remember who threw him overboard,"

Lillie said. "And the videos will connect Juliette with the two men, proving they were up to something on the ship."

Flint smiled at his sister. "That is exactly what I'm hoping." And praying.

"Going somewhere?"

Juliette looked up in surprise. She'd been packing her rental car. After she'd gotten Flint's message she'd known she had to move fast. "Good afternoon, Deputy." She'd seen this one around. He wasn't bad looking. A little pudgy for her taste, but every time she'd seen him around town, he'd definitely shown an interest in her.

"Leaving, are you?" he asked, seeming amused.

She stepped closer to read his badge. "Deputy Cole." She stopped within inches of him, knowing instinctively that it would make him nervous. It did. "Were the suitcases the dead giveaway?" She ran a finger down his smooth cheek. "Have you been watching me?"

His Adam's apple bobbed and he took a step back. "The sheriff asked me to keep an eye out and let him know if you decided to skip town."

"Is that what you think I'm doing?" She laughed, shaking her head. "What does the *H* stand for?"

"Huh?"

"The *H* in Deputy H. Cole. What does it stand for?"

"Harper."

"Harper?"

"But everyone calls me Harp."

Definitely nervous. She had that effect on men.

"I would think you might want to see your husband. He should be here soon."

"Why would I? He's the one who hasn't called me or even

let me know where he is. According to his *girlfriend*, he has no desire to talk to me, let alone see me."

"On the contrary, I know for a fact that he's looking forward to seeing you."

She shook her head. "Really?" She saw him reach for his cell phone. No doubt to call the sheriff. "Well, I'm not leaving town." Deputy Harp Cole eyed her suitcases. "So you can call your boss and tell him that my offer to have my marriage annulled still stands. Maybe AJ would like to chip in for the cost since she apparently is quite close to my husband."

"The way I hear it, you won't be needing much money in prison. I'm sure Cyrus won't have any trouble getting your so-called marriage annulled once you're indicted for murder and attempted murder."

She cocked her head at him, seeing that she was no longer intimidating him. "I have no idea what you're talking about. Anyway, like I said, I'm not leaving town. I'm only moving to other accommodations. It's too noisy in the hotel."

"That's good to hear."

"Now, if you will excuse me," she said.

As she started to load the suitcases into the car, the deputy said, "Let me help you with those."

"You are such a gentleman." He blushed. "Maybe you'd like to come into the hotel bar and have a drink with me."

"I'm a married man," he said as if shocked that she would ask. "Also I'm on duty."

"I see. Well, I can save you from having to watch me. I'm moving to those cabins at the edge of town."

"The Happy Holiday Cabins and Kitchenettes?" he asked in surprise.

"Delightful name, wouldn't you say? Yes. So you can tell your boss for me." She winked at him and turned back into the hotel. She needed a drink before she could face the Happy Holiday.

AFTER A LONG day of flying across the country and then driving two hours, AJ announced that they were almost to Gilt Edge. Cyrus saw that it was nearly dark. The sky to the west burned a bright orange, highlighting the mountains around the small western town as she drove into the outskirts.

Escaping the Caribbean and the island, Cyrus thought he would feel less anxious. But he was going home to Montana to a family he didn't know. Worse, to a wife that he couldn't remember marrying—and suspected she'd tried to kill him not once but three times.

"It's going to be all right," AJ said, letting go of the wheel to reach over and squeeze his hand.

He smiled at her. What would he have done without her? He couldn't have stayed on the island but he also couldn't have left without identification.

Thanks to her, he knew his name. But he still didn't know who he was and feared he might never know. That dark hole in his memory had teased him when it came to AJ. But other than her, he'd felt nothing when he had looked at the photos of his family. Now he was about to meet them in the flesh. They would be expecting him to know them.

He'd hoped his memory would come back in a brilliant flash, filling in all the blanks, the moment he reached Montana or saw Gilt Edge. But as he looked around, he felt no recognition at all. The frustration made him angry and gave him a headache.

"Don't push it," AJ said. "Pretend this is the first time you've ever been here."

His laugh held no humor. "As far as my memory is concerned, it is. I hate the thought of disappointing my family."

"They understand the situation. They'll give you time and if you never remember, you'll get to know them fresh. They love you and you'll love them. I've certainly fallen for them."

"And for me?"

She smiled over at him. "What do you think?"

He smiled, feeling a little better. At least he wasn't facing this alone. He wasn't sure he could do that. He felt like a newborn, completely lost in a world that had been going on without him.

Stretching his legs, he realized that his body ached from sitting this long in planes and an automobile. The hard physical work he'd done on the island had helped him recuperate and get stronger. This day had been hard. They'd landed in Miami and quickly gotten on a commercial flight to Minneapolis, where they'd boarded yet another plane to Billings where AJ had a rental car waiting.

From there it had been another two-hour drive to Gilt Edge. AJ hadn't been kidding about how hard it was to get to his home. Apparently the town was in the middle of the state, and only accessible by two-lane roads from what he could see.

He felt as lost as he had when he'd crawled up the beach on that island. He didn't know where he was, nothing looked familiar, all this immense wide-open country with no one for miles made him feel as if he was on the moon. Had this really been his home?

He could feel AJ's gaze on him. She'd been watching him. He could feel her hope, the strength of it making him weak. He wanted to please her more than take his next breath. But he wasn't remembering. He might never remember.

That thought terrified him because he feared AJ would never be able to live with that and he would lose her.

"So where's the ranch in relation to town?" he asked, needing to say something. Needing to show an interest.

"It's set against the Judith Mountains overlooking the town." Clearly she hadn't understood his question.

"So it's not so isolated?"

She laughed. "Yes and no. You love riding up in the mountains where you aren't going to see another person all day."

"So I've always liked solitude?"

"And hard manual labor. You said only your brother Hawk could string barbed wire fence faster than you."

"So I have always worked with my hands," he said, looking down at his calluses. "And we raise cattle."

"Black Angus."

Just outside of town he'd seen a pasture full of rust-and-white cows. Herefords. His eyes widened. "Those cows right outside of town? Were those Herefords?"

"Yep." She froze for a moment and then glanced away from her driving for a moment to stare at him. "You know Herefords?"

"Apparently."

She broke into a smile that lit up her face. Could she be any more beautiful? "Progress," she said and nodded, still smiling.

"Maybe," he said and looked ahead. "How much farther?"

JULIETTE EMPTIED THE drink in front of her and looked around the cabin, feeling sick to her stomach. She'd had a drink at the hotel and then headed for the liquor store where she'd bought herself a bottle of gin and some tonic. At the grocery store, she'd bought limes and a little food for her kitchenette.

That her life had come to this frightened her more than the thought of coming face-to-face with her...husband. If her family could see her now, wouldn't they have just loved to see how far she'd fallen. She poured herself another drink, even as she warned herself she would need her wits about her when Cyrus arrived. He'd probably bring his sheriff brother with him.

She groaned at the thought as she started to lift the drink to her lips. Her phone rang. Putting down the drink, she pulled out her cell, feeling a little sick and hating that apparently she couldn't hold her alcohol anymore. She saw who was calling with a sense of relief. At least she could put off dealing with Cyrus for a little bit longer.

"Could use a little good news," she said, picking up. "Cyrus and his girlfriend are headed home. Unless they aren't... Tell me the sheriff's information is flawed."

"Sorry, but we couldn't stop them," Otis said.

She swore, leaning against the makeshift bar for support. This whole thing had been a gigantic nightmare. "I should have listened to Arthur."

"Or me," the ex-cop said. "But it's not too late to cut your losses and get out."

"That's your sage advice?" she snapped. "Let's not forget how little money I have in the bank, shall we?"

"Go to the south of France, some fancy resort. Put it on a card and pick yourself up another sugar daddy. Or marry me and stop all this foolishness."

She laughed. "And how will we live?"

"We aren't that broke."

"I don't want to live like that anymore. I can't." She shook her head and felt dizzy. That drink was probably a mistake. She hadn't been feeling good all day. Her stomach. She blamed this town, this situation, this mess.

"I don't think we really have a choice at this point," Otis said. "Cyrus could already be in Montana. Depending on what flights they managed to get, he could be in Gilt Edge by tonight."

She swore and stumbled over to one of the threadbare chairs to sit down. "I thought you said you hired some islanders to take care of this?"

"Two of the locals were almost killed trying."

She couldn't believe this. "Are you trying to tell me that Cyrus, in the shape he's apparently in, fought off these men?"

"Maybe it was his girlfriend," he joked.

"You think this is funny?"

"Julie…"

She got up, feeling light-headed and nauseous. She stepped into the first bedroom. She just needed to lie down. "You should have taken care of it yourself. You know how hiring someone to take care of these things often gets…messy. What if they sing like canaries?"

"Neither of them are credible and both have iffy relationships with the law, so I'm not worried about that."

"What do you know?" she demanded angrily.

"His girlfriend purchased plane tickets to San Juan and from Miami to Minneapolis with the final destination Billings, Montana."

"Wait how are they getting from San Juan to Miami?"

"Private jet I would imagine. Apparently his girlfriend has money."

"Are you just trying to piss me off?" she demanded.

"Just trying to warn you. With any luck, they could be in Gilt Edge at any time."

She lay on the bed, staring up at the cracked ceiling as she tried to get her stomach to settle down. It felt as if the room was going to start spinning.

"I don't know what more we can do, Julie. If you're determined to play this out, when they get back to Montana, I think things could get worse. Much worse unless you do something drastic."

"Drastic? Like hire someone here to take care of them? In Cyrus's hometown where his brother is sheriff?"

"No, I'm telling you I think it's a mistake not to end this and cut your losses. I told you to pass this one, but you thought he would be easy pickings."

"He should have been," she said under her breath. "Otis, I need you."

He chuckled. "I do like the sound of that. But it would be dangerous, me coming there."

"More dangerous than leaving me in the same small town as Cyrus and his girlfriend?"

"I think you need to find out just how much he remembers," Otis said. "He either doesn't remember anything or he has his reasons for not talking. Otherwise, we'd all be in jail right now. I suspect that blow to his head when he hit the railing jarred something loose and he doesn't remember what happened."

She scoffed at that. "If so, that doesn't mean his memory won't come back and when it does... We can't let that happen," she said, closing her eyes. "Cyrus must still be in bad shape if it has taken this long for him to return home. A man like that could be suicidal, don't you think?"

He groaned. "You're talking about taking a hell of a chance."

She sat up abruptly and felt the room spin. Had she caught some bug going around?

"You still there?" Otis asked.

"Yes." The room had stopped spinning. At least for the moment. "We can't have Cyrus Cahill testifying against us. It would be the final nail in our coffins. So far the investigations in Arizona and Florida have hit dead ends. Okay, I screwed this one up, but I need your help to fix it."

"But what about his girlfriend?"

"I'll take care of her. She's really been a fly in the ointment. So she's mine," Juliette said, realizing she needed to get off the phone because she was going to throw up.

CHAPTER NINETEEN

AJ COULD SEE that Cyrus was nervous as she drove into Gilt Edge. Cyrus was staring out the window at the small western town as if he'd never seen it before.

She tried to imagine what it would be like to have no memory of any of this. Not knowing your name or your family or anything about who you were. Her heart went out to him at just the thought of how hard this must be for him.

Cyrus seemed to be worried about what kind of person he was. Before all of this, she would have said he was down-to-earth, responsible, solid. A man who didn't make hasty decisions. A man a woman could depend on.

Had there been a side to Cyrus Cahill that no one, including his family—and especially her—hadn't seen?

She braked for a stoplight along the main street of town. "Your brother Flint said he'd be waiting for us at the sheriff's office—"

"I want to see Juliette."

"Juliette?" she asked, surprised and a little taken back. He wanted to see his wife first? "Have you remembered her?" A sharp blade of jealousy cut into her heart.

"No. But she's supposedly the reason I ended up on a cruise ship, married and later near drowned after going overboard. I want to see her." He looked over at AJ. "I have to know how I could have fallen for another woman when it was clear to me that I was falling for you before I left Montana."

She smiled at him, even though her heart felt close to breaking. He could say that now, but who knows how he felt the night he met Juliette at the bar after a couple of drinks. Being in a large city where no one knew him, it was hard to say how he could have reacted to Juliette making a pass at him. Or how he would have felt the next morning.

"Okay, Juliette first." She was terrified of what would happen when he saw the woman he'd married. Would he take one look at the woman and remember everything? Was that what he was hoping? "It's just that your family is anxious to see you." The light changed and she drove on through the intersection. "But we can start wherever you want. I can drop you at her hotel—"

"I want you to come with me."

AJ shot a look at him. "Me?"

"Yes, if you don't mind."

It took her a moment. "Not at all. Actually, the last thing I want you to do is be anywhere near that woman alone. Once you get your memory back—"

"Nothing will change," he said as he touched her shoulder. He gave it a squeeze. "Where is she staying?"

"At the hotel."

AJ pulled the rental car up in front of the hotel, cut the engine and looked over at Cyrus. He looked as nervous and anxious as she felt. "Are you all right?"

She'd driven the two hours since Cyrus had no idea where they were headed even if he'd had a valid driver's license on him. If Juliette really had filed the death certificate, then it might take a while to get him identification even if he remembered who he was.

Nerves jangling at the thought of what would happen when he saw his wife again, she said, "I can wait here for you." Would he instantly remember Juliette? AJ tried not to think about it. So much was riding on him remembering, and at the same time if he remembered Juliette would that mean that he had fallen in love with her?

"I was hoping you'd come with me," he said.

She shot him a look. "You want me to go with you?"

"Is that asking too much? You've already done—"

"No, I'd be happy to."

He smiled. "Thanks. I figure this can go down one of two ways. I don't know her from Adam."

"Or you recognize her and remember why you married her," she said, looking away.

"I don't think either of us believes that is going to happen." His voice was as soft as his touch. He brushed his fingers over her cheek. She swallowed the lump in her throat and turned to him. "I know this is hard on you and I'm so sorry about that."

She couldn't speak. He looked out at the lights of the town. She followed his gaze, feeling as if she was seeing Gilt Edge with different eyes. She'd fallen in love with this place and the man next to her. Now she was taking him to see his wife? "I'm not sure I can do this," she said, her voice breaking.

He reached over and put a hand on her arm. "Trust me."

She shot him a look. Something in his voice… "Are you remembering something?"

He shook his head. "Maybe I'm starting to trust that I'm the man you believed in. That man wouldn't have done what I'm told I did. Isn't that why you came looking for me? Because you didn't believe it."

She nodded. "I felt that something was wrong with the story."

He smiled at her. "I'm so glad you did. You're so strong."

"I wish I was as strong as you think I am," she said with a chuckle as she turned to look at the old brick hotel.

"Oh, you've already proved that."

AJ tried to relax. There was still so much on the line, but he was right. She was strong enough to see this through and Cyrus wanted her to trust him. She realized she would trust him with her life.

She straightened her shoulders and looked over at him. "Ready?"

He smiled at her. "Let's get this over with."

She opened her door and he did the same. Stepping out she looked up at the towering structure. Cyrus's reaction to Juliette would confirm her greatest hope—or fear.

But she was also anxious to see Juliette's reaction to seeing Cyrus. That he'd changed was impossible not to notice. Some of his scars had healed, but there were others that she feared might never heal. Nor was he the easygoing shy cowboy AJ had known and fallen in love with.

This Cyrus was wary, suspicious. He was more direct just as she suspected he was more dangerous. But there seemed to be an even greater strength to him. He was ready to face whatever had happened to him. The man she'd found had been scared. This man was determined. If he feared what was ahead, it didn't show on his face.

He led her through the front door of the hotel. At the main desk, he asked for Juliette's room.

"Last name?" the clerk asked.

"Cahill."

"I'm sorry, Mrs. Cahill has checked out."

She shot Cyrus a surprised look.

"When?" he asked.

"Earlier today."

Today? The day Cyrus was returning? AJ wanted to scream.

"Did she mention where she was going?" Cyrus asked.

"I'm sorry," the clerk said, shaking his head.

As they turned and walked out, Cyrus said, "She must have known I would be coming by to see her."

AJ had been afraid of what would happen when Cyrus and Juliette came face-to-face. Now she was just angry. "This proves that she's guilty as hell."

Cyrus seemed more amused than angry. "You said she's trying to get money out of my family. If so, then she hasn't gone far or if she has, she'll be back."

She was boiling mad as she slid behind the wheel.

As Cyrus climbed in, he said, "Let's go see my brother, the sheriff. Maybe he knows where she's gone."

"He said he'd be waiting for us at his office."

At the sheriff's office, they walked in and Deputy Harper Cole came rushing over. "Cyrus, unbelievable," Harp said. "You really did survive falling off a cruise ship?"

"So it would seem," Cyrus answered.

"Wow, what a story you will have to tell," Harp said, clearly excited. Cyrus, she realized, was now a local hero.

"The sheriff is waiting on us," AJ said, anxious to get to Flint's office. This was hard enough on Cyrus.

"Well, it's good to see you." Harp went on out the door, but kept glancing back at him.

"Does everyone know?" Cyrus asked.

"It's a small town," she said.

As they neared Flint's office, Cyrus seemed to slow his steps. Her heart went out to him. She couldn't imagine how hard this was for him. Everyone was a complete stranger whether friend or family. They had expectations that Cyrus couldn't meet. Might never be able to meet.

She took his hand and squeezed it before starting down the hall, knowing that Flint had been waiting for this for a very long time.

FLINT HAD JUST glanced at his watch, anxious and getting more worried, when he looked up to see AJ standing in his office doorway. His heart took off like a wild stallion in a storm as AJ stepped in. He stared at the open doorway, afraid for a moment that Cyrus wouldn't appear in it.

Several heartbeats later, a man filled the doorway. The hair was bleached lighter from the sun, the skin a deep, dark brown, the body leaner. A quarter moon scar marred one cheek and there were lines around his eyes that Flint didn't remember.

But the biggest change was the gray eyes themselves. He looked into his brother's gaze and felt his heart break at what Cyrus had been through. There was no recognition. Just pain. Flint couldn't bear to think about what horrifying things had happen to him and what he was still going to have to face.

The sheriff blinked. AJ had said that Cyrus had changed but still it came as a shock. His heart though instantly swelled to overflowing. He pushed himself up out of his chair and rushed around his desk to throw his arms around his brother. It didn't matter that Cyrus stiffened in his arms. Nothing mattered now that his brother was home, alive and safe. At least for the moment.

"Oh God, Cyrus, I can't believe it. I thought you were gone." Flint's voice broke. He pulled back to look into his brother's face. He looked into those familiar gray eyes and saw absolutely no recall. He couldn't help the part of him that winced. He hugged him again and stepped back.

"Sorry," Cyrus said and tapped his temple.

Flint nodded. "It's okay. I'm just glad that you're alive." He cleared his voice. "It's a miracle." He couldn't help staring at his brother. "Can I get you anything?" Cyrus shook his head. "Have a seat. Did you have any trouble getting here?" he said and stepped to AJ to give her a hug and whisper, "Thank you. Thank you so much."

AJ pulled up a chair, Cyrus remained standing. "We were attacked twice in the past twenty-four hours on the island," she said as Flint took his seat again behind his desk.

"But you're all right."

AJ nodded. "Someone definitely didn't want us to leave the island alive. Both of the men who attacked us…" Her voice broke. She glanced over at Cyrus. "Juliette had to be behind it."

Flint shook his head. "This has been such a nightmare."

She nodded, tears in her eyes as she reached for Cyrus's hand. "Sorry, it's just been… I'm not used to people trying to kill me."

"I'm not sure it's something you get used to," Flint said and looked at his brother again. Cyrus was so different. Wary, like AJ had told him. He now looked as if wired to spring at a moment's notice. There was distrust in his gaze and almost an expectation that someone would try to harm him again.

"We stopped by to see Juliette," AJ said into the tense silence that had fallen in the room. "She checked out earlier today."

Flint nodded. "Sorry, I should have told you. I had a deputy watching the hotel. She hadn't gone far."

"She doesn't know he has no memory of what happened?" AJ asked.

Flint shook his head. "But she's suspicious. Probably because she's done this before and knows that if the police aren't at her door arresting her, then there's a problem. I'm not sure she believes Cyrus is really alive—let alone that he's well enough to return."

He reached into the file he'd started on Juliette and pulled out two photographs. "We've been going through the surveillance videos from the ship. We've been able to find Juliette talking to two different men on board. It appeared that she knew them both. Once we were able to identify them, it turns out that she does know them."

Flint slid the photos across the desk. AJ picked up the one of Otis Claremont, a dark-haired man with a mustache. "That's the former detective from Arizona. He worked in Scottsdale when one of Juliette's husband's died. That's where the investigation is continuing. Otis quit a few months after the murder."

"He was on the ship?" Cyrus asked and took a seat next to AJ. She handed him the photo. He stared at it for a long time.

"Do you recognize him?" Flint asked.

He shook his head and picked up the second photo.

"That's Arthur Davis. He was Juliette's first husband back when her name was Julie," the sheriff said.

Cyrus studied the photo and asked, "She didn't kill him?"

"He didn't have any money. He was also on board the ship and we have him talking to Juliette," Flint said. "But while suspicious, it's not evidence. Do you recognize either of them?"

His brother shook his head and put down the photos.

AJ looked as disappointed as Flint felt. "You know their being on the ship isn't a coincidence. They had something to do with Cyrus being thrown overboard on her orders while she holed up in her cabin pretending to be knocked out on seasick medicine so she'd have an alibi."

Flint nodded. "Like I said, she has experience at this. But we have no proof." He was glad that she was a lawyer and wasn't demanding he arrest Juliette on circumstantial evidence like his family had been doing. He looked to his brother.

"I'm sorry," Cyrus said. "I know how important it is that I remember." He shook his head. "Believe me, I've tried. I need to know what happened, starting in Denver and ending up half-dead on that island." His eyes hardened as they met Flint's. "It seems pretty clear that my…wife is behind all of this."

Flint nodded. He looked from AJ to his brother again. "I'm not sure if you want to hear—"

"Whatever you found out, I need to know."

"I believe AJ has told you what we found out about Juliette." He couldn't help staring at Cyrus and at the same time marveling that he was still alive. "Have you heard the term *black widow*?" he asked as he pulled the file over and opened it. "She's gone through a variety of names over the years. She was born Julie Barnes in a small town in Idaho. Most recent name, Carrington. Married the first time at sixteen, faked a pregnancy. That marriage ended about the time she met her first husband with money. He had an accident involving a ladder. Four marriages followed, with more husbands making her a widow. Each time, she moved up financially."

"So I was just one of a long line," Cyrus said.

"All of Julie's husbands, except for the first one, died under suspicious circumstances. Unfortunately, it is hard to prove she was involved because she has been very careful and made sure she always has an alibi."

"So she married me to kill me," Cyrus said and frowned. "But I'm not wealthy. Far from it, right?"

"I think there's a chance she overheard you talking about buying a three-hundred-thousand-dollar bull," Flint said. "Juliette said you met in the bar that night. I contacted the man you bought the bull from. He said the two of you had a couple of drinks in the hotel bar to celebrate the deal. He said he noticed a nice-looking blonde and that she approached you as the two of you were leaving the bar."

"So he saw her," Cyrus said. "Did he say what happened after that?"

"He left but he thought the woman was hitting on you. She

had her hand on your arm and she was leaning into you, whispering something into your ear."

Flint saw AJ tense. "The next day you were on a ship, married and, twenty-four hours later, you were missing. Man overboard."

Cyrus sighed and shook his head. "There has to be more to it. I might not know who I am, but I can't see myself marrying anyone that quickly." He looked over at AJ. "Nor could this Juliette have stolen my heart."

The sheriff reached into the file and pulled out a copy of the photo the police commissioner had sent him. It was of Cyrus and Juliette being married by the ship's captain. "You can see that the day and time were stamped on it."

"That's my wife?" Cyrus asked. "No." His brother stared at the photo for a long moment. "There is something wrong," he said and looked up at Flint.

"You look drunk. But you might have been drugged. I'm sure AJ has probably told you that you hit a lower railing when you fell from the ship and left blood that the FBI had examined to make sure it was yours. They also did a toxicology screen and found drugs in your system," he said.

Cyrus shook his head. "Even drunk and drugged, I still wouldn't have married her."

"How can you be sure of that?" Flint asked.

His brother got to his feet. "I need to see her. You said you had a deputy watching the hotel? So you know where she went."

"I'll see if she's there to save you the trip," Flint said, "since it's getting late." He called Juliette. Her phone rang four times before she picked up.

"Hello?" She sounded like she'd been asleep. He wondered if she was a drinker. Something told him she liked being in control too much to lose that control with alcohol or anything else.

"Juliette, it's Sheriff Cahill. I just wanted to let you know that

Cyrus is back in town. He's anxious to see you. He stopped by your hotel but was told that you have checked out."

"Yes, it was too noisy, but you already know that since I told your deputy Harp. We had a nice talk. How sweet of you to have a deputy watching my every move. I'm staying at the motor court on the edge of town. The one with the small cabins."

"The Happy Holiday Cabins and Kitchenettes," he said. "Maybe he could meet you somewhere else."

The chuckle was filled with amusement. "If he's so anxious to see me, I would think my little cabin here would be perfect."

"Why don't I have him give you a call and the two of you can set up a time to meet." He hung up.

AJ had leaped to her feet when she'd overheard the conversation. "Juliette? The same Juliette I met when I was here is staying out there in those old cabins?" she demanded. "Why would she leave the hotel?"

"She said the hotel was too noisy."

AJ's eyes widened. "Noisy? For her to move to a place like that... What is she planning to do, kill someone else?" She'd let out a cry. "Oh my God, she is."

"We aren't going to let that happen," Flint assured her and Cyrus. "I have a deputy watching her cabin. But still, I want the two of you to be careful. It would be better to call her and meet somewhere else besides the cabin. In a public place or..."

Cyrus was shaking his head. "I want her to feel safe. I want her to think she's going to get away with this. We know how dangerous she can be if she doesn't." He got to his feet. "If you don't mind, I'd prefer to see her without the law being with me."

Flint wanted to argue, but he could see that his brother was determined to do this—and his way. So maybe this Cyrus wasn't that much different from the old one.

"We passed a motor court on the way in with small cabins," Cyrus said.

"That's the one," Flint said.

"You can't be serious," AJ said to Cyrus. "She's already tried to kill you three times. Those cabins probably stay empty this time of year and being on the edge of town…"

"It's all right," Cyrus said and smiled at her.

Flint saw how close the two had become. "Just be careful. There's a deputy watching the place and I'm only a phone call away. And don't forget, this woman is a ruthless killer."

"I'm not likely to forget that," Cyrus said. "It wasn't that long ago that I came to in the dark sea half drowned and completely alone. If I hadn't latched onto a buoy that had come loose in the storm, I would be another of her dead husbands."

CHAPTER TWENTY

"I CAN'T COME the rest of the way to Montana."

"What?" Juliette snapped into the phone. She'd known there was a problem when Otis had called back so quickly. She had enough problems.

"I just got a call from my friend at the department," he said. "There's a BOLO out on me. Seems Sheriff Flint Cahill wants to know where I am."

She swore under her breath. "Does that mean what I think it does?"

"It means that he knows about me and you. That's all he can know. We were careful on the ship. We made sure that we weren't caught on the surveillance camera that night. But the last thing I can do is come up there. I can't fly, rent a car or even drive to get to you since all a cop has to do is run my plates and I'll get picked up for questioning."

She couldn't believe this. After all this time, trapped in this horrible place with it snowing almost every day. She'd had the nightmare every night and would wake up in a cold sweat. She hadn't dreamed about her childhood in years and now this had brought it all back.

"What am I supposed to do?" she cried. This was the lowest she'd felt in years.

"If you're determined—"

"We need the money," she snapped. "And we can't chance that Cyrus will remember. Once he's gone, we'll be safe. I can't do this anymore."

"I hope that means that you are finally ready to settle down. With me."

She looked in the discolored mirror on the cabin wall. Somewhere along the way to this point, she'd lost her youth. There were fine lines around her eyes and mouth. She was almost forty-five. She still pass for thirty-five or younger, but her days of picking up the really wealthy men were behind her. Even with one foot in the grave, they could get the twentysomethings and she couldn't pass for that anymore.

"This is the last con."

Otis let out a pleased sound. "Then get Arthur to take care of it."

"Arthur?" She practically choked on the word. "You can't be serious."

"He can handle this. I'll walk him through it from here."

She tried to relax.

"Have you seen him?" Otis asked.

"No, not yet. But I moved out of the hotel and into a cabin in a stand of pines at the edge of town."

"Why would you do that?"

"For obvious reasons. If there is going to be a problem, I don't want witnesses."

"Good thinking."

She rolled her eyes. She'd always been the brains in this outfit. Otis and Arthur were the muscle. "Just make sure Arthur doesn't screw this up."

"You'll need to pick him up. He's flying into Billings tomorrow night using his fake ID. He should be fine as long as you keep him undercover until it's time. But given this new problem, Julie, I wish you'd change your mind."

"My plan is going to work," she said. "I have a new angle."

"A new angle?"

"I don't want to talk about it because it might jinx it."

He laughed. "You've never been superstitious." He had no idea. "I'm worried about you."

She shook her head and felt nauseous again. "Otis, please—"

"Julie, when this is over—"

"We'll talk." She'd put him off for years and knew that she couldn't keep telling him they would eventually get married. "I have to go." She disconnected and raced to the bathroom to throw up again.

AJ FELT AS IF she couldn't breathe. The weight on her chest made even walking from the car to the front door of cabin number seven feel impossible. When Flint had told them that Juliette had moved to the Happy Holiday Cabins and Kitchenettes, she'd thought he was joking at first.

Until she'd realized the woman's real reason.

And now they were about to step into the black widow's web.

"You okay?" Cyrus asked now as they neared the front of the cabin. It sat back in the pines, rustic and a little worn.

She nodded, unable to speak. It was a cold night in early March, the snow deep from a long winter, the kind of night that made her think spring would never come. But the weather was the last thing on her mind.

The big question hung between her and Cyrus. Would he

take one look at Juliette and remember everything? Remember that he'd fallen in love with her?

"It's going to be all right," he said. He'd been partway to the door, but had turned and come back to her because she'd stopped to stare at the cabin, suddenly too scared to move.

"Are you sure you shouldn't go in alone?"

"The only reason my brother the sheriff isn't here with us is because I needed to do this and not with a lawman but with someone I trusted. Someone who Juliette won't feel threatened by."

She met his gaze. "When I get around her, believe me, I want to do more than threaten her. But what if—"

"We can stay out here all night going over the what-ifs. How about we get this over with?"

She swallowed, shivering from the cold and the fear. "I'm scared." She knew he had to be just as nervous, just as anxious, probably even more than she was. But he hid it well.

"She isn't going to do anything to either of us. I'll protect you."

AJ laughed and shook her head. "That isn't what I'm afraid of."

"I know. But I'm not afraid. You know why?" He went on before she could answer. "Because my heart tells me that it's you I've been in love with for a very long time."

She eyed him skeptically.

"I'm not just saying that."

From behind him there was a sound of a door cracking open a few inches and then closing again.

"Let's do this," he whispered.

"Juliette isn't going to like me being here," she whispered back.

He took her hand. "Like I care. I love you."

I love you, she mouthed as the cabin door opened again.

"Are the two of you going to stay out there all night whispering or are you going to come in?" demanded a strident female voice.

Cyrus chuckled. "You didn't mention how delightful my wife is." He turned then and, holding AJ's hand, drew them both toward the open doorway.

She saw Juliette's gaze go to their entwined fingers as she moved to let them enter the cabin before she scowled and shifted her gaze to Cyrus.

"Cyrus," she cried. "I can't believe it. But it's really you."

CYRUS STARED AT the woman in the stark overhead light of the rented cabin. The photo of her at their wedding hadn't done her justice. She was tall, blonde and blue-eyed with a classically beautiful face. She could have been a model, she was that exquisite and she knew it.

She rushed to him. As she neared he saw that she wasn't as young or as flawless closer up. She threw her arms around him. He felt AJ extract her hand from his as Juliette kissed him passionately on the lips.

As he started to shove her back, she quickly let go. "I'm sorry. I hope I didn't hurt you. I heard that you've been recuperating on some island. Are you all right?"

"I'm fine." He looked into her soulless blue eyes—so different from AJ's—and then he turned to see AJ hanging back as if edging toward the door to escape. All the color had drained from her face. He moved to her. His gaze locking with hers.

He could see the question in her expression. He shook his head and, taking her hand again, turned and said to Juliette, "I'm sure you've probably heard, but AJ saved my life down in the islands."

Juliette's expression was all venom as it shifted to AJ but she managed a sneer of a smile. "Yes, but I was hoping we would have some time alone, but if you need your…nursemaid, by all means."

He felt AJ tense. He squeezed her hand and they moved to the sagging couch. "I have so many questions," he said as he and AJ sat down.

"I feel the same way," Juliette gushed. "I've been going mad worrying about you," she said as she closed the door. "Imagine how I felt when I was told that you were alive but that I couldn't talk to you, couldn't even know where you were? After all, I *am* your wife."

"Yes," Cyrus said. "That's something I want to talk to you about. Why don't you sit down and tell me everything."

Juliette stiffened. "Can I offer you something to drink first?"

"No," he said, and saw that she liked to be in control. But how did she get control over him in Denver. That was the question. He wouldn't have taken this woman's bait. He was sure of it. So how did he end up marrying her?

Juliette sighed and sat in one of the chairs facing them. "I'm sure AJ has filled you in on my part." She made a pointed glare at their hand-holding and AJ pulled free. "I want to know what happened to you."

"I was hoping you would tell *me*," he said.

She shrugged. "I would think AJ would have told you."

"I've heard the version you gave the ship's captain and the FBI," he said.

"There's no other version."

"Really? How about starting with Denver."

Juliette drew back in surprise. She let out a nervous laugh. "You don't remember?" There was definitely relief in her voice. She glanced at AJ. "Surely you don't want me to tell it in front of your…nursemaid."

"AJ isn't my nursemaid."

"Fine, your girlfriend, because it's clear that the two of you have become very close. You're making dissolving our marriage much easier every minute."

"Denver," he repeated.

"It was love at first sight."

He shook his head. "I don't believe that. You're not my type."

Juliette's gaze went to AJ. "I don't know what she's been telling you—"

"Let's pretend that it was love at first sight. Then why was it AJ who came looking for me believing I was alive," Cyrus said and met the woman's blue gaze, "and not my loving wife? Why didn't you come looking for me?"

Juliette wet her lips and then looked at him with doe eyes. "Everyone said there was no way you could have survived..." She pretended to tear up, and then met his gaze. When she saw that he wasn't buying any of it, she started to say something, but then quickly excused herself and rushed down a short hallway. A moment later he heard her throwing up.

He and AJ exchanged a look. As Juliette continued to heave and gag, AJ got to her feet.

"I didn't fall for this woman," he said. "She's lying."

"Then how did you end up married to her?" AJ asked. He shook his head. "She's just going to keep lying," she said as she walked nervously around the cabin's main room as if unable to sit still any longer. "Maybe you should have come with Flint. Or—" She stopped at a trash can at the edge of the apartment-size kitchen.

He was about to apologize for putting her through this, when he saw her eyes widen in alarm as she reached into the trash and lifted out a small box with bright lettering on it. She peered inside and let out a curse.

The bathroom door opened and Juliette stepped out. She was

apologizing as she touched a tissue to her lips, but then she saw AJ and what she was holding and froze.

AJ held up the box, her face white as the snow outside. "You're pregnant?" she cried.

CHAPTER TWENTY-ONE

"THIS IS NOT the way I wanted to tell you," Juliette said quickly and glared at AJ before rushing over to Cyrus and dropping on her hands and knees in front of him. She pursed her lips in what she must have thought was a cute little girl pout.

"It's a miracle," Juliette was saying. "Remember, I told you that I didn't think I could have children."

"No, I don't remember," he said.

"Well, it's true. Imagine my surprise."

AJ dropped the pregnancy test back into the trash with distaste and fought tears. She told herself it couldn't be Cyrus's baby. She felt as if the room was spinning and just wanted out.

Turning, she charged the door, fumbled with the knob and finally got it open before racing out into the winter evening gasping for air.

Behind her, she heard Cyrus arguing with Juliette, who wanted him to stay so they could talk about this amazing thing that had happened between them. She heard Cyrus coming after her.

"It's not my baby," he said, catching up to her.

"You don't know that," she said as he turned her to face him, surprised that she was crying.

"AJ, I couldn't have purposely married that woman. Are you listening to me? She's a con woman. This is just another con."

"No, Cyrus. It's not." All she could think about was the pregnancy test results she'd seen in the trash. "She's really pregnant. I saw the test. It was positive."

He looked shaken. "Well, it can't be mine." But his voice lacked his earlier conviction.

"It is yours," Juliette said from the open doorway of the cabin.

For a moment they'd both forgotten about her.

AJ pulled free of Cyrus and went to the rental car, opened the door and climbed behind the wheel. As she started the engine, she was shaking so hard her teeth chattered. She turned on the heater, knowing it would be a few minutes before it blew anything other than cold air, but didn't care.

Cyrus had moved back to the open doorway and Juliette. She couldn't hear what he was saying to the woman. She watched Juliette look hurt and start to cry and had to look away.

A moment later, Cyrus climbed into the passenger side of the car. "Let's get out of here."

IT HAD BEEN a long couple of days, Cyrus thought and then laughed to himself at how ridiculous that thought was. Since he'd woken up alone in the dark in the ocean gasping for breath and having no idea how he'd gotten there, his life had been a terrifying nightmare.

He looked over at AJ. She was staring straight ahead and driving as if not really knowing where she was headed, just driving. "I can't see the rest of the family now," he said.

She glanced over at him and blinked. Clearly she'd been reliving what had just happened in that cabin back there. "Where—"

"Can you drop me off somewhere? At a motel or how about

that hotel where Juliette had been staying. I'm afraid I'm going to have to borrow some money though."

She stared at him for a moment before turning back to her driving. They hadn't talked about what would happen when they got back to Montana. Had she thought he would return to his room at the ranch as if nothing had happened? Or had she thought he would stay with her?

That's what he wanted but she lived upstairs over the saloon that his sister and brother owned. He couldn't very well go there without seeing the family and he wasn't ready. He needed some time. He said as much to her.

AJ turned down the street to the hotel. "I understand."

Did she? He hoped so. "I'll call you first thing in the morning from my room." She nodded. "I never slept with that woman."

"You can't be sure of that. You shared a berth on the ship even before you were married." She didn't look at him, as if she couldn't bear it.

"I love *you*." He saw her face crumble, her fingers gripping the steering wheel so tight her knuckles went white as she pulled up to the hotel and stopped.

"I love you," she said and reached for her purse. As she started to give him money, he put his hand over hers.

"We're going to figure this out." She nodded as he took the money, thanked her and climbed out. "I'll call you in the morning," he said again and closed the door.

AJ BURST INTO tears as she shifted the car into gear and drove to her apartment over the Stagecoach Saloon. She'd heard that the saloon had reopened after Ely's funeral. She parked in the back, hoping that she could sneak in and not be seen in the condition she was in. But as she opened the back door, Billie Dee saw her and dropped what she was doing to rush to her.

In the arms of the large loving cook, she began to cry again.

"What is it?" Billie Dee said in alarm.

"It's Juliette."

"Oh her," the cook said. "What matters is you're home. Where is Cyrus?"

"At the hotel."

"The hotel? What is he doing there?"

AJ shook her head as she looked at the older woman. She and Billie Dee had hit it off. AJ loved her like a second mother. Billie Dee was the reason she'd come to Montana to begin with. She'd tracked down the cook after finding out that she was Gigi's birth mother. She'd had to do it on the QT since Gigi said she had no interest in meeting her birth mother.

AJ had wanted to meet the woman first before she told her friend what she was up to. She'd fallen in love with Billie Dee and had eventually told her best friend. It still warmed her heart that she'd been able to bring the two together.

"Juliette," she repeated.

The cook narrowed her eyes. "What's she done now?"

"She's pregnant and she says it's Cyrus's!"

"SHE'S PREGNANT?" FLINT swore when his brother called to tell him.

"I'm telling you, it's not mine," Cyrus said, clearly upset.

Flint groaned. "But you can't know that."

"I *do* know that. I wouldn't have fallen for that woman, let alone marry her. I was in love with AJ."

The sheriff didn't know what to say. "You're sure she's pregnant?"

"She has morning sickness and AJ saw the pregnancy test and said it was definitely positive," Cyrus said. "Isn't there some test to prove that the baby isn't mine?"

Flint was counting the weeks since he'd gotten the call about Cyrus going overboard. "She isn't far enough along, I don't think, for another week or two. The earliest prenatal paternity tests are eight to nine weeks, I think. We can check at the hospital. You realize that if it is your baby it gives her even more leverage."

His brother swore. "That's why I thought for sure that it was a trick. I told her I want a divorce. She pretended that she cared, but said she'll give me a divorce."

Flint scoffed at that. "What she's saying is that she'll give you a divorce for a price. She'll keep bleeding you dry with child support after that—if that baby is yours."

"It's not."

He couldn't help being skeptical since they still didn't know how Cyrus had gotten involved with the woman to begin with and he was no help since he had no memory of it.

"If this woman is a con artist and is being investigated for killing at least two of her husbands—"

"No charges have been brought against her," Flint said. "Just because she's being investigated doesn't mean anything. Innocent until proven guilty. Conning men into marrying her, unfortunately, isn't a crime."

"Killing them for their money is," Cyrus argued.

"Unfortunately both investigations have stalled. The detectives in both cities were hoping you would remember how you ended up in the ocean. With your testimony..."

"Don't you think I've tried to remember? I've tried for weeks. I thought maybe seeing Juliette would do the trick, but I felt nothing. More than nothing. I hated the sight of the woman."

"But you felt something with AJ."

"I did the moment I saw her even though I didn't trust her. I love her. I'm kicking myself for not acting on how I must have obviously felt sooner."

"You don't remember that, either?"

"No. She told me that we went for a horseback ride. I almost kissed her. Maybe if I had..."

"It would have been Hawk who went to Denver to buy the bull. Hawk who is happily married and madly in love with his wife, Dierdre. So Juliette would have probably stayed clear of him."

"It wasn't love that brought Juliette into my life in Denver," his brother said angrily. "Nor infatuation or seduction."

"Then what?"

"That's what I need to find out before this goes any further. We know she drugged me, but she couldn't have kept me so drugged up that I didn't know what was happening. There has to be another explanation."

"Where are you now?" Flint asked.

"I'm staying at the hotel. I needed time alone to think. I know the rest of the family is anxious to see me, but can we please do this tomorrow. It's been a very long day."

"I know it has. Get some rest. I'll let everyone know."

"I have to find out the truth."

"But not alone. The woman tried to kill you."

"Three times," Cyrus said. "But she can't take that chance again."

"I wouldn't be so sure about that. Please stay clear of her. The next time you go to see her, I want to come with you."

"I appreciate your concern, but she isn't going to say anything in front of you. With me alone with no witnesses, she might be honest."

"I wouldn't count on that. If anything, she's in the clear—as long as you don't remember. But if you start... I'm not going to be able to hold off the family much longer. What do you say about breakfast at the saloon tomorrow? I'll pick you up." He could hear his brother hesitate.

"Okay. What time?"

"Not too early. Ten. I would imagine you're still on island time."

Juliette ground her teeth at the memory of AJ standing in this cabin. She swore. The woman had seduced her husband! No wonder it had taken so long to get Cyrus back to Montana. The two had been frolicking on the beach. Jealousy and anger made her rigid for a moment until she remembered that she didn't give a damn about this man. But now she had a way to get a divorce without coming off as the gold-digger wife. Her husband had cheated on her.

She stood in the center of the room and smiled to herself. She still hated AJ, but she had to admit, things couldn't have gone better if she'd planned it. She laughed at the memory of AJ's face when she'd looked into the pregnancy test box. It was priceless.

Juliette grabbed her phone and called her lawyer. "I want to settle. Now. Get the Cahill family to make me an offer I can't refuse," she said without preamble.

"Nice to hear from you too, Juliette. Has something changed?"

"My husband's been cheating on me and I'm pregnant."

Silence. "I see."

"Doubtful. They are going to want a DNA test. I will lose the baby before then, but if Cyrus wants to be free of me, then he is going to have to pay for the privilege."

"I'll see what I can do."

"Tonight. Tell them, otherwise I will leave town and he will never be free to marry his girlfriend."

"And the baby?"

"I will get rid of it and he will never know if it was his or not."

"That's pretty cold."

She laughed. "Trust me, the man's in love and he can't remember a thing. He'll do anything to be free."

Her attorney sighed. "It is always a pleasure doing business with you, Julie," he said facetiously. "I'll get back to you."

She disconnected and looked around the cabin. No more living like this, she told herself. She would go somewhere warm and cheap to live out the rest of her life. Placing a hand over her stomach, she had a moment of weakness when she could see herself with a child in some tropical place. It surprised her.

Just like it surprised her that she could see both Arthur and Otis making good fathers.

She blinked and removed her hand. As if she could stand a squalling baby and being married to either man. No, once she had the money, she would leave the country and neither of them would see her again.

But first, they had to help her take care of Cyrus Cahill.

CHAPTER TWENTY-TWO

THE NEXT MORNING at the Stagecoach Saloon, Billie Dee was making Mexican quiches along with Texas-style biscuits and gravy and slabs of ham for the family breakfast. She was as anxious as the rest of the family to see Cyrus. She wanted everything to be perfect.

Her fiancé, Henry, stopped by to see how she was doing. "Who all is coming?"

"Just immediate family to begin with. Flint thought that would be easier for Cyrus. Then the spouses for the actual breakfast. Please be here for moral support for me."

"Only if you tell me the wedding is still on," her cowboy said as he nuzzled her neck. She still couldn't believe she'd gotten so lucky. She'd come to Montana on the run only to see a sign in the Stagecoach Saloon window that a cook was needed. Staying here had been the smartest thing she'd ever done. Not only did she find a family in the Cahills, but also she'd met Henry Larson and fallen in love. He'd saved her life literally as well as figuratively.

"You drive a hard bargain, but you're on," she said now. "I

talked to Gigi." Billie Dee had only recently been reunited with the daughter she'd given away at birth. "Her restaurant is open and everything is going smoothly again. She said to just tell her when the wedding is and she'll be here. She's been worried about AJ though. She was overjoyed to hear that her best friend found Cyrus and the two of them are back in Montana."

"And Juliette?" Henry asked.

"Ugh. I'd like to forget about her. Well, at least with Cyrus alive, she can't demand his share of the ranch," the cook said.

"I doubt it will be that easy," he said. "So don't be surprised if it takes money to get her out of his life."

"Not if she was the one who shoved him overboard."

"Let's hope Flint can prove it. She doesn't seem like a woman who will walk away with nothing."

Billie Dee shook her head angrily. "How did he get involved with her?"

Henry shrugged. "Hopefully he'll remember."

"Well, you can bet that his story will be a whole lot different from hers."

"For AJ's sake, I hope that's true."

Her face fell. "It is breaking my heart. Now the awful Juliette is pregnant? It can't be his baby. AJ loves him and I thought he was falling for her, as well. I'm usually not wrong about these things."

He smiled at her. "I'm sure you aren't." He kissed her. "I can't wait to make you my wife. Soon."

She smiled. A wedding might be exactly what this family needed, but she realized that couldn't happen until Juliette was out of their lives.

Soon, the family began arriving.

CYRUS WAS WAITING outside the hotel when Flint drove up. Only in Montana could the weather change so drastically. It was

March but it felt more like spring. The temperature was expected to reach high fifties. The snow that had been falling for weeks was now melting. Not that the piles that had been plowed up over the winter were going anywhere until June.

Flint breathed in the day, feeling blessed in so many ways. Montana's big sky was a robin's-egg blue without a cloud anywhere. The sun was warm with the promise of spring. It was a good day for Cyrus to get reacquainted with his family, he thought, and hoped it went well.

Cyrus hopped into the patrol SUV. He didn't look like a man who'd noticed the beautiful March day. February was now behind them. Spring was coming.

"Are you all right?" the sheriff asked.

"I keep running into people who say they know me and know about my 'ordeal.'"

So that was it. "It's a small town and everyone knows you," Flint said.

"So I'm finding out." He didn't sound happy about that. He buckled up as if just wanting to get this over with. If he didn't get his memory back, would he leave here? Flint couldn't stand the thought and yet it seemed more than possible. He could see how hard this was for his brother.

And now they were headed for brunch with the family. He remembered how disappointed he'd been when Cyrus hadn't remembered him. But it would be nothing like his little sister, Lillie, would experience when Cyrus looked at her and didn't have any idea who she was.

"I can't imagine how difficult this is for you," Flint said, "but there's someone I want you to see before we meet the family at the saloon." He looked wary. "It's a local doctor. I've told him about what happened..." He rushed on before Cyrus could argue. "It's important that we know what we're up against, okay?"

Cyrus nodded. "Why not? I keep thinking my memory is going to just miraculously return. But since it hasn't..."

THEY WERE LED right into the doctor's office. Flint watched as Dr. Brady examined his brother. "Amnesia is a form of memory loss that is usually temporary. Common causes are trauma or a head injury. I understand you hit your head on the railing of the ship."

Cyrus nodded. "That's what I've been told."

"But it wasn't enough to knock you out?"

"Maybe for a few seconds. But not more than that. Otherwise, I would have drowned."

The doctor nodded. "A lot of things could cause memory loss. Given what you've been through, I'm not surprised. In your case, I think your memory loss might be psychosomatic."

"What does that mean?" Cyrus asked.

"Psychological."

"In other words, it's all in my head?" his brother joked.

"The trauma of what happened to you has caused you to forget everything. It happens. It's rare. But if this is the case, then there is a good chance that your memory will come back. Either gradually or possibly all at once under the right stimuli."

"And if not?" Flint asked.

"In cases of retrograde amnesia like your brother's, the memory loss could also be due to a lack of adequate oxygen to part of your brain when you almost drowned. In which case, your memory might not return."

Cyrus sighed. "Great."

As they were leaving, Flint said, "I believe it was the trauma and your memory will return. Let's hold on to that hope. After all, you remembered AJ, right?"

"Not exactly. With her, it was just a feeling. At first I thought

I had reason to fear her." Cyrus shrugged. "I can't tell you how badly I want to remember, *need* to remember."

"I know. This has got to be incredibly hard on you," Flint said as he drove toward the saloon. "People here care about you. Your family loves you. We're going to be with you through this no matter what happens."

Cyrus nodded. "The problem is that you're all strangers to me and while I appreciate everything you've done and are doing..."

"Just give it time," the sheriff said quickly. He didn't mention that Juliette's lawyer had called first thing this morning demanding a settlement to get her out of their lives. He'd had to tell the lawyer that they couldn't raise that kind of money. Not without selling the ranch.

I suggest you do whatever you have to do, the man had said. *You've met Juliette. She's serious.*

So time wasn't necessarily something they had if they hoped to free Cyrus of this woman who'd already proved how far she would go.

As they drove up to the side of the saloon, AJ came out and hopped in the back. "Have you said anything to the family?" Flint asked her. She shook her head. "Let me go in first, then?"

"I know how hard this must be for all of you," his brother said.

"I don't want you feeling bad about any of this, okay? It isn't your fault that you don't remember."

Cyrus said, "Maybe that's true. But I married the woman trying to take the ranch away from you."

Flint laughed. "Hell, she tried to take something even more valuable from us. You. We have you back."

"That's just it," he said, meeting the sheriff's eyes. "You don't."

"Not yet," AJ said. "But I have faith that you will remember. I have enough faith for all of us."

He smiled back at her sadly. "I hate hurting these people. I can see that they care..."

"Don't worry about us," Flint said. "We're a tough resilient bunch. Look at you. Look what you were able to survive. We're Cahills. It's what we do."

CYRUS GOT OUT and climbed into the back of the SUV with AJ. "I tried to call you last night," he said.

She nodded. "I turned my phone off. I just needed to—"

"Be alone. Me too." He took both her hands in his. "But I was worried about you."

AJ nodded. "I was worried about you too."

"I'm a Cahill. Tough and resilient apparently."

She smiled. "Yes, you are. They're just happy you're alive. They'll give you the time you need."

"And if I never remember?"

"Like I said, then you will fall in love with them all over again."

He looked over at her. "I don't know what I would do without you."

"You'll never have to."

Her words hung in the air. Both of them looked toward the back door of the saloon. Neither said the obvious. Cyrus wasn't just married to another woman, but now she was pregnant. He was convinced that the baby couldn't possibly be his.

But what if he hadn't been tricked? What if he'd married this Juliette woman because what she said was true? That one look at her and he'd been caught in her spell?

At the back door of the saloon, Flint appeared and waved for them to come on in.

"I'm here for you," AJ said as they got out of the SUV and headed inside.

Cyrus smiled over at her. "You are something, you know that?" He grabbed her before they reached the back door and pulled her into a kiss. "I love you, AJ Somerfield. Don't lose your faith in me, okay?"

She shook her head, tears in her eyes as she met his gaze. "Never."

IT FELT SURREAL introducing Cyrus to his family, Flint thought. Cyrus looked a little shell-shocked. Lillie, of course, broke down, hugging her brother and crying. But Cyrus was great with her.

He could tell though, that like him, they'd hoped each of them would be the one who made him remember. It did his heart good though to see all the love in the room and he could tell that Cyrus was touched by it. If he wanted to know what his life was like before, he'd gotten a taste of it this morning.

Billie Dee had greeted Cyrus with a huge hug before all the food was brought out and the spouses arrived. Flint didn't bother with introductions. It was clear that Cyrus was overwhelmed enough.

They ate and the mood lightened up. There was laughter and joking and talk about everything from cattle to Billie Dee's chicken and dumplings—which would be served tomorrow. Cyrus seemed to be taking it all in, especially the stories about him growing up.

"I can't even remember ever riding a horse," he said at one point.

"It's like riding a bike," Hawk said. "Once you're in the saddle again..."

Cyrus nodded. "I look forward to that day." They all knew he wasn't talking about being on a horse again. He'd looked over at AJ seated next to him.

Flint saw the way the two of them looked at each other. He wasn't sure what had happened down on the island, but there was no doubt that they were in love.

He thought about Juliette, but waited until the breakfast was over and the spouses left before he brought up the subject.

"I hate that we have to talk about this, but Juliette is pregnant," the sheriff said after the dishes had been cleaned away and only the immediate family was left.

Everyone looked at Cyrus who said, "It's not mine." He looked to Flint. "How soon can we prove it?"

"I checked," Flint said. "We can get a paternity test as early as eight weeks into the pregnancy. It's a simple blood test. So I would think in a couple of weeks."

Cyrus seemed relieved.

"In the meantime, Juliette's lawyer is willing to rush through an annulment if some sort of remuneration is offered."

"What does that mean?" Lillie asked.

"She wants us to buy her off," Hawk snapped. "Like hell."

Flint looked to Cyrus.

"How much does she want?" he asked.

"She was asking a million and a half."

Cyrus looked around the table. "Do I have that kind of money?"

"That's what her attorney feels your part of the ranch is worth," Flint explained.

"It would mean selling the ranch to raise that much money," Hawk said.

Cyrus looked over at AJ. "As badly as I want to be rid of that woman, I can't ask you to do that. I got myself into this somehow. I have to try to get myself out of it." He looked at Hawk. "I assume that I have a vehicle?"

"Your pickup is at the ranch," his brother said. "Along with your room, if you're interested."

Cyrus nodded and looked around the saloon at his family. "I'm sorry I don't remember any of you, but I can see that we were a close-knit family. I want that back." He turned to AJ. "Would you give me a ride out to the ranch?"

She nodded and looked to Hawk.

"I'll meet you both out there," he said.

"Cyrus, I'm not sure what you're planning…" Flint realized that his brother was staring at his badge. "Cyrus? Is something wrong?"

His brother blinked.

"You were staring at my badge."

Cyrus blinked again and shook his head. "I felt as if I was remembering something." He shook his head again. "It was probably nothing." He got to his feet. "Thank you all. I apologize for putting the family through this."

They all quickly told him that they didn't believe it was his fault. But the only person at this point who knew how Cyrus had gotten into this mess was Juliette.

Flint couldn't help but wonder what Cyrus was planning. He'd seen the glint in his brother's eye. The family had enough trouble without him doing something rash.

"WAS IT AWFUL?" AJ said as she drove Cyrus out to the ranch.

"No. They seem like nice people."

She laughed. "They *are* nice people. Once you get to know them…" She shook her head. "Once you remember…"

"Let's not count on that," he said. "So this is the ranch."

"From down there all the way to the mountains and from over there to the edge of town. It's been in your family for several generations."

He nodded but said nothing as they pulled up to the house. It was big and rambling, a large old farmhouse that had a history. AJ had loved the place the first time she saw it. She would love to live in a house exactly like it. She'd lived most of her life in a penthouse overlooking Houston.

The Cahill home felt warm and worn compared to the clean, cold, modern minimalistic style of her parents' penthouse. She wondered what it had been like growing up here with all this space to roam.

"So this is where I was raised?" Cyrus said, taking in the house.

"You loved it. You spent most of your time on your horse. You love this ranch." Her voice broke. "It's your life."

He said nothing as he nodded.

"Cyrus, what are you planning to do?"

"Get free of Juliette, no matter what I have to do."

"But you wouldn't make your family sell the ranch," she cried.

He looked away for a moment before he opened his door. "I hope it won't come to that."

CHAPTER TWENTY-THREE

JULIETTE WAS SURPRISED to open her cabin door and find Cyrus standing outside. She was even more surprised to realize that he'd come alone.

"Where is your...nursemaid?"

He didn't take the bait. "I thought we should talk."

She hesitated, giving Arthur long enough to hide in the second bedroom at the back of the cabin.

"I guess we do have some things to talk about," she said and stepped back to let him enter. "How about a drink?" she asked as she closed the door and saw that he'd taken a seat on the couch. "I was just about to tell you to make yourself at home," she said with a chuckle.

"Should you, with the baby and all?" he asked.

"I'm having sparkling water. It helps the nausea. But I have your favorite brand of gin."

"You remember what I drink?"

She smiled. "Of course. Gin and tonic with a twist of lime. You got me hooked on them on the ship."

"Now that you mention it, why don't you tell me what really happened on the ship. It's just the two of us. How about the truth?"

Juliette laughed as she poured them both a drink. "Are you wearing a wire?"

"You watch too many crime dramas. I'm not wearing a wire. But you're welcome to search me."

She had her back to him. She finished making his drink before she turned from the makeshift bar and shot him a leering look. "If you're suggesting what I think you are, I'm already in enough trouble, wouldn't you say?"

"Don't kid yourself. I've never slept with you. Nor will I ever. That's why I know the baby isn't mine," he said as she handed him his drink.

As she sat down at the other end of the couch and tucked her legs under her, she tried not to take his words personally. With regret, she saw him put the drink she'd made him aside on a marred end table without taking even a sip.

"Just because you don't remember doesn't mean it didn't happen. After that romantic moonlit night we had on the ship locked in our cabin? We couldn't keep our hands off each other."

He shook his head. "I don't think so."

"But you can't know for sure, otherwise you wouldn't be here." She took a sip of her sparkling water. "You really can't remember anything?" she asked as she ran her finger along the rim of her glass. "Not even the night we met in Denver?" she asked, raising her gaze to meet his.

She noticed that he still hadn't touched his drink she'd made him. Had he seen her doctor it?

"Tell me how you did it," he said.

"Did what?"

"Convinced me to go on a cruise with you, let alone marry you."

She chuckled and tilted her head back to touch the sweating

glass to her throat. Slowly, she slid it down the opening in her shirt, stopping just short of the rise of her breasts peeking from her blouse. She'd been seducing men since she was twelve. Did he really think he wasn't susceptible?

"How do you think I did it?" she asked in a throaty voice that had always worked wonders for her.

"Not *that* way," he said, making her glare at him as she pulled the glass away from her chest and sat up straighter. "I said the *truth*. You didn't seduce me."

"But your precious nursemaid did?" she snapped, telling herself not to let him get to her.

"Let's keep AJ out of this."

"Kind of hard to do. You had an affair with her in the islands. Don't deny it. You're in love with her."

"I don't deny it."

She pretended to pout. "You're my husband and I'm carrying your child."

He got to his feet. "If you keep lying to me, I'm going to leave. I thought if I came alone we could cut the bullshit. Just tell me what really happened and how much it's going to cost to make you go away."

She laughed. "What does it matter how it happened? You wouldn't believe me anyway."

"Try me."

She shook her head as she got to her feet and set down her glass on the table at her end of the couch before turning to him. "The end result is that you and I got married on a cruise ship," she said as she stepped to him.

"And somehow I ended up in the ocean in the middle of the night and you and the ship just kept going," he said but didn't move as she placed her palms on his chest.

"Whatever you were doing since I last saw you, it looks good on you," she said as she unbuttoned his shirt and checked for a wire. "AJ must have been excited to see you," she said as he stood perfectly still while she ran her hands around to his back and then checked the waistband of his jeans before running her hands down each of his legs.

"You don't mind, do you?" she asked as she unbuttoned his jeans and checked his crotch. He didn't move, nor did he respond to her in any way other than to stare at her unfeelingly as she searched him.

She stepped back. No man had ever ignored her like this one. It irked her that even in Denver she'd gotten nowhere with him—just like now.

CYRUS BUTTONED UP his jeans and smiled "Satisfied?"

"Hardly," she said with a sneer.

He could tell that she was furious and at the same time thrown off balance by his complete lack of interest in her. What did she expect? She'd tried to have him killed.

"Isn't it enough proof that I'm carrying your child?" she demanded.

"A DNA test will prove otherwise. A simple blood test can be done in two weeks. But what's the point? We both know that isn't my child you're carrying. I would think you'd want this over as quickly as I do. What is it going to take to get this... marriage annulled and you out of my life?"

"My lawyer—"

"I heard what your lawyer is asking, but we aren't paying that. Otherwise we can wait for the DNA test and for my memory to return. But when that happens, I suspect you'll be going to prison given what I've heard about your past."

"You shouldn't believe everything you hear," she said but she didn't sound so sure of herself. "And what if your memory never returns? In a case of head trauma like yours—"

"Actually, I'm told that it could be psychosomatic because of the trauma. For some reason I'm suppressing the memory, in which case, I could remember at any time. But if you're long gone by then..."

"You're offering me a deal, is that it?"

"Who said you weren't sharp?"

She glared at him. "You don't have to be nasty."

"I didn't throw *you* overboard."

"I couldn't lift you, let alone throw you overboard."

"Only because you aren't strong enough. That's why you have your accomplices Otis and Arthur do your dirty work. So can we please quit playing this game?"

She tried a different tact. "Why don't we sit down and I'll tell you everything? You haven't even touched your drink I made special for you."

"I'm sure it is special. I'm not going to drink it, so if that was your plan..."

"You want to know how it worked?" she snapped angrily. "Fine. It will just be my word against yours."

He heard a sound from the back of the cabin. Juliette heard it too because she tensed. He took a step toward the back.

"This is ridiculous. I'm your wife. We fell in love and now I'm carrying your baby."

He strode toward the back of the cabin where the sound had come from. She tried to stop him, grabbing his arm. He shook her off and kept going, glancing into several bedrooms before seeing a small enclosed sleeping porch and a back door. The door was ajar.

He pushed through onto the back porch and through the door. There were footprints in the snow. Man-size. But whoever it had been was gone.

Closing the door, he walked back into the cabin. He didn't see Juliette but he heard her in the bathroom throwing up.

When she came out, he said, "I can wait you out and I will. My memory is going to come back. It is already starting to. I remember how much you disgust me." With that he left.

JULIETTE WATCHED HIM drive away, fearing he was right. She was still shaking inside. Her stomach roiled again. She still couldn't believe she was pregnant. How had she let that happen? Maybe Otis was right and they should pull the plug.

What if it was just a matter of time before Cyrus remembered on his own? She told herself that he was bluffing. If he was going to remember, he would have already. He was threatening her because he feared he would never remember. The only reason he was pushing her was because he wanted her out of his life so he could be with his girlfriend.

She gritted her teeth at the thought of AJ Somerfield and realized the girlfriend, as much as she despised her, was her ace in the hole. If Cyrus thought AJ was in danger, he would fold first. Or there was always the option of extorting money from his girlfriend. AJ admitted that she came from money. Hell, had bragged about not touching her trust fund. How much would she pay to have Cyrus divorced and baby-free?

She smiled, feeling a little better. If she played this right, she was going to get her payoff and then she was out of here. She'd deal with the baby issue later. No hurry since she couldn't be that far along.

Cyrus had been gone for about five minutes when she heard the back door open and close.

Arthur came in looking upset. "You weren't really going to tell him, were you?"

"Of course not. You almost got caught. That was a stupid move making noise back there."

"I was trying to save you from yourself. You wanted to tell

him. I could hear it in your voice. Damn it, Julie, what's happening with you?"

"Nothing." She could feel him staring at her.

"You're *pregnant*? Or just pretending to be pregnant?"

She raised her gaze to him. She should have known he was listening to all of it. "I might have messed up."

He shook his head. "Whose kid is it?"

She shrugged and gave him her best sad smile. The smile had worked on him since they were kids. She'd wrapped him around her finger ever since.

"Oh hell, it's not the cop's?"

"What if it is?"

He swore and looked as sick to his stomach as she'd been. "So what are you going to do?"

"Finish this and get out of the country."

"And the baby?"

She shook her head. "I don't know yet. Cyrus is going to cave and pay me off. Once the marriage is annulled and I have the money…"

"I think you're kidding yourself. He didn't sound like a man who was ready to give in."

"We'll see. I have a plan."

He swore. "These people are onto us. He knows about me and Otis."

"But he has no proof of anything. As long as he doesn't remember… I have something I need you to do tonight at the Stagecoach Saloon. Cyrus's girlfriend lives upstairs."

Her ex-husband was shaking his head. "I'm not sure I can do this."

She stepped to him to cup his jaw in her hand. Arthur still had his good looks from when they were teens. "When this is over…" She pressed her lips to his ear and whispered exactly what she knew he wanted to hear.

FLINT WAS AS worried about Cyrus as the rest of the family. He'd known his brother was up to something when he'd asked about his vehicle. Hawk had called to say that once he'd handed over the keys to Cyrus's truck, he'd left.

"Any idea where he went?" he'd asked Hawk even though he had a pretty good idea.

"We can't stop him from forcing us to sell the ranch, can we?" Hawk had asked.

"It won't come to that."

"I hope you're right, but he doesn't know us. He doesn't care about the ranch. Flint—"

"I know." He was scared too, but didn't want to admit it. "We just have to hope his memory comes back." And soon.

Now as he walked into his office, she saw that his sister was waiting for him.

"We need to get Cyrus to a doctor," Lillie said, jumping up as he walked in. "We have to do something to help him remember."

He went around his desk and sat down. "Lillie, I already took him to Dr. Brady. He said time—"

"Flint, I know it will take time, but we have to get our brother back."

"We will," he promised. "But we have to be patient. He's dealing with a lot right now."

"Juliette." She said it like a curse. "What if she really is pregnant with Cyrus's baby?"

"She's not," he said. "But if she was, we'd deal with it."

"So let's pay her off and get her out of our lives. Trask and I talked about it after breakfast this morning. He is willing to sell off some of our ranch and mortgage the rest."

Flint smiled at his sister. "Sis, that's very sweet. But let's hope it doesn't come to that. This woman belongs behind bars, not paid off for trying to kill our brother. She wants more than we can pony up without selling off the family ranch."

"But if she is as dangerous as—"

"She isn't going to do anything crazy, not here in Gilt Edge."

His sister gave him a disbelieving look. "She tried to kill him. What makes you so sure she won't again?"

CHAPTER TWENTY-FOUR

"YOU NEED TO get back to work," Billie Dee said as AJ paced the saloon kitchen.

"I need to help Cyrus."

"You *have* helped him, but now you need to let him help himself," the cook said. "You can't keep trying to protect him. Neither can his family. He has to be his own man."

AJ knew she was right. "How do I do that?"

"Put on your apron and go back behind the bar and go to work. If Cyrus needs you, I'm sure he'll let you know."

She nodded. "It can't be his baby."

"Flint said we should know in two weeks, maybe less—especially if Juliette is lying about when she conceived. And since she apparently lies about everything, I think we can assume she didn't get pregnant on the ship."

AJ hadn't thought of that. Juliette could have gotten pregnant before she even met Cyrus. If she was too far along for it to be his, they'd have proof that she was lying. "If true though, she isn't going to be anxious to have the test."

"Nope. My guess is that she'll want to make a deal though."

"So it keeps coming back to money for Cyrus to be free of her." She shook her head. "We know she's a black widow. We know she's killed before and tried to kill Cyrus but we can't prove any of it? There must be something we can do."

Billie Dee was shaking her head. "Whatever you're thinking about doing, don't. Like you just said, the woman is a killer. One look in her eyes and you can tell she's ruthless. Are you listening to me?"

"I'm going back to work," AJ said, grabbing one of the aprons and tying it around her waist. "If you need me, I'll be behind the bar."

The cook eyed her skeptically. "I know that look and I want you to know, you're scaring me."

CYRUS LOOKED UP from where he stood just inside the stables to see his brother Hawk headed toward him.

"You know what you're doing?" Hawk asked and grinned.

"I'm saddling a horse," he said. "How am I doin'?"

His brother stepped over to check the cinch and raised a brow. "Not bad," he said stepping back. "I see you saddled your own horse."

"Don't be thinking that I remembered which horse was mine," Cyrus said quickly. "AJ showed me a photo. As for saddling it..."

"Let me guess," Hawk said. "You quit trying to remember and just let it happen. Muscle memory."

"I reckon," he said. "Now if I remember how to ride."

His brother laughed. "You never were that good."

Cyrus had to smile. "Something tells me that you and I have been competitive at some point in our lives."

Hawk grinned. "Because you can't stand the fact that I'm better than you at most things. Except computers. I'll give you that one. But ranching and horses? I got you beat."

"That sounds like a challenge. Even if you have an advantage over a man who can't remember his own name?"

"I figured you'd try to play that sympathy card." Hawk shook his head. "It's wasted on me, brother. Hope that horse doesn't buck you off." He turned to leave, and then turned back and tossed Cyrus his cell phone. "Just in case you can't get back and need my help."

"It might help if I knew your number. Also where I was going," he said after catching the phone.

Hawk took the phone back, put in his number and tossed it again. "I put my number under the word *Help*." He grinned. "As for where you're riding to, there are trails, but all that land halfway up that mountain, that's our ranch. From there to the top is Forest Service. Good luck." Hawk turned and walked off whistling.

Cyrus stood for a moment next to his horse before he swung up into the saddle. His horse shimmied under him and, for a moment, he thought the mare might buck. But when she didn't, he gave the reins a tug and she headed toward the mountains. Apparently she knew the way, even if he didn't.

AJ WORKED ALL afternoon and evening, telling Darby she would close up so he could go home to his pregnant wife and son.

It's good to have you back, he'd said. *We are all indebted to you for going to look for Cyrus. I think about what could have happened if you hadn't been so determined…*

He's going to get his memory back.

Darby had nodded. *Hawk called earlier. Cyrus saddled his horse and rode up into the mountains. He always did that when something was bothering him. It's a good sign*. She'd been surprised. *He is going to come back to all of us.*

Did she dare hope? Juliette's pregnancy had thrown her even with Cyrus being so determined that the baby couldn't be his.

Her heart ached. She'd dreamed of having his babies, of the two of them living on the ranch, of their children growing up with all their cousins.

A hard lump formed in her chest. Juliette couldn't be having Cyrus's baby. Cyrus was so sure. And yet he'd married the woman, whether he remembered it or not. AJ couldn't explain away that and neither could Cyrus.

If he never remembered… They would never know the truth. Unless Juliette was really carrying his child. In that case, they would both have to accept that Cyrus had fallen for the woman.

Now as the last of the bar crowd left, she locked up the front door and turned out the exterior lights for the night. Billie Dee was right. It felt good to be doing something besides worrying. Fortunately, the saloon was busy her entire shift so she hadn't had time to hardly think.

She finished up behind the bar and, after turning out the lights and locking the back door, she headed for her apartment upstairs remembering what Darby had told her about Cyrus going for a horseback ride. Darby and Hawk seemed to think that was a good sign. She tried to breathe easier. For weeks she'd been telling herself that he was alive. She'd believed that once she found him everything would be like it was.

Now she questioned if anything would be the same.

AJ shoved those thoughts away. She couldn't lose faith now. Cyrus was home. Juliette was lying about everything. That's what AJ had to believe. What she had to hold on to. Otherwise…

Apparently Cyrus had moved back to the ranch. Maybe sleeping in the house he'd grown up in…

As she climbed the stairs, she tried to hang on to that thread of hope, the one that had sent her to the Caribbean to look for Cyrus. Back then, it had been a feeling in her heart that told her he was alive.

Now he had taken all of her heart, every bit of it. She thought about being in his arms as she pushed open her door and stepped into her apartment.

She heard a scraping sound and started to turn, but the man was on her before she could. All she caught was a glimpse of a black ski mask covering his face before he threw her to the floor.

CHAPTER TWENTY-FIVE

"HOW WAS YOUR RIDE?" Hawk asked as Cyrus came through the door of the house they'd grown up in.

He stopped in the doorway to take in the large living room and the blaze popping and cracking in the huge rock fireplace. This was home? He closed the door and moved toward the fire, feeling chilled. He'd been fine when he was out riding, but when the sun had gone down and darkness moved in, the night had grown cold.

"I was starting to worry about you," Hawk said. "Not enough to go look for you but close."

Cyrus chuckled. "There's a full moon out tonight. Riding through the pines with the moon like that..." He couldn't put the feeling into words. "Sorry I was gone so long. I didn't mean to make you worry." He reached into his pocket and handed his brother his cell phone. "I didn't have to call for help anyway."

Hawk chuckled. "I suppose that's something. Sounds like you remembered how to ride."

"My horse was kind enough not to buck me off. It's beautiful country. I can see why I liked it."

"You loved it. You always said that it would take dynamite to get you out of Montana," his brother said. "Apparently you were wrong."

Cyrus shook his head. "I didn't fall for Juliette. And before you ask, I have no idea how I ended up on a cruise ship married to the woman. But I will remember and when I do..." He balled his hands into fists. When he saw Hawk noticing, he spread his fingers and tried to still the anger in him but it was difficult.

While he didn't know how all of this had happened, he was sure of one thing. Juliette had set him up somehow, trapping him and then doing her best to kill him. As it was, she'd taken everything he'd apparently once loved from him—his family, his life here—and was doing her best to take AJ from him as well by pretending the baby she was carrying was his. He wasn't going to let her get away with it, because in his heart of hearts, he knew she was lying about all of it.

"I just came in to give you back your phone," Cyrus said. "Is it all right if I stay here tonight?"

"Bro, it's your house too. Your room is at the top of the stairs, second door on the left."

"I'll be back. I have to go see AJ."

AJ KICKED AND screamed and clawed at the man as he threw her down and tried to press her to the floor. She knew no one would hear her screams but it didn't matter. She feared she was fighting for her life.

"Shut up!" the man snarled as he tried to roll her over onto her stomach.

She managed to elbow him hard in his side and heard his sharp intake of breath. She elbowed him again and spotted the cowboy doorstop within reach. Grabbing it, she swung it hard. He got a hand up so instead of the heavy iron doorstop hitting him in the ribs, it ricocheted off his arm and hit him in the head.

He let out of howl of pain. Wresting the heavy iron object from her and for a moment, holding it in the air as if he wanted to hit her with it. With a growl, he threw it across the room.

It gave her a little advantage and she took it. She brought her knee up and caught him in the groin. He backhanded her hard as he fell forward on top of her. His body was large and heavy. She tried to shove him off. She couldn't breathe.

He was groaning and swearing. She grabbed hold of a handful of his hair and tugged hard, desperate to get him off her so she could catch her breath.

She could feel his anger. He was sweating profusely. She felt the heat of that fury and smelled it on him.

"You bitch," he spat out as he grabbed both of her wrists and pinned her to the floor. There was a gash on his temple where the doorstop had opened his skin. Blood ran down his cheek and splashed on her throat. "You are going to pay for that."

"YOU KNOW WHAT time it is?" Hawk asked, glancing toward the clock next to the fireplace.

"I know it's late, but I have to be sure she's all right or I won't get any sleep tonight," Cyrus said. "She is devastated about Juliette's pregnancy."

His brother lifted a brow. "I would imagine she is."

"It's not my baby." Hawk said nothing. "I know how hollow those words sound. But I've never been more sure of anything in my life."

"Let's hope you're right. If the baby is yours, she will milk you out of every dime you have and then some."

"I'm sorry that I've jeopardized the ranch."

Hawk shrugged. "We're family. We'll get through this."

Cyrus felt his heart swell. "Thanks. For that, I won't wake you up when I come back."

"If you come back," Hawk said with a grin.

He drove through the moonlight toward the Stagecoach Saloon, glad he'd been paying attention earlier on how to get there. The night sky was bright making the mountains that surrounded the small town a deep purple. He thought of his horseback ride, that feeling of freedom. It had felt familiar.

As he drove, he realized a lot of things were feeling familiar, including driving down this road as if he'd done it a thousand times. He was sure he had. And sparring with his brother Hawk. Even the house, the big fireplace, being back in the saddle. Was he starting to remember?

Ahead he could see only one light shining at the Stagecoach Saloon—in the upstairs apartment. AJ was still up. Hadn't he known she would be? Like him, she probably was having trouble sleeping. He pulled in along the side of the building, cut his engine and climbed out.

As he neared the back door, a dark figure came charging out and took off at a run into the woods behind the saloon. Startled, he realized the man had been wearing a black ski mask. He looked toward the back door of the saloon, now standing open.

AJ! "AJ!" He raced to the door and up the steps, calling her name, fear making his voice crack. He shoved open the door into the second-story apartment. She sat on the floor, something clutched in both her hands, her back to the wall. He rushed to her, dropping to his knees.

"Are you all right?" he cried, seeing that she held a cowboy doorstop. Also noticing that there was blood on it. His heart took off at a gallop.

She looked up at him, tears running down her face and said, "I'm all right. Now that you're here."

He gathered her in his arms, holding her tightly. Hawk was right. He wouldn't be returning to the ranch tonight. But first, he had to call his brother the sheriff.

Flint listened to AJ's version of the night's events. He could tell that she was still shaken, though thankfully not hurt. He'd bagged the doorstop with the blood on it. If the man who attacked her had a record, then his DNA might be on file. Otherwise it wouldn't be of much use.

"You know who's behind this," Cyrus said. "Juliette. She did this to force me to pay her off to get rid of her."

He nodded, thinking his brother was probably right. "Like everything else, what we don't have is proof. We know that she was working with Otis Claremont and Arthur Davis. I have a BOLO out on them both, but still no word on where they might be."

"At least one of them is in town."

Flint listened as his brother told him about hearing someone at the back of Juliette's cabin.

"There were footprints in the snow. Man-size ones," Cyrus said. "She isn't alone."

"Even if one of them is in town, the best I can do is pick him up for questioning. I know it's frustrating, believe me. But I need proof." He turned to AJ. "You're sure you didn't get a good look at him?"

She shook her head. "He was wearing a black ski mask, like I said. I never saw his face. Just his eyes. Brown, small."

"I saw him run into the woods," Cyrus said. "He was about six foot maybe taller, and big."

His brother's description matched AJ's, but both Otis and Arthur were good-size men. He closed his notebook. "AJ, maybe it would be a good idea for you to come stay with Maggie and me tonight."

"I'm staying with her," Cyrus said. "Anyway, I don't think he'll be back. He's injured."

Flint nodded. He'd seen the blood on AJ as well as drops on the apartment's wood floor and a few on the stairs. The man hadn't been injured badly though. But any injury would make it easier to pull him in for questioning.

"I'll lock up behind myself, then," he said, getting to his feet to leave. He could see Cyrus was beside himself with fury. "Don't be thinking of doing anything that could end you up in my jail, please."

His brother shook his head. "Don't worry. I'm told that I'm cautious to a fault. I never do anything without thinking it out first."

Flint laughed, glad to see his brother hadn't lost his sense of humor. "Right. Like I said…"

"YOU'RE BLEEDING ON my floor," Juliette snapped. "What the hell happened?"

"You should have warned me about her," Arthur snapped back. "She almost killed me."

"Seriously? You couldn't handle a woman you outweigh by a hundred and fifty pounds?" She grabbed a hand towel from the bathroom. "Here, put this on it. What did she hit you with?"

"How would I know? An iron cowboy. Some stupid thing and then she kicked me in my balls."

Juliette stood looking at him, shaking her head.

"You think this is funny?" he demanded. "I would have killed her if her boyfriend hadn't shown up."

"Wait. What?"

"I had the bitch down. I was going to choke her scrawny neck and watch the life drain out of her, but then I heard a vehicle pull up outside."

"Did he see you?" Her voice came out high, scared.

"No—at least, I don't think so. I still had my mask on anyway. I ran into the trees behind the saloon. He went upstairs to check on his girlfriend."

Juliette fought to control first her fear that the fool had been seen and then her anger. "I told you, AJ was mine. I didn't send you to kill her."

He pulled the hand towel away from his head, thrusting it at her to show her the blood. "I'm the one bleeding. I'm the one who got my balls jammed up my—"

"This is about your inability to control your temper," she snarled. "I don't know why I trusted you with this." She spun away from him afraid she would grab something and hit him.

"You trusted me because you don't have anyone else," he said behind her. "Where's Otis anyway?"

She took deep breaths, trying to calm down. Everything was fine. Arthur hadn't screwed things up too badly. But after this, he was going to have to go. She knew he wouldn't go without a fight. That meant he'd have to be taken care of before she left the country.

Juliette turned slowly around to face him. "I'm sorry. You're right. Let me bandage your head." She led him over to a chair and went to get the first aid kit she'd seen in the bathroom. He came like a lamb. That was the problem with Arthur. Most of the time he was a wimp. But when he lost his temper... She reminded herself to keep that in mind in the future. If he ever turned that temper on her...

Once he'd gone to bed, she called Otis. "I need you. Get here any way you can. Arthur is going to blow this whole thing."

THE MOMENT FLINT LEFT, Cyrus locked the apartment door. AJ was curled up in a chair hugging herself as if cold. His heart was in his throat. He'd come close to losing her. Anger made it hard for him to breathe. This was Juliette's doing. She was trying to force his hand.

He wanted nothing more than to pay her off. If it meant selling the family ranch, he didn't give a damn. Whatever it took.

But even as he thought it, he knew he couldn't do that to this family that he could see loved him.

But if he could get his hands on Juliette right now, he would ring her neck and then go after the man who'd attacked AJ.

AJ. Taking a deep breath, he blew it out and pushed all thoughts of Juliette away. Right now, he had to take care of the woman he loved. Walking into the bathroom, he turned on the shower, letting it run until the room was warm and steamy.

When he came back out, he lifted her into his arms and carried her into the bathroom and closed the door. She locked eyes with him as he carefully undressed her and helped her into the shower before stripping down and joining her. He held her as the warm water cascaded over their bodies.

He gently soaped her, caressing her smooth skin as he washed away what he could of the man who'd hurt her. She leaned her back against him, closing her eyes. She quit shaking after a few minutes, her lashes heavy with water droplets.

"I thought he was going to kill me."

"That's what he wanted you to think." He turned off the water and reached for a towel, and then began to dry the body he knew as well as his own.

"No," she said, shaking her head. "I made him so angry..." She shuddered and he enveloped her in her silk robe hanging by the door. After drying himself off, he wrapped a towel around his waist, and then picked her up and carried her out to the big bed with the stack of quilts on it.

"No one is going to hurt you," he said as he tucked her into the bed. She stared up at him with such a loving gaze that he felt himself melt inside. He dropped his towel and climbed into bed next to her and eased off her robe. Taking her in his arms, he said, "I'm going to put an end to this one way or the other."

AJ looked into his eyes, worry creasing her brow. "I can't lose you."

“You aren't going to lose me. Ever.” He kissed her, drawing her to him, their naked bodies melding together into a perfect fit as if only they were made for each other.

CHAPTER TWENTY-SIX

FLINT HAD PLANNED to pay Juliette a visit first thing this morning, but he got called out on a semi jackknifed on the road north and a one-car rollover. With law enforcement few and far between in a state the size of Montana, everyone had to pitch in when there was trouble.

It seemed sometimes as if trouble came in threes. Before he'd left the office this morning he'd gotten a call from Logan Sparks, a local rancher.

"Someone stole my snowmobile," Logan had said. "That old one I keep in my barn. Only use it to check the cows sometimes in the winter, but I'd like to have it back."

Flint had asked when he thought it had gone missing.

"Had to be last night. Figure it was kids. Little devils."

"I'm headed out to an accident scene on the highway and I'm a little short on deputies..." He'd remembered Harp. He'd had him watching Juliette's cabin, who'd gotten called off last night on a domestic. Unfortunately, if Cyrus was right and one of Juliette's male accomplices had attacked AJ last night, then there wouldn't have been a deputy on duty to have seen the man come or go from Juliette's cabin.

With no options since he was short on manpower, he'd tell Harp to go out to the Sparks ranch. The deputy was perfect for a job like this, since he'd been complaining about how boring watching a cabin was. With luck, Harp wouldn't be able to foul this up. Not that the deputy hadn't been better this past year…

"I've got a deputy I can send out," Flint had said. Then he'd called Harp on the radio and told him. He'd had to listen to Harp grumble a little about the exciting cases he got to cover.

"Just find the man's snowmobile. It shouldn't be that hard," Flint had snapped. "Follow the damned trail it left."

At the scene, Tucker took photographs and measurements from the one-car rollover accident while the sheriff called the ambulance.

"I'm sure Cyrus is right and that attack on AJ was Juliette's doing," Flint said as he disconnected and flagged a car racing up on the accident as they waited for the ambulance and wrecker to arrive. From the smell of alcohol and the beer cans littering the highway, the driver had been drinking—and not wearing his seat belt. He'd gone through the windshield, probably dying on impact.

"You think she's trying to scare Cyrus into settling," Tucker said.

"That's what he thinks and I have to agree. I keep hoping that either Arizona or Florida arrests her, but it doesn't look good. I talked to one of the detectives and told him what was going on here. He thinks she is just trying to get enough money to leave the country—and there is no way to stop her. Unless Cyrus remembers what happened."

"But what if it turns out that he did marry her and that baby she's carrying is his?" Tucker said.

Flint shook his head. "I know it looks bad, but there's no way.

Not my brother. Anyway, it's obvious that he's crazy about AJ. You can bet there is more to the story."

The sheriff hoped he was right for all their sakes, but especially AJ's. He couldn't imagine how devastated she would be if she found out that Cyrus really had fallen for Juliette that night in Denver.

AJ WOKE TO an empty bed. She found Cyrus's note on the nightstand next to her. "Billie Dee is downstairs so you aren't here alone. I had to go but I'll see you later."

She hated to think where he'd gone. Juliette… She swung her legs over the side of the bed, surprised that she hurt all over. As she dug in her bureau for clean clothing, she caught her image in the mirror and froze.

Her cheek was badly bruised where the man had slapped her. She touched it gingerly, remembering how terrified she'd been. Cyrus thought Juliette was behind it. AJ didn't doubt that, but Cyrus hadn't seen the fury in the man's face. He would have hurt her badly if Cyrus hadn't driven up when he did—or worse, killed her.

At the sound of footfalls on the stairs, she froze for a moment and looked around wildly for something she could use as a weapon.

"AJ? Are you awake?"

Relief flooded her as she heard Billie Dee's voice. "I'm awake."

The cook gently pushed open the apartment door with the edge of the tray she was carrying. "I brought you breakfast."

"You didn't have to do that," AJ cried. "I was coming down."

"Don't be silly, I—" The older woman's voice caught at the sight of her.

AJ's hand went to her cheek. "It's not as bad as it looks."

"Oh, sweetie," Billie Dee said, putting down the tray and

coming over to hug her. "He must have scared the life out of you."

She nodded into the cook's soft shoulder and tried to swallow the lump in her throat.

"Well, you're safe now. Have some breakfast," her friend said as she pulled back.

"Would you mind if I brought it downstairs?"

Billie Dee glanced around the room as if realizing that the apartment probably didn't feel all that safe right now. "Of course not."

AJ insisted on carrying the tray and the two of them tromped back down to the warm saloon kitchen. At the table, AJ ate the quiche with a side of fruit while the cook sat across from her, sipping her coffee.

"Did Cyrus say where he was going?" she asked.

Billie Dee shook her head, but AJ knew they both had a pretty good idea of where he'd gone. "Don't even think about following him," the cook warned her.

She knew the woman was right. She couldn't protect him any more than he could her from the horrible Juliette and her thugs. Once Juliette had set her sights on Cyrus…

JULIETTE PRETENDED TO be surprised to see Cyrus standing on her doorstep early the next morning. Fortunately Arthur had left on an errand. She'd thought she'd be seeing Cyrus so she'd told her ex-husband to be sure when he returned to look to make sure that the cowboy's pickup wasn't out front.

Arthur had been getting on her already frayed nerves. Why the man didn't give up on her, she'd never understood. She'd asked him once why he stayed around when all she did was use and abuse him.

You need me, he'd said simply. *You've always needed me. I'm the one person you can count on when things get bad. And they are going to get bad, Julie, if you don't stop this.*

Juliette, she'd snapped. *I'm Juliette. Why can't you remember that?*

He'd smiled his goofy smile. *You'll always be Julie to me.*

Like that was a good thing, she thought now. The man was impossible. She'd married him to get out of a bad situation she'd gotten herself into. Arthur had helped dispose of the problem. She'd divorced him when she'd met a man with money. It hadn't taken long before she was sick of that man and wanted rid of him. Arthur had been there, as always, ready to clean up her messes.

Otis had come along later after he'd been part of the investigation involving one of her deceased husbands. He'd seen right away that it would be much more lucrative to join her than stay with the police force.

But like Arthur, he wanted more than she had to offer and that was becoming more of a problem, especially now. Otis had called earlier. He'd stolen a pickup and new identification and would see her soon, he'd said.

She kept telling herself that when this was over, she would free herself of both of them.

First she had to free herself of Cyrus Cahill, something she thought she'd done that night on the ship when Arthur and Otis had returned saying her husband had gone overboard.

"Good morning, my husband," she said brightly now.

Cyrus scowled and pushed his way past her. "Where is he?"

"Where's who?" She closed the door and turned, folding her arms over her ample chest, to look at him. Clearly, Cyrus was upset—just as she'd planned. His precious AJ had been victimized. Juliette smiled. Shouldn't he have realized by now that she didn't play fair?

"Otis. Or was it Arthur?"

"I'm not sure I know what you're—"

Cyrus swore and moved to her so quickly that she choked on the last of her words. Seeing the look in his eyes, she stumbled back, banging into the door behind her. He stood so close she could see the flecks of gold in his gray eyes. Maybe there was more to this man than she had originally thought.

"You've misjudged me," he said quietly. "I might have come like a lamb to the slaughter for some reason when we first met, but that man drowned at sea. If you or one of your hoodlums ever touch AJ again, I will kill you."

She tried to laugh, but he grabbed her by the throat with one large hand, strangling the laugh before it reached her lips.

"I have no life. No memory. I have nothing to lose."

Juliette knew that wasn't true. She grabbed his wrist and with great effort pulled his hand from her throat and shoved it away. She coughed and said, "You still have AJ. You kill me and you lose her forever."

He smiled. "If I married you without you holding a gun to my head I will lose her anyway, let alone if that baby inside you is mine."

She met his gaze and couldn't help smiling again. He wasn't so sure now, was he. "Then you've lost her."

Cyrus shook his head. "Not yet. We're ending this today. Let's do the blood test. It's a little early, but I'm betting that baby was in there before you met me."

Juliette hadn't expected this. "What will you do when you find out it's yours?"

"I'll cross that bridge when I get there. Grab your coat. It's getting colder outside. I heard there is another storm coming in," he said.

The last place she wanted to go was a hospital lab. "I'm not going anywhere with you."

"Funny, but I thought you might say that." He reached into his pocket and pulled out a check.

She felt her eyes light up. "What's that?"

"It's a check for every dime I have."

Instantly, she knew it wasn't going to be enough. She wanted his part of the ranch. She started to tell him as much when he laid the check down on the small table by the door next to the Happy Holiday Cabins and Kitchenettes notepad and pen. The amount was better than she'd thought.

"Take the check," he said, seeing her eye it. "It's all you're going to get. Once we get the results of the blood test and I prove that baby isn't mine, if you haven't signed the annulment papers that will be delivered today, I'm going to stop that check and you'll get nothing. Now get your coat. If I have to, I'll drag you down to the lab or I'll find a way to take your blood right here in this cabin."

She could see that he was dead serious. She was trying to come up with a way to put him off when she heard the sound of the back door of the cabin opening onto the sleeping porch. A moment later, Arthur called, "I looked all over for that face cream you wanted, but—"

He stopped in midsentence when he saw them and, dropping the two bags of items he'd bought, turned and crashed out the back door at a run.

She grabbed Cyrus's sleeve, holding on tight enough that he had to waste valuable seconds getting her off him. He tore after Arthur, busting through the bags on the floor, sending the contents shooting in all directions. He hit the sleeping porch door at a run. It banged open and then he was gone.

Juliette stood holding her breath. If he caught Arthur...

ARTHUR DAVIS CRASHED through the trees ahead of him and dropped out of sight. Cyrus had recognized him from the photos Flint had shown him. He ran into the pines, shoving branches aside, determined to catch the man. He hadn't gone far though when he realized why he'd lost sight of Arthur.

The land behind the cabins dropped down to a creek. He could see where Arthur had fallen, rolling through the snow to the bottom of the steep hillside. From there the man's tracks crossed the frozen creek and disappeared in the adjacent woods.

Cyrus grabbed a tree limb to keep from falling down the steep hillside as Arthur had done. He stood, his heart hammering in his chest. What would he have done if he'd caught the man? The violence Juliette and her crew brought out of him scared him. He didn't know who he was, but he was sure he was not this man. He shook his head and turned back to the cabin, half expecting Juliette to be gone.

Opening the back door, he walked through the screened-in porch, kicking the bags of groceries and sundries aside as he stalked in. He found Juliette in the bedroom packing.

"Going somewhere?" he asked from the doorway. She had been throwing things into the suitcase.

Now she jumped, dropping something on the floor in her surprise.

He saw a flash as light caught what had fallen from her fingers. She was quick, but not quick enough. He got to the object before she could retrieve it from the floor.

Picking it up, he stared at the FBI badge in his hand. Blinking hard, he slowly looked up at her. It was as if his mind had been closed off and suddenly opened. First Arthur's voice. Now this badge.

"I remember," he said. "I remember it all."

CHAPTER TWENTY-SEVEN

"I REMEMBER." CYRUS stared at the woman standing in front of him, all of it coming back in a hot rush. Once the door opened, memories rushed in at breakneck speed. The doctor had said it might happen like that because of the trauma he'd experienced. But he'd been afraid the memory loss was due to striking his head on the railing as he fell and lack of oxygen before he'd surfaced at sea. He remembered those frightening moments in the rough ocean, the waves trying to push him under again, the terror that he was going to die.

"The hotel bar," he said more to himself than to Juliette. He could see it so clearly, it was like he was there again. The smell of alcohol. The dim lighting. He hadn't wanted a drink but the breeder who'd sold him the bull insisted. All he really wanted to do was go upstairs to his room and pack. If he left early, he would be home by supper tomorrow night.

Billie Dee was making his favorite. Her version of chicken and dumplings. AJ said if he was late that she'd save him some. Just the thought of her made him even more anxious. He hadn't been able to get her off his mind since he'd left Montana.

Being away from her had made him even more convinced about how he felt for her. He was in love. He'd been so happy that evening, anxious to get home and see her. He knew he had to tell her how he felt and, even though that scared him, he couldn't wait. He'd never felt like this before.

Now he looked down at the FBI badge in his hand. Then up at Juliette. "I saw you when I came into the bar. You were sitting alone in a booth."

She said nothing, merely stared at him as if frozen in place. Had this been her fear? That he would remember? That he would know that she'd tricked him?

He saw himself walking into the dark hotel bar. He couldn't wait to get the drink over with. The breeder was a large, jovial man with a ruddy complexion and clearly enjoyed the celebrating-over-a-drink part of the bargain. Cyrus had never been much of a drinker. A few beers around a campfire in the summer. A gin and tonic at a wedding or a cattlemen's meeting dinner.

But that night, he agreed to have one drink before going upstairs to pack. If only he had turned down the drink. If only...

His memory felt almost painful. He could smell the alcohol in the dimly lit bar. The breeder, a man named Harry Winston, slid into the booth next to the blonde's and waved to the bartender.

Harry was a talker. He pulled out the check Cyrus had written him and grinned. "Best damned bull I ever raised. Worth every penny of the three hundred grand you paid for it." He nodded and put the check away as the bartender came over to see what they wanted.

Cyrus started to order a beer, but Harry reminded him that they were celebrating and he ordered a gin and tonic with lime. Harry ordered a rum and cola, light on the cola he told the bartender with a wink and pulled out a hundred dollar bill to pay.

"You overheard the conversation," Cyrus said to Juliette now and shook his head. "You targeted me." If Harry had kept his mouth shut about the damned bull, none of this would have happened.

Juliette seemed to defrost. She pushed past him.

"You're not going anywhere," Cyrus said, still holding the badge as he followed her.

She stopped in the middle of the room. All the haughtiness was gone. She looked scared.

After two drinks, he'd managed to get away from Harry. As the breeder left, Cyrus had started out of the bar when the blonde from the next booth stood and caught him by the arm. It happened so fast and was so out of the blue that all he'd been aware of was the pressure of her fingers on his arm and her whispered words as she leaned closer to his ear.

"FBI. Come with me quietly. See the man in the lobby in the dark suit? He's also an agent."

He'd looked up and seen Otis. He'd looked so much like law… "What is this about?" Cyrus asked, glancing toward the man waiting just outside the bar at the edge of the lobby. He saw the man signal the blonde.

She flashed her badge with her free hand so only he could see. "I'll be happy to explain. You don't want me to have to draw my weapon. Let's just walk out of here so I don't have to use the cuffs and make a scene."

He looked at the badge again now. It said Federal Bureau of Investigation on the top. It was gold. And the words Department of Justice were printed on the bottom of the badge. It and her credentials had looked real, right down to her agent number. But then again, it was the first time he'd laid eyes on an FBI badge.

"I bought it, hook, line and sinker," Cyrus said now. "If I had checked it out with your field office…but you didn't give me a chance, did you? I had no reason to question your badge or anything you told me. You played your part perfectly."

"No, not perfectly obviously or you wouldn't have figured it all out and forced my hand," Juliette said.

"You took me into custody on some trumped-up money laundering scheme." He frowned, remembering her reaching into the pocket of his coat after the three of them were in the elevator, and pulling out a small thumb drive.

"You had the thumb drive in your hand the whole time, right?" She didn't confirm or deny it. "Was there anything on it?" Juliette gave him an impatient look. "I kept asking for a chance to call my lawyer." He frowned. "Then you made me a deal. Help you catch the man who'd set me up by putting that drive in my pocket, the real person you were after."

"I can be quite convincing."

"Apparently."

"All that was required was your silence."

"I signed something saying I would never divulge any of it." He shook his head and laughed. "You had me spotted as a fool right off the bat."

"Actually, you were one of the tougher ones I've had to deal with. Arthur kept saying we should cut you loose."

"Oh, you cut me loose, all right. When you had them throw me overboard."

"You were getting too close to the truth," she said as if killing people were something she did on a regular basis. Apparently it was.

"Well, you had me."

"At least for a while," she said.

"You got me on the flight to Miami and then onto the cruise ship," he said and frowned. "You told me I had to take part in some operation to prove my innocence."

"I told you I needed a cover and that I thought the captain of the ship was in on the money laundering since he was able to move from country to country without any suspicion."

He chuckled. "Which explained the marriage. You told me it wouldn't be legal. And I bought that?"

"You were being to doubt all of it. That's why I drugged you and forced you to go along with it, promising that your part would be over and you could fly back to your precious Montana."

Cyrus thought about all of it, remembering how real it had felt. "I admit, I was scared. I'd never been in trouble with the law, let alone the FBI." He laughed and shook his head again, furious with himself. "You got me to marry you, telling me it was all fake, all part of the plan. I even believed that there were other FBI agents aboard the ship, all waiting to take down the money laundering criminals in this huge string you had going. How could I have been so stupid?"

"You were naive, yes, but not stupid. And Otis and I were very convincing."

"So you planned to kill me all along."

"Not as quickly as we had to. You were asking a lot of questions. We knew we had to move fast."

"So all of this was just about money?" he asked, still having a hard time believing it.

Juliette glared at him. "Spoken like someone who has never had to worry about money. You were born on a ranch. You had food and clothes and a good standing in the community."

Clearly she didn't know about his father, Ely, who was considered the town nutcase. He felt a stab of pain as he realized that his father was gone. Dead and buried while he'd been lost at sea and beyond.

Juliette was angry, seething as she glared at him. "I grew up with nothing. I went to bed hungry. I was cold and miserable. My clothing, like my bedding, was threadbare." She lifted her chin and he saw that there were tears in her eyes. "I never had a new piece of clothing until I ran away from home. So yes, it was all about money. Money I thought you had."

He stared at her. "You're a monster."

Juliette wiped at her eyes. He watched her bite her lower lip for a moment. "I swore when I left home that I would do whatever I had to do to never be cold or hungry again. Unless you've been in my shoes…"

He glanced around the cabin. "Well, you have guts. You really came back here pretending to be my wife to con money out of my family?"

"Oh, we are husband and wife. That at least is real."

"Not for long. After what Flint has discovered about your past, I get the picture. Well, take the check, Juliette. It's all I have. You don't deserve a dime of it. But it's worth it to get you out of my life."

Her laugh was bitter and sharp. "It wasn't even about you. It was the ranch I wanted. I thought anyone who could afford a three-hundred-thousand-dollar bull was worth my effort. I should have asked how many siblings you had. But still, I almost talked your family into paying me over a million for your share of Cahill Ranch."

"But then you found out I was alive."

"Yes, that was unfortunate, but it wasn't personal."

"Not personal?" He laughed as she launched herself at the couch where she grabbed her purse and began to dig in it.

Cyrus caught her in two long strides. He grabbed her arm and squeezed until she dropped the gun she'd pulled from her bag. He emptied the bullets in the gun, dumped the weapon back into her purse and tossed it to the other side of the room.

She glared at him and rubbed her arm. "You hurt me."

"Seriously?" He shook his head. "You're lucky we're landlocked. If we were near an ocean, you'd be getting some of your own medicine."

"I can't swim."

He smiled at that. "I'd toss you a buoy to try to hold on to for hours and hours."

"If you're waiting for me to say I'm sorry—"

He loomed over her. "Don't bother, we're way past that." He shook his head, studying her. A chunk of memory fell into place making him frown. Drugged, he would have appeared drunk. Which would explain why the stewards thought he had a drinking problem while on board the ship.

AJ had said that it was suspected he'd climbed up on the railing drunk and had gone overboard. And at that hour of the night, no one had witnessed it.

He saw her look at the clock on the wall. "Expecting company?"

She didn't bother to answer. They both knew it would be a lie anyway. "We realized you were going to have to be taken care of. You'd gotten wise to me drugging you. You pretended you were knocked out in our cabin and later followed me up to the deck."

He nodded. "Let me guess. You were with Otis and Arthur, your criminal masterminds."

"There was a scuffle. We couldn't let you go to the captain. I was afraid you'd already made a call from the room to either the authorities or your girlfriend. We had no choice."

"No choice but to throw me overboard." He laughed. "Come on, Juliette. Admit it, you were planning to kill me even if I hadn't discovered what was going on."

"If I had planned to throw you overboard before our 'honeymoon' was over, I would have made sure you were too drugged up to have survived," she spat at him.

"That's the loving wife I remember," he said. He chewed at his cheek for a moment. "So from the very beginning you planned to trick me into marriage and then kill me."

"You're wrong. Yes, I was desperate for money and I thought you had more than you do. But the last thing I needed was another dead husband," she said.

"Then how did you think you were going to get away with all this?"

She shrugged. "I was going to divorce you once we got back to the States. It would be my word against yours. You think anyone would believe some story about me pretending I was FBI to get you to marry me? Especially when there were witnesses on the ship who would testify that you seemed to be drunk most of the voyage. Unfortunately, you became a problem for us on the ship and had to be disposed of."

"Disposed of. You really are a heartless—"

"If you hadn't survived, I would have gotten away with it because I even had your family believing that you'd had too much to drink and must have climbed up on the railing that night."

"AJ never believed it," he said.

"AJ." Juliette swore. "I really didn't plan on her. You weren't wearing a wedding ring. When we interrogated you, we confirmed that you weren't married. You never mentioned a girlfriend. Then along comes AJ determined that you're alive. That you had to have survived. She suspected right from the start that something was wrong with the entire story."

He smiled. "Thank God for AJ. She knew I was alive. She… felt it. That's true love, not that I think it is something you have ever experienced or ever will."

Cyrus realized the gun in her purse hadn't been the only thing she had gone for. She pulled out her cell phone and hit a few numbers.

As he pocketed the FBI badge, he said, "Give me that."

When she didn't hand it over, he grabbed it out of her hand to stop the call from going through to whoever she'd been dialing.

"What are you doing?" she demanded.

"What do you think? I'm calling Flint. He's going to love locking you up."

"He won't believe you."

"I think he will, especially when I show him the badge you used."

"I wouldn't do that," Juliette said as she got to her feet an instant before Cyrus heard the creak of a floorboard behind him.

He spun around into Otis Claremont's big fist.

"I WAS AFRAID you weren't going to get here in time," Juliette cried and threw herself into Otis's arms.

"And leave you here alone with Arthur? Not a chance."

"The damned fool just about got caught over at the saloon and now he didn't check to see if Cyrus was here and came in the back door flapping his lips... Cyrus went after him but didn't catch him, thankfully. But when Cyrus came back, I could tell his memory was coming back. Then he saw my FBI badge. I was packing, planning to get make a run for it." She groaned. "He remembered everything."

"I heard."

"What are we going to do with him?"

Otis looked down at Cyrus. He had quickly gagged and handcuffed him, binding his ankles with tape. "What we planned all along. I got here late last night. Heard something on the radio that got me thinking. Found this little canyon... I've got it covered." He grinned.

"It has to look like an accident or suicide or something. And we have to get rid of his girlfriend. I want her dead." She looked down at Cyrus who was struggling to get out of his bondage. The blow had only stunned him long enough for Otis to get the cuffs on him. She'd had to help hold him down to get his ankles bound and the gag on him. "But isn't that going to look suspicious?"

Otis touched her cheek. "I told you, baby. I've got it all figured out. Call Arthur. I'm going to need his help. The place I found is perfect. We get rid of both of them. Make it look like they took off together. When they're found..." He grinned again and she realized that he'd seen the check Cyrus had written her. "We are going as far as this will take us," he said, picking up the check and waving it like a fan. "Warm weather, ocean breezes, you and me."

Juliette studied him, feeling as if she'd gone from the frying pan into the fire. She raised an eyebrow as he pocketed her check. "Any trouble getting here with that BOLO out on you?"

"Borrowed a vehicle and an ID."

"And you had time to scope out a perfect place to finish this?" she asked, feeling the hair rise on the back of her neck. Sometimes he scared her.

"To take care of things. I couldn't leave it to Arthur."

She looked into his handsome face and felt a shiver. She knew he would double-cross her in a heartbeat if the money was right.

"Once he and his girlfriend are dead, you get everything Cyrus had," Otis said.

"And where will you be?"

He pulled her to him. "Sweetie, I can't stick around here. I'll take care of Arthur and then I'll meet you somewhere sunny and warm. Isn't that the way we always planned it?"

"Take care of Arthur?"

"It's time to lose him. It's been time for a while, don't you think? But first call him. Get him back here. I need his help. Then call the girlfriend. Get her over here and then bring her out to the spot I found. I'll draw you a map." He stepped to the small table by the door and picked up the notepad there and began to draw. "If she ever wants to see Cyrus alive, she'll do what you say."

"Where's this perfect spot?"

"Not far from here, actually. Back in the mountains."

On the floor, Cyrus was staring daggers at her. If looks could kill…

CHAPTER TWENTY-EIGHT

AJ JUMPED WHEN her cell phone rang. She'd been on edge since waking up to Cyrus's note. She'd seen how furious he was last night. And how frustrated. He'd brought this woman into their lives and he had no way of getting rid of her—short of selling his family's ranch.

She could tell that as badly as he wanted free of Juliette, he couldn't do that to the Cahills. Even if he couldn't remember his family, he had seen how much they cared about him. If push came to shove, they would give up the ranch to save him.

So she hoped he wouldn't take things into his own hands with Juliette. The Cyrus she'd known had been strong but gentle. He wasn't a killer. Neither was AJ. But Juliette had changed that, hadn't she?

There were times when she relived that night on the trail down from the hot springs. She saw herself lifting the rock and bringing it down. She shuddered at the thought. She'd saved Cyrus. Fortunately, she hadn't killed the man. She didn't want to be faced with such a decision again before this was over. She feared neither of them would ever be the same and worried where that left their relationship. They couldn't look at each other without remembering what they'd had to do to survive.

Nerves jangling, she pulled out her phone and was surprised to see who was calling. "Juliette?" she said without preamble.

"I thought we should talk. I was hoping you'd come by my cabin."

"Have you seen Cyrus?" AJ asked.

"No, why?" Juliette said.

"I thought he might have stopped by."

"Really? If this is about the baby—"

And then there was the baby, AJ thought with a silent groan. She told herself that Juliette was lying, like she did about everything. But what if she wasn't? She pushed the thought away. "Last night someone attacked me in my apartment."

"That's awful!" Juliette cried. "But you're all right?"

"A little bruised, but fine. You wouldn't know anything about it I'm sure."

"No, this is the first I've heard," Juliette said. "How frightening. Well, I can tell you I'm going to make sure I lock my cabin door tonight. I thought Gilt Edge didn't have any crime."

AJ gritted her teeth.

"Still, you and I need to talk," the woman said. "It's about Cyrus. I think I have a plan that might put an end to all of this. I know how much the two of you want to be together. I can make that happen."

"For a price."

"Please. Let's just sit down, girl to girl. Maybe I'm not as heartless as you think I am."

AJ wasn't about to touch that line. Heartless, soulless, evil. "I'll be right there." She disconnected, wishing Cyrus had a cell phone. That should have been one of the first things they picked up for him when they returned to the States. Not that he would think he needed one, she was sure.

Grabbing her coat, she ran downstairs. She wasn't looking forward to this meeting with Juliette, but if there really was a way to get the woman out of their lives, she would jump at it.

"Where are you off to?" Billie Dee asked, looking worried as she stepped to her to gently touch the side of her face. "That bruise is awful. If that man comes back around here, I'd like to take a rolling pin to him."

AJ laughed in spite of her sore cheek and jaw. "If you hear from Cyrus, would you tell him Juliette called and wants to talk about freeing him from their marriage. At least I hope that's what she meant."

"Do you think that's a good idea going over there alone? You know what that woman is capable of doing."

She hugged Billie Dee. "That's why I'm telling you where I'm going. I think Juliette is beginning to realize she can't win this one."

The cook looked skeptical. "That man who attacked you last night—"

"He might not even know Juliette."

"We both know better than that. I'm sorry, but that woman isn't the kind to give up. Gigi's father was like that," she said of the man who'd fathered her daughter. "Even after all these years, if he knew where I was now, he would make trouble for me and worse for Gigi. Those kind never give up."

"I hope you're wrong about Juliette because I'm afraid of what Cyrus will do."

DEPUTY HARPER COLE groaned inwardly at he took down the information from Logan Sparks about his missing snowmobile.

"So what would you say the value of your machine was?" Harp asked the elderly rancher.

"Value? To me? Priceless. On the open market?" Sparks laughed. "Hell, doubt I could give it away. You're missing the point, son."

"I know. You just want it back," he said before the old man could lecture him. "Can you describe it?"

He listened as Sparks told him what he'd suspected. The snowmobile was so old they didn't even make that brand anymore. The seat was cracked on it, the paint faded, the short windshield broken off and the body dented and rusted.

"But it still runs," the man said. "And I still use it."

Harp groaned inwardly. "When did you last see it?"

"Was in the barn yesterday evening."

"With the key in it?" the deputy asked.

"Of course the key was in it. You think I want to be carrying the key around? Wasn't like I thought anyone was going to steal the damned thing. You have to pull start it. Weren't easy, either. About jerked my shoulder off sometimes getting it started but once I did, it ran just fine."

Harp looked from the barn where they stood to the house. "I would imagine it was noisy running."

"Deafening. I hear the newer ones aren't quite so loud."

"But you didn't hear it being taken?"

"Yep, see what you're getting at. I sleep like the dead. Especially with my hearing aid out."

Harp nodded and put his notebook away. "So the snowmobile was parked here." He pointed to a spot not far into the barn where the dirt was displaced by the track and skis on the snowmobile. Glancing out the barn door he could see the tracks heading toward the south. He figured he would find the snowmobile buried in a drift where some kids had gotten it stuck and couldn't get it to go any farther.

He sighed. "I'll see if I can find it and let you know."

"You find it and I'll identify it," Sparks said. "Doubt there's another one like it still running."

Harp nodded and began following the fresh snowmobile tracks through the snow, telling himself that he deserved better than the kind of cases the sheriff sent him on. He knew Flint resented him from the start. The sheriff had inherited him when he'd taken the job. The fact that Harp was the mayor's son had kept Flint from getting rid of him from the get-go.

Admittedly, he'd made some mistakes. He hadn't taken the job seriously for a while. But now that he was married, had a son and a wife who was expecting again, he was a changed man.

Not that he thought Flint was ever going to trust him with real lawman work. What did he have to do to prove himself? He'd helped solve a half-dozen cases. What more did Flint want? Harp had settled down. He was doing his best to prove himself. Didn't that show that he was trustworthy?

Suddenly the snowmobile tracks stopped so abruptly that Harp stumbled to a halt and blinked. "What the hell?" He'd been so sure it was kids who'd stolen the old snowmobile. But as he stared at the track at the edge of a small secondary snow-covered road, it took him a moment to realize what he was seeing. He couldn't help being surprised since as Sparks had said, the snowmobile wasn't worth anything.

But darned if someone hadn't pulled up to the edge of the road, backed up against a snowdrift and driven the snowmobile up into the bed of a pickup. He could see the indentation of the pickup's bumper in the snowbank.

He bent down and realized that wasn't all he saw. The license plate had also been pressed into the snowbank. Harp let out a laugh as he pulled out his cell phone and took a photograph of the plate complete with numbers. He was going to find Sparks's snowmobile. Another crime solved. So there, Sheriff Flint Cahill, he thought as he called in the plate number and let out a low whistle when he heard the news.

The pickup had been stolen from a barn down by Red Lodge. This case was getting more interesting, he thought as he noticed that the truck hadn't headed toward the main road, but had driven toward the road to Horse Thief Canyon.

AJ PULLED UP in front of Juliette's cabin and felt a shiver as she looked around, thinking about what Billie Dee had said. This place was definitely isolated. The office was six cabins away and up by the main road while this last cabin was back in the pines by itself. She didn't think it was coincidence that Juliette had chosen it.

The woman's car was parked out front. Next to it, there were tracks in the snow where someone had also been here. Cyrus? Had Juliette lied about not seeing him this morning?

Why had Juliette gotten her out here? Just then, the door of the cabin opened. The blonde stuck her head out and gave her an impatient nod to come in before closing the door. AJ noticed that the woman's rental car was covered with snow. It appeared she hadn't been anywhere recently.

She took a breath and let it out, just wanting to get this over with. If there was a way to free Cyrus of this woman, she had to try, she told herself as she climbed out and walked toward the cabin.

It was one of those March days when the weather didn't seem to know what it wanted to do. This time of year in Montana it could snow two feet just as easily as it could be sunny and warm. Today it was overcast and the weatherman had mentioned another storm coming in.

The snow in the mountains was deep this time of year. Down here in the valley, there was a good foot of it. Everywhere there were piles of snow that had been removed from the streets and deposited around town in high mountains that the local kids played on until June when the snow finally melted.

AJ felt the cold dampness as she tapped on the cabin door. A few flakes began to fall around her, growing more dense quickly.

She started to reach for the knob, wondering what she was doing here. Did she really believe they could work something out?

The door opened so fast that she was taken aback for a moment. Juliette had clearly been impatiently waiting for her just inside the door. AJ hoped that was a good sign. Maybe she really did want to settle and be on her way.

She started to step in when she noticed that Juliette was wearing her coat and boots. She stopped in the doorway. "Were you coming or going?"

Juliette smiled, reminding her that the woman was attractive when she wasn't scowling. "Just waiting on you."

"With your coat on?" Juliette appeared a little nervous. AJ got the impression that she was lying about something, but then again most things out of the woman's mouth were a lie. "Maybe this wasn't a good idea," AJ said and started to step back outside when Juliette pulled the gun from her coat pocket.

"*We're* going out," the woman said. "You're driving. Cyrus is waiting for us."

AJ looked from the gun to Juliette as her mind reeled. "I thought you said you hadn't seen Cyrus?"

"My mistake," the blonde snapped and pointed the barrel at AJ's chest.

A thought streaked past. *Run!* Juliette appeared to know how to use a gun, but even she couldn't be that accurate firing at a running target with a pistol.

She started to take a step back, when Juliette said, "Cyrus dies if you don't come with me. Yes, Cyrus was here earlier. But so was a friend of mine. If you want to see your boyfriend alive, then you will come with me quietly."

"How do I know you aren't lying?" AJ demanded.

"Are you really willing to take the chance?"

BILLIE DEE HAD gone back to her cooking after AJ left, but she couldn't quit worrying. AJ was young. She still believed that good could overcome evil. Not that Billie Dee didn't believe that, as well. But as Henry had taught her, sometimes good needs a helping hand—the kind that plays just as dirty.

She put down the spoon she had been using to stir her chili with and wiped her hands on her apron. Pulling her phone, she called the sheriff's office.

Flint was out of the office. She left a message and then tried his cell. It too went to voice mail. She left another message and pocketed her phone, telling herself Juliette wouldn't be foolish enough to hurt AJ. Not in broad daylight. Not in Gilt Edge, Montana.

Billie Dee pulled out her phone again. She thought about calling Henry, but he'd gone down to Billings with his sons for the day to pick up ranch supplies. She was glad he was spending time with them.

After another moment's hesitation, she called the Cahill Ranch. Hawk answered.

"Hawk, I'm probably just being a silly old woman, but I don't know if you heard what happened here last night?"

"I heard. Is he there again?"

"No. But...well, AJ just left here to go see Juliette after the woman called her wanting to meet. I called Flint but he wasn't in and he isn't picking up his cell..."

"I can see why you're concerned. They're meeting at the cabin Juliette is staying in on the edge of town, right?" Hawk asked.

"That was my assumption."

"Maybe I'll just drive by and check on her."

"Thank you," Billie Dee said on a relieved breath. "AJ is so sure that Juliette wouldn't do anything..."

"But you and I don't believe that. Don't worry. I'll head out right now."

THE FALLING SNOW was thick now, the visibility getting worse, as AJ drove south away from Gilt Edge. The wind whipped the snow, sending it whirling around the car. Next to her in the passenger seat, Juliette sat holding the gun pointed at AJ.

"Where are we going?" she asked, praying she wasn't making a mistake. What if they weren't going to see Cyrus? It wouldn't be the first or the last time Juliette lied. And yet, AJ knew after what had happened last night in her apartment that Cyrus would have gone to Juliette today.

She knew he would have tried to do whatever it took to get the woman to stop. If Juliette really was taking her to Cyrus, then things must have gone horribly wrong.

"Turn right up here onto that road that heads back into that canyon," Juliette said. AJ realized the woman was looking at a piece of notepaper on which someone had drawn her a map.

AJ didn't know the road, but as she slowed to make the turn, she could see two sets of tracks in the fresh snow. She also saw a sign posted on a tree next to the road in. CLOSED to All Outdoor Use. AVALANCHE DANGER. There had been a chain across the road but it appeared to have been cut and now lay across the road in the snow. Ahead, all she saw were snow-laden pines. Past them, along the ridgeline of the mountain, huge cornices hung over the edge. Carved by the wind, they looked like pristine white waves that were about to break over a beach.

Except these waves hung out over the edge of the mountain, both beautiful and dangerous. It would take so little for one of them to break off and careen down the mountainside taking anything in its path with it.

"Go!" Juliette shouted, making AJ realize that she'd stopped only a few yards onto the road. The snow was deep and she could see from the tracks of the vehicles that had come in ahead of her that they'd slid some trying to bust through the deep, untracked snow. She was glad that she'd bought a four-wheel drive SUV before she'd come to Montana. She'd just never dreamed she would need it for this though.

Juliette prodded her with the gun. "You want to see Cyrus?" she demanded.

AJ pushed down on the gas pedal and, tires spinning, the SUV started up the narrow road. Dark pines, capped with snow, lined each side of the road making it feel like a tunnel. Large snowflakes fell from a low, sullen sky. AJ shivered. What was Juliette planning to do? This seemed an odd place to bring her. Was Cyrus really waiting somewhere ahead?

"Cyrus remembered."

She swung around to look at Juliette. The woman nodded and smiled in answer.

"Watch where you're going!" Juliette cried as, for a moment, AJ had lost control of the SUV. The right front wheel dropped out of the tracks and into the deeper snow at the edge of the road. But she was able to pull it back up onto the tracks left by whomever was ahead of them before the SUV got stuck.

"I figured Cyrus would remember one day," Juliette continued. "His head injury couldn't have been that bad or he would have drowned. So the memory loss was apparently psychosomatic. My mother had that for a while when I was young. Just seemed to forget everything. Couldn't blame her since her life was a living hell in that dilapidated farmhouse where we lived hand to mouth. I wished I could catch the memory loss from her."

AJ looked over at Juliette. It was the first time she'd heard anything about the woman's younger years. "Just because you were poor—"

"Poor?" Juliette scoffed. "Poor in a way you never could even imagine. One look at you and I knew you were born with a silver spoon in your mouth. Bet you've never gone hungry or been cold or had to wear clothes that had been handed down so many times you could see right through the cloth."

"I'm sorry, still—"

"I don't want to hear your pathetic excuses," Juliette snapped and looked ahead through the pines, the gun resting on her thigh, pointed straight at AJ. "I do what I have to do. Someone like you could never understand. If it makes you happier, Cyrus was a huge mistake." She shook her head. "I was so sure he would have drowned. But you just had to go find him, didn't you?" She cursed.

That the woman could be so cold and uncaring chilled her more than the winter storm outside.

"Once you found him... Well, then, you gave us little choice. He could have gone years without remembering. Or not." She glared at AJ. "You could have done yourself and me especially a favor and not gone looking for him."

AJ shook her head, thinking if she hadn't at least Cyrus would be safe on the island. "What have you done with him?"

"Don't worry. He's alive. You'll have your reunion. Turn up here."

AJ slowed to make the turn onto an even smaller road that had been cut through the snow and pines. She could see where someone had cut a Christmas tree. Ahead she saw two pickups, Cyrus's and one she didn't recognize. Cyrus's was parked in the middle of the road. The other one had managed to get turned around and now was backed up against the mountain, the tailgate down and a snowmobile in the back.

AJ looked past them to the warming hut. It also had the closed sign on it along with the avalanche warning. Ahead she could see a deep gully where the road dropped down into an old avalanche chute.

"Stop here," Juliette ordered.

CHAPTER TWENTY-NINE

FLINT GOT THE message from Billie Dee on his way back from another winter vehicle accident. He quickly called to see if AJ had returned.

"I haven't seen her," the cook said. "I'm worried. I didn't like her going out there alone."

"You have good reason to worry. I'll try to call her," the sheriff said. "What about Cyrus?"

"He left early this morning. I haven't seen him since. But I know AJ thought he probably went to see Juliette after what happened last night."

Flint swore. He knew his brother even if his brother didn't know him. Of course Cyrus would confront the woman. To threaten Juliette? Or try to reason with her? He doubted either would do any good.

"I'm on my way into town now," he told Billie Dee. "If you hear from either of them, call me back. Otherwise…"

It was the otherwise that worried him as he tried AJ's cell. It went straight to voice mail. He disconnected and, turning on his lights and siren, sped toward town.

DRIVING THROUGH THE falling snow, Hawk pulled into the Happy Holiday Cabins and Kitchenettes. He realized he should have asked what cabin Juliette was staying in. Parking in front of the building marked office, he jumped out and ran up to the door. The snow was coming down in a wall of white. He could barely make out the other cabins along the tree line.

He tried the door. Locked. He knocked, and waited, but soon realized no one was going to be coming to the door. It was off-season. He wondered how Juliette had been able to rent one of the cabins. The woman was very persuasive. If she flashed around enough money… Or batted her eyelashes…

Running back to his pickup, he climbed in and started it up again to clear the windows before he drove slowly along the line of the cabins, following the older tracks in the snow.

Juliette's rental car was parked outside of number seven. But he could see that it hadn't been moved since the snowstorm had started. Nor were there any lights on inside the cabin. Still, he jumped out and ran to the door. Locked. He pounded on the door, but when he got no answer, he hurried back to his truck.

AJ wasn't here. But that didn't mean that she and Juliette hadn't left in her car. That seemed unlikely. If so, where would they go? He checked his watch. Early afternoon. He supposed they could have gone somewhere for coffee to *talk*.

As he was debating what to do, he heard the sound of a siren. A moment later he caught the blur of flashing sheriff's department lights coming out the highway. The vehicle slowed to make the turn into the cabins and came flying toward him. The sound of the siren grew louder as the patrol SUV came to a snow-boiling stop just feet from his pickup.

Hawk had been worried before, but Flint's appearing like this made his stomach roil. He hadn't heard from Cyrus and with AJ now missing too…

THROUGH THE PINES, AJ stared at the huge cornice of snow hanging from the ridge at the top of the mountain directly over the narrow avalanche chute. It looked like a giant white wave that could break off at any moment and come barreling down the mountainside. Every year a snowmobiler or skier got caught in an avalanche in this area. With the latest snowfalls, it was no wonder the area had been closed.

"Shut off the engine," Juliette ordered as AJ pulled up behind Cyrus's pickup.

She stared at the warming hut for skiers and snowmobilers when the area was open to recreation. It was small, built of wood and simply a place to get out of the cold and snow. AJ couldn't imagine why Juliette had brought her. But everything about this made her skin crawl. She knew she'd driven into a trap, but she didn't know what else to do if she had any hope of helping Cyrus. Right now, even if he was here, that seemed impossible. Juliette had a gun on her and from the look in the woman's eyes, she knew how to use it.

Now that she was here, she had no idea how she could save either of them if Cyrus was here, if he was still alive. At least Billie Dee knew where she'd gone. Not that it would help much if both she and Cyrus were dead. The thought that Juliette might get away with this made her blood boil.

"I said shut off the engine." Juliette jabbed her with the barrel of the gun. "You have been nothing but a pain in my ass. If you had just left well enough alone... *Turn off the damned engine.* I'd just as soon shoot you here. Then I'm going in there and telling them to kill Cyrus." AJ turned the key. The engine died. "Leave the keys. Now get out."

She climbed out of the SUV. If she was going to run, now would be the time she thought as Juliette awkwardly climbed out of the passenger side into the deep snow, trying to keep the gun on her prey and still stay on her feet.

But AJ didn't run. Couldn't. Juliette was right. If there was even a chance of seeing Cyrus again, let alone a chance that the two of them could somehow get out of this alive... Without him, nothing mattered. She'd given him her heart. There was no getting it back. There was no future without him.

She headed toward the warming hut with Juliette bringing up the rear. Before she reached the door though, it flew open. AJ recognized the man standing in the doorway as Otis Claremont. He looked past her to where Juliette was tromping through the snow toward them. He motioned AJ inside, moving back to let her in and give her a view of the small building.

On the floor behind Otis was Cyrus, bound and gagged—but alive! His gaze met hers in a mixture of relief and fear for her.

FLINT SWORE AS he got the call from Deputy Harper Cole.

"You're going to find this interesting," Harp said without preamble. "Sparks's snowmobile—"

"Not now." He disconnected as Hawk climbed out of his pickup and slid into the passenger seat of the patrol SUV next to him.

"Have you seen either Cyrus or AJ?" Flint asked already knowing the answer from the expression on his brother's face.

"No one was here when I arrived, but there were two sets of tracks out," Hawk said.

Flint swore. "Let's have a look inside."

"The door's locked," Hawk said.

"Not for long." Flint opened his door, grabbing what he needed from the vehicle. It didn't take long to break in the flimsy front door.

"Something tells me this isn't legal," Hawk said as they entered the cabin.

"It is if I thought I heard a distress call. Apparently you didn't hear it."

"What happened to my brother Flint, the brother who always goes by the book?" he asked as they quickly searched the place.

"Last year I almost lost Maggie. This year we lost Dad. I'm not going to lose my brother and the woman he loves," the sheriff said. "Find anything?"

Hawk shook his head as they met back up in the living room area of the cabin. He moved to one of the end tables by the couch where he stopped by a scratch pad and pen. He picked up the notepad. He could see the indentations made on the top sheet where someone had drawn something. Directions?

"Find me a pencil," he said to his brother as his phone rang again. He couldn't believe it. Harp again? He started not to take it. "What?" he snapped as his brother came back with a pencil. He began to carefully brush the lead over the top sheet of the notepad.

"The stolen snowmobile. They loaded the snowmobile on the back of a *stolen* pickup," Harp said before the sheriff could hang up on him again. "They headed toward Horse Thief Canyon."

"It's closed because of avalanche danger."

"That's where they're headed. Tell me that isn't suspicious."

Flint blinked. "Where are you now."

"At the road into Horse Thief Canyon. There are three sets of tracks going in."

"Cyrus and AJ are missing," the sheriff told him. "Nor can we find Juliette."

Flint looked down at the map that appeared beneath the faint pencil strokes in front of him and swore. "Stay right there. We're on our way."

AJ RUSHED TO CYRUS, dropped beside him and removed his gag.

"Oh, AJ," he said with a groan. She could hear the pain in his voice at seeing her. "This is all my fault. I got you into this. I'm so sorry."

"It's going to be all right," she whispered.

He shook his head. The look in his gray eyes said it wasn't.

She turned to Otis. "Take these cuffs off of him!" she demanded.

"Would you listen to her," Otis said.

"Believe me, I *have* listened to her," Juliette said as she entered the warming hut and shut the door behind her. She stood shivering. "Let's get this over with. I just want this done so I can get out of this godforsaken cold country."

Otis shook his head. "I need you to go back to the cabin. Ditch her car at that old closed convenience store on the way back. You need to be at your cabin to get the bad news later today. So you'd better get moving."

Juliette glared at her. AJ could tell that she didn't want to miss what happened next. "Can't you just shoot them and get it over with?"

Otis pulled her over to the door and whispered something to her.

"Fine," the woman said, though she didn't look happy. "Just end it."

AJ turned back to Cyrus, realizing that they had probably only minutes left together. She touched his cheek and fought back tears. He looked as bad as she did, only the skin around his eye was just starting to turn black and blue. Hers was black and blue and purple this morning from where she'd been hit last night.

"You aren't going to get away with this," she said, turning to see Otis grab Juliette and kiss her hard.

She heard him whisper, "This is almost over, then it's just you and me, baby." He gave her a loud slap on her behind as she turned to leave.

"We've already gotten away with it, no thanks to you." Juliette hesitated for a moment in the doorway and then went out. "Make sure she suffers for putting me through this."

AJ looked to Otis as the door closed. "Please. Take off his cuffs. I know you're going to kill us but at least give me a moment in his arms before you do." She sounded close to tears. She was.

Otis laughed and shook his head. "You're a lot more romantic than Juliette."

Juliette was a heartless, cold bitch, but she didn't tell him that. If he didn't already know, he would soon enough. They deserved each other.

"Please. You've taken so much from him. At least give us a few minutes together," she said.

"You are awfully demanding," he said as he stepped toward her and Cyrus. "No wonder Juliette is so fond of you. You know she wanted to kill you herself, but it didn't work out. You should be damned glad of that. Okay, why not? Stand over there," he said to her as he knelt down and reached for his keys to the cuffs. "Make a move and I'll shoot him in the head and then turn the gun on you. Got it?"

She nodded and pressed herself against the wall as he'd ordered.

Cyrus was looking at her as if he hoped she knew what she was doing. Not half as much as she hoped she did. The moment she'd come into the warming hut, she'd looked around for something she could use as a weapon.

Unfortunately, there wasn't much. Someone had left a pile of garbage in the back corner. There was a broken ski pole lying next to it. Closer was the tip end of a broken cross-country ski. It wasn't much, but it would have to do, she thought as she waited for Otis to dig out his handcuff keys.

She watched Otis kneel on the floor next to Cyrus.

"You pull anything and I'll blow your head off," Otis said, brandishing the gun in his left hand as he rolled Cyrus over to get to his cuffed wrists at his back.

The moment he turned the key and the cuffs fell away, she made her move. The warming hut was small enough that all she had to do was take a step to reach the broken ski tip. She snatched it up, disappointed immediately to feel how light it was. It wouldn't make much of a weapon, after all.

But she was committed now and had no choice. She swung it with all her strength. It caught Otis in the side of the head. The sound it made was more impressive than the damage it did. He swayed a little and let out a curse as he started to grab for her.

The blow slowed Otis enough that Cyrus was able to spin around. He brought up his knees, his ankles still bound, and kicked Otis hard in the chest. AJ had to jump out of the way as Otis went sprawling on his back.

AJ saw the man raise his gun. She leaped on him, grabbing the gun as she tried to wrest it away from him. Cyrus rolled over and grabbed Otis's arm, the three of them wrestling on the floor, when the door of the warming hut burst open.

CHAPTER THIRTY

THE GUNSHOT TOOK them all by surprise. Dust and wood splinters filled the air around them. Cyrus turned toward the doorway to find Arthur Davis waving a gun. The man raised it as if to fire another shot into the ceiling.

"Arthur, stop!" Otis ordered as he wrestled the gun from AJ. He swung it. Cyrus ducked, but still caught enough of the barrel against his head for the light to dim for a moment as he fell back. Otis gave AJ a shove that sent her falling back onto the wood floor. "Keep your gun trained on them." He got to his feet, wiped at the blood running down his cheek and swore. The metal edge of the cross-country ski tip had torn into his flesh. But the wound was obviously only skin-deep.

Cyrus reached for AJ, taking her in his arms. He couldn't believe her bravery. His love for the woman swelled until his heart was bursting. He wished there was some way to save her. He didn't see any way out of this now. He'd managed to get the tape off that had bound his ankles. But there was no way he could launch an attack on the two men holding guns on them.

"If we're going to die, I want you in my arms," he whispered in her ear as he held her tight. "I'm so sorry, AJ."

She shook her head, tears running down her face as she drew back to look at him as if suspecting, like he did, that it would be the last time.

Otis sighed and said, "Let's get this over. If either of them move, shoot them."

Out of the corner of his eye, Cyrus saw the former cop reach into his pocket and bring out a syringe. So that was the plan? Not shoot them?

Otis stepped to them, grabbed a handful of AJ's hair, and dragged her from Cyrus's arms. "Shoot her first if Cyrus moves," the ex-cop ordered.

Cyrus had no doubt that Arthur would do it. The man seemed to be the loose cannon of this bunch. But as Otis went to jam the needle into his arm he pretended to flinch and managed to move enough that even though he felt the prick of the needle, the ex-cop had trouble emptying all of the drug into him. Otis swore and kicked him in the thigh hard enough to make him double over.

"Did you get enough of the drug into him?" Arthur asked.

"I think so. Won't make any difference in about twenty minutes anyway," the former cop said. "Go get ready. You think you can handle this?"

Arthur smirked at him. "You just do your part." He turned then and left.

Cyrus could feel the drug racing through his system. He realized that they weren't going to dope AJ. He was afraid of what Otis had in mind for her. The former cop seemed distracted, no longer worried about Cyrus, no doubt knowing that the drug would soon leave him unable to defend himself. He could already feel its effect weakening him. He just hoped that he'd managed to get so little of the drug that it wouldn't render him useless for long.

But even as he thought it, he felt himself drifting, his body feeling as if he was floating. He tried bunching his hands into fists. It was as if his brain and his body were no longer connected. Had they used this drug on him on the ship, he thought, he wouldn't be here now. And neither would AJ.

"HERE IS WHAT we're going to do," Otis said as from outside came the loud rat-a-tat-tat of a snowmobile engine coming to life. "You're going to help me get your boyfriend here out to his pickup. Or I shoot you here. Your choice."

AJ moved from the wall where she'd been standing and the two of them helped Cyrus to his feet. Otis kept the gun clutched in his free hand and she could feel him watching her, looking for an excuse to get back at her for hitting him with the ski. The cut on his scalp where she'd hit him with the ski was still bleeding. She'd hurt him and he wasn't one to forget it.

He kicked open the door of the warming hut and they stepped out into the heavy snow. Cyrus's now leaden body shifted and she almost fell into a snowdrift under his weight. Otis managed to pull him back and they made it the few steps to Cyrus's pickup. The ex-cop opened the passenger side door and ordered her to go around to the driver's side.

Cyrus fell face-first into the pickup. Otis grabbed his legs with effort and shoved him in the rest of the way.

As AJ slid behind the wheel, she tried to imagine what the man had planned for them. None of this made any sense. If he was going to kill them, then why not get it over with and just shoot them?

He slammed the passenger side door and she saw her chance. She reached down to start the pickup. If she could get away fast enough... The key wasn't in the ignition. Her door flew open.

Otis jangled the keys in front of her, laughing as her slim hope of escape evaporated.

"Scoot over," he ordered. There wasn't much room in the cab with Cyrus slumped over. Otis helped her shove him into a sitting position and had her put his seat belt on.

She watched as he put the key in the ignition and started the engine. What did he plan to do? Plug the tailpipe and let them die of carbon monoxide poisoning? She'd heard of it happening in the winter. Drivers went off the road and kept their vehicle engines running while they waited for a wrecker, not realizing that the car's tailpipe was in the snow and the vehicle was filling with the deadly gas.

But that didn't seem to be the plan, she thought as he got out, stood in the open doorway and honked the horn. The noise of the snowmobile could be heard in the distance. It had quieted some she realized—until Otis honked the horn. He reached over and honked the horn twice again. She heard the snowmobile rev up in the distance.

"What are you—"

"I'm giving you a chance to save yourself and your boyfriend," Otis said. "Drive down the road through that gully. Here's your chance to live. If you make it to the other side and up that mountain, then I won't come after you and shoot you both. You'll live." He reached down to wedge something against the gas pedal. The engine howled. He shifted the truck into gear and jumped back as the pickup leaped forward.

AJ was so stunned it took her a moment before she grabbed the wheel and slid over under it as the truck roared down the steep road out of control. She started to touch the brakes but remembered what Otis had said. The engine was revved so high she couldn't hear herself think. She shifted the truck into Neutral, but the pickup had already dropped over the edge of the ravine and was now careening downward.

She pumped on the gas pedal trying to get it to come up. The pickup was bouncing down the mountain at breakneck speed through the pines and snow. It was all she could do to keep it on the road and not crash into the pines as snow rose in the air and blew over the windshield.

Ahead, the trees opened into the bottom of the gully. That's when she knew what Otis had planned. Avalanches over the years had barreled down the gully, clearing out the trees and anything else in their paths. The gully was now an avalanche chute and with the heavy cornices at the top of the mountain…

That's when she heard the roar. Arthur had taken the snowmobile up on the mountain to set off the avalanche. They would be buried alive in it if she didn't reach the other side of the gully.

Her gaze shot to Cyrus's passenger side window. A wall of white was rushing down the mountainside headed right for them. She had no choice. She shifted back into gear. The pickup leaped forward as she raced toward the other side of the gully, knowing she wasn't likely to make it, but having to try.

CHAPTER THIRTY-ONE

OTIS WAITED UNTIL he saw Cyrus's pickup disappear under the mountain of snow before he climbed behind the wheel of the stolen truck. He'd promised Arthur that he would wait for him. He'd lied. Just as he'd lied to Juliette. He had the check in his pocket. He had a friend who would cash it for him and then he was out of the country. He already had a new passport and identification in another name.

"You should have listened to me, Juliette," he said, smiling, as he started down the road out of the canyon. He told himself that he wasn't worried about Arthur surviving and turning state's evidence against him. Arthur was so sure he could start the avalanche without getting caught in it.

But Otis had known the man for years. Arthur couldn't do anything right. By now he would be under all that snow along with the stolen snowmobile. Otis smiled to himself. He just wished he could see Juliette's face when she realized what had happened. If she talked, she would only incriminate herself.

Anyway, she hated the cops. All the times her mother had called the police when she was a kid and they showed up but did nothing about the woman's abusive husband. It was just a matter of time before he killed her and he did. He would have killed Julie too if she hadn't gotten out of there and reinvented herself as Juliette.

He almost felt sorry for her. But his own father had been a real bastard so he couldn't work up much sympathy for her. Did she really think he wanted to run away with her and marry her? He must look like a fool in that case. He'd seen into her heart. She could never love any man. She was busy destroying every man she could snare as if killing her father over and over again.

Otis shoved away the past, like swatting away a pesky fly. If his plan worked, it would appear that AJ and Cyrus had gotten caught in an avalanche. It would look suspicious, but there would be no proof that any of them had been involved.

He would get rid of the stolen pickup as soon as he reached Billings. In a city that size, it was just a matter of wiping it down and leaving the keys in it. Soon he would be a free man. Free of Juliette and Arthur. In the spring they would find Arthur's body. If Juliette wasn't already behind bars, they'd suspect her. But with her luck, she'd probably skate. She had a knack for getting away with murder.

Otis couldn't wait to get out of the country. He'd saved every dime he could of the money he'd made with Juliette. He had a nice nest egg, enough that he could live comfortably where he was going. He thought about sun on his face, a cold beer in his hand, a pretty woman on his arm. Hasta la vista.

HARP HAD WAITED at the entrance into Horse Thief Canyon. He'd kept looking at the tire tracks in the road until he hadn't been able to stand it any longer. It wouldn't be the first time that he'd disobeyed a direct order. But it could be the last, he'd thought as he pulled out his shotgun, made sure it was loaded and then took his handgun from its holster and laid it on the passenger seat next to him.

He'd glanced down the road up to the canyon. Still no sign of the sheriff. True, it had only been a few minutes since he'd made the call. No way could Flint have gotten here yet. Harp's gut instinct had told him not to wait. He wasn't sure he could trust it, that's why he hadn't disregarded the order to wait right after it was given.

Now as he shifted the patrol SUV into gear, he told himself he was taking a hell of a chance. There'd been a time that Sheriff Flint Cahill had just been itching for an excuse to fire him. And he'd come close more times than Harp liked to remember. But there'd been those other times when Harp had followed his gut instinct and saved the day. Not many of them.

But today, he felt like if he waited things could go very wrong.

Tromping on the gas, he thundered down the narrow road through the pines. The deep snow flew up over his SUV, making it hard to see at times, but he didn't slow.

As he came around a bend in the road, he saw the pickup headed right for him. A second later a bullet shattered his patrol SUV's windshield. Harp didn't let up on the gas. The pickup and the patrol SUV were on a collision course, but he wasn't going to be the one to turn away. He grabbed the handgun on the seat and fired through a hole in his windshield.

The pickup suddenly veered to the left and crashed into the pines.

Harp hit his brakes but he was going too fast. He tried to get past the tail end of the pickup sticking out in the road. Unfortunately, the road wasn't quite wide enough. He heard his mirror fly off as the pickup scraped down the side of his SUV.

But somehow, he managed to get past the truck and was now barreling toward the warming shack, afraid of what he would find. Ahead, he saw something that made his heart race with worry. Snow rose from the gully next to the warming hut in a billowing cloud that seemed to obliterate everything ahead.

CYRUS OPENED HIS EYES. For a moment, he saw nothing but white. He blinked and tried to move his body. His fingers twitched. Then his arm jerked. He looked down. He was sitting up in what appeared to be his pickup, strapped in by the seat belt. Through the windshield, he could see nothing but snow. It was at his side window, as well. It seemed to be packed around him. He tried to open his door, feeling as if he needed fresh air. It wouldn't budge.

He was trying to make sense of it when he looked over and saw AJ slumped against the door. He unhooked his seat belt and reached for her as he tried to shake off the fuzziness of the drug. She stirred.

"What happened?" he asked. He could see that their air bags had deployed, he realized. He shook his head in confusion.

"Avalanche," AJ whispered as she leaned into him.

He saw that she'd hit her head on the side window. There was blood running down the side of her face. He pulled her to him, wiping at the blood with his sleeve. "Avalanche?" It was freezing in here.

"Otis." She met his gaze, tears brimming in her eyes. "The truck was caught in the avalanche."

He felt his eyes widen in alarm. "We're under the snow?"

She nodded and he felt his heart take off like a shot as he realized there was little chance of digging themselves out. They had no idea which way was even up. Just as there was little chance they would be found. Soon they would be out of oxygen.

AJ looked at him, her blue eyes wide and scared, but her expression accepting. She knew that they weren't going to survive this.

He wanted to break a window and try digging them out, but

he knew it would be fruitless and waste what little oxygen they had left. He hugged AJ to him and breathed in the sweet scent of her hair, his heart full of regrets.

"Juliette said you remembered."

He nodded. "It all came back." He told her about the FBI badges, the thumb drive someone had slipped into the pocket of his jacket, and how Juliette and Otis had taken him upstairs at the hotel. "I was such a fool. But they were so believable." He shook his head. "They said they believed me that I was innocent and had no idea how the thumb drive had gotten into my pocket. They said the only way they could help me was if I helped them."

"That's how you ended up on the ship," AJ said.

He nodded. "All of it including the wedding was supposed to be a ruse to catch the real criminals. I got swept up in it. I thought I was helping my country. I was suspicious that they'd set me up. But I still believed they were FBI. I heard them make calls to their superiors supposedly. It was all very real."

"But at some point, you caught on to them."

"Yes, and that's when I was thrown overboard. The wedding was supposed to be part of the ruse. And all of it was just an elaborate plot to get the ranch. And it would have worked if you hadn't believed I was alive and come looking for me."

He pulled her to him and kissed her. "I'm so sorry. I got you into this—"

She touched a finger to his lips and snuggled against him. "We're together. No couple knows how long they have together."

Cyrus shook his head. He'd never met anyone like her. "They can't get away with this."

"I heard Otis whisper to Juliette how they plan to make it look like we ran off together. She won't give up trying to get the ranch."

He hugged her, realizing it was getting harder to breathe. He couldn't do anything about Juliette or the ranch or getting out of this pickup. He thought of his family. He remembered them all and felt a lump form in his throat that they would never know how much he loved and appreciated them.

Looking at AJ in his arms, he said, "I love you." He started to say that if they got out of this… But he couldn't bring himself to say the words. They could no more dig themselves out of this than he could change the past.

"I love you," she whispered.

He could tell she was getting sleepy from lack of oxygen. He thought of all the ways they could have died. At least, like she said, they were together.

HARP PULLED UP in front of the warming shack and jumped out. Light snow fell around him as if someone had set off a chalk bomb. As it settled though, he could see the tracks down into the avalanche chute. They stopped abruptly at the edge of the massive snowfield that now filled the gully.

He ran down the road, slipping and falling and getting back up. When he reached the edge of the avalanche, he climbed up the mountain of snow. He didn't know what he was looking for until he saw it.

Red metal. Part of a vehicle was wedged against the other side of the gully. It had been caught in the avalanche and had been swept down the gully twenty yards to be deposited against the mountainside. He ran back to his SUV and put out an urgent call, before grabbing the small shovel he carried to get himself out of a ditch in the winter and ran back down.

As he uncovered more of the pickup, he could see where the cab was in relation to where he'd dug and quickly moved to the spot. He didn't know how much air there was in the cab. If one of the windows had been down or broken during the avalanche, then the cab could be stuffed with snow and there was no saving anyone.

But he kept shoveling, telling himself that if there was even a chance they were still alive, he had to take it. He'd dug down until he could see part of the driver's side window. He could see AJ lying in Cyrus's arms. Neither was moving. He shoveled harder until he had enough snow moved that he could break the window and get them air.

He called to her but with all the snow still covering the truck, she apparently didn't hear him. Or she was already gone. He tried not to think about that as he swung the shovel. It bounced off the window ineffectually. He started to try again when he heard the sound of a snowmobile in the distance.

FLINT AND HAWK raced down the road toward Horse Thief Canyon. All the way, he told himself that the missing snowmobile probably had nothing to do with the missing Cyrus and AJ, let alone Juliette. But the fact that the pickup involved with the stolen snowmobile was also stolen made him think that Harp might be onto something.

Anyway, it was all he had to go on at this point. As he reached the entrance into the canyon, he saw the chain was down that had blocked the road. There were multiple tracks in the road. And there was no Harp.

Flint swore. "I knew he wouldn't wait. I swear I'm going to fire him." Giving the patrol SUV gas, he started up the road through the dense snow-filled trees. They hadn't gone far when he saw the wrecked older pickup in the trees. Stopping, he jumped out and waded through the snow. Otis Claremont lay over the wheel, a bullet hole in his chest. He appeared to still be alive, but barely.

Back at the patrol SUV, he called for an ambulance and was

told that Harp had already made the same call only he also had called for help shoveling out victims from an avalanche.

"Hell's bells," Flint said as he disconnected. He could see where Harp had driven on past the pickup. Flint had no choice but to do the same thing and with probably the same results. He winced as the rear edge of the pickup scraped down the side of the SUV. Once past, he drove into the canyon, terrified of what they would find.

Ahead, he spotted Harp's SUV parked by the warming shack. But there was no sign of the deputy. As he and Hawk climbed out he saw the tracks down to the avalanche. Tire tracks—and boot tracks. That's when he heard the snowmobile headed toward them. A moment later a bullet whizzed past.

HARP SWUNG THE shovel again. The side window shattered. He quickly squatted down and looked in. Cyrus was holding AJ. They both appeared to be asleep. Harp swore as he reached in and shook the cowboy's by his sleeve.

"Wake up!" he yelled. "Wake up." He pulled on Cyrus again. As oxygen began to fill the pickup's cab, the rancher stirred. "Cyrus!" he called and tugged on his sleeve until he turned to blink at him. "Come on, I can get you out the window. Can you get AJ to move? Shake her. Hurry."

He watched as Cyrus shook AJ. For a moment, it appeared that she was already too far gone. But then she let out a gasp. "Drag her this way, closer to the window." Both seemed disoriented. Harp realized they were probably suffering from hypothermia along with lack of oxygen.

Cyrus helped get AJ through the window and then crawled out himself. Both were shivering. But Harp could hear a siren in the distance.

The sound of gunshots reverberated through the pines and across the expanse of the avalanche area. He looked up at the top of the mountain. One large cornice had broken off and swept down. But there were others. Anything could set them off.

"Come on," Harp said as he and Cyrus got AJ to her feet. "We have to get out of here."

FLINT DREW HIS weapon as the snowmobile barreled down through the pines at them. He recognized Arthur Davis. Resting his arm on the roof of the SUV, he fired. The bullet caught Arthur in the shoulder. He saw the man's surprised expression. But the snowmobile kept coming. Arthur tried to raise the gun in his hand but couldn't. Nor did he seem able to stop the snowmobile. At the very last minute, Arthur rolled off the speeding machine into the snow. The snowmobile crashed into the side of the patrol SUV. The sheriff swore as he holstered his gun.

Hawk had taken off down the road toward the avalanche. Now Flint saw him coming through the pines. He and Harp were helping AJ and Cyrus. Behind him he heard the sound of the ambulance.

He retrieved Arthur, locked him in the back of the patrol SUV and rushed to his brother and AJ.

"They were caught in the avalanche in Cyrus's pickup," Harp said. "They're suffering from hypothermia. We need to get them to the ambulance."

"He saved our lives," Cyrus said, coughing as he still fought to breathe in the cold mountain air. He pulled AJ to him as the ambulance arrived, lights flashing, siren blaring.

CHAPTER THIRTY-TWO

"I'M AFRAID I have bad news," the sheriff said, taking off his Stetson as he stepped into Juliette's cabin later that evening. "I'm sorry, but were you expecting me? You don't seem surprised."

She looked flustered for a moment, but quickly checked herself. "Honestly? I wasn't surprised to see you at my door. I've had a terrible feeling since seeing Cyrus earlier," Juliette said. "He was so distraught. He finally remembered everything, us falling in love, getting married, our baby... I knew he didn't want to believe it because it meant losing AJ. He was going to find her when he left. I was so afraid that when he did, she would end it, and as despondent as he was... Tell me he didn't kill himself."

Flint looked down at his Stetson in his hand and said nothing.

"Oh no, I knew it. I feared he'd do something like this. I knew he loved AJ..." Her eyes widened in alarm. "When he left here, he was going to find her. I was afraid if he did... He didn't hurt her, did he?"

"Juliette—"

"As much as she seemed to love him, the news had to be devastating for her."

"Juliette, they're both alive."

"What?" She blinked, her expression one of disbelief. She was shaking her head. "But I thought you said..."

"I said I had bad news. It wasn't Cyrus and AJ. It was your ex-husband, Arthur Davis."

She frowned. "Arthur?"

"And a friend of yours, Otis Claremont."

"Are you telling me that they're..."

"Both were shot. Otis is dead. He died at the scene, but Arthur is going to survive. He's at the hospital. He's already agreed to turn state's evidence against you and Otis. Right now, the FBI is at the hospital taking his statement. The real FBI. Have you heard the expression, 'sing like a canary'?"

Her mouth formed a hard straight line. Her blue eyes were cold as ice chips. "I have nothing more to say to you without a lawyer present."

"Oh, you've said quite enough. I know you were expecting Cyrus and AJ to be dead. A double suicide, isn't that what you'd hope for? Or at best an accident? Sorry. They're both suffering from hypothermia and lack of oxygen but the doctor said they'll be just fine.

"The bad news for you though is that when Arthur finishes telling the FBI everything he knows, investigators from Arizona and Florida will be flying in. They'll be taking Cyrus's statement as well as Arthur's. This time, Julie, you aren't going to get away."

He stepped to her, spun her around and cuffed her as he read her her rights. With luck, she would spend the rest of her life behind bars. Still, she would get off better than almost all her husbands.

CYRUS REACHED ACROSS the space between the two hospital beds to take AJ's hand. The doctor had said that if either of them had been alone, they would have died of hypothermia before their oxygen ran out. But together they'd stayed warm enough until almost the end. In the ambulance and later at the hospital, their body temperatures had been brought slowly back to normal.

The doctor had wanted to keep them overnight, saying it could take twelve hours before full cognitive function returned. He was more worried about their extremities. "You both had low pulses and difficulty breathing in the ambulance on the way in. Now I just want you to get plenty of fluids and rest."

Cyrus had insisted at the hospital that they be put in the same room. "I never want to be away from that woman again."

"I can't believe we're alive," AJ said now as she squeezed his hand.

He smiled at her, wondering how he'd gotten so lucky to find a woman like AJ. "Only because of you."

"I believe the credit goes to Deputy Harper Cole," she said.

"That time, yes," Cyrus agreed. "I keep thinking about what would have happened if you hadn't come looking for me."

She shook her head. "Me too. I just felt it in my heart that you were alive. Everyone thought I was crazy." She laughed and then coughed. "There were times I thought the same thing. I was ready to give up and then I saw you."

"I'm so glad you're not the kind of woman to give up on anything, especially me," he said and smiled over at her. He could tell that she was still shaken from their latest brush with death. Earlier in his pickup under all that snow, they'd shared what they thought were their last moments together.

They turned at a knock on the door. Flint stuck his head in. "Good news. The doctor said the two of you are going to be released in the morning."

"I'm hoping you brought us even better news," Cyrus said. "Juliette?" His greatest fear was that she would escape, skip the country, do this to someone else.

"Under arrest," Flint said. "I put the cuffs on her myself. She's now behind bars. And more good news. The FBI is interrogating her ex, Arthur Davis, after he was treated for his gunshot wound to his shoulder. He's agreed to turn state's evidence against Juliette. Meanwhile, the investigators from both Florida and Arizona would be coming to take statements from the two of you."

Cyrus lay back on the bed and tried to relax. He'd lived with this nightmare for so long, he'd thought it would never end. "So it's over?"

"Yes," Flint said. "And now that you have your memory back…"

Cyrus smiled at his brother. "I remember all of you. I owe you all such a huge debt. If you hadn't held Juliette off—"

"I doubt Hawk will ask you to go after any more bulls though," Flint joked.

"What about the baby Juliette's carrying?" AJ asked.

"She has agreed to put it up for adoption," Flint said.

"And Juliette is okay with this?" AJ asked.

"Apparently, she wasn't planning on keeping it anyway."

She shuddered. "The woman is soulless. I've never met anyone more inhuman and yet when she was telling me about her childhood… I felt sorry for her."

Cyrus shook his head. "Looking back, I know it seems impossible that I wouldn't have seen through them."

"No," Flint said. "I saw the badges and identification they were carrying. They'd both dealt with enough FBI, I'm sure they were very convincing."

"Hopefully I'll never be detained by a real FBI agent," Cyrus said with a curse. "I really will end up in jail because there is no way I'm going anywhere with that agent."

AJ met his gaze. "I suggest you stay close to home."

He smiled at her, their gazes locking across the space between their beds. "Trust me, you aren't getting me out of Montana or far from you ever again." He looked up at his brother. "I'm going to marry this woman. That is, if she'll have me."

AJ's eyes filled as she nodded and smiled through her tears.

"But what about your honeymoon?" Flint asked. "We were going to chip in on a Caribbean cruise."

"Funny," Cyrus said, even though he could laugh now that it was over. He'd been through so much. He wondered if he would ever get over it. He looked to AJ and knew that with her by his side though, he could overcome anything.

"The only way you could get me back on a ship is hog-tied, but I'd let Hawk lasso me if it is what you want," he said to her.

AJ laughed and shook her head. "I'm thinking something a whole lot closer to home. But first we need to get Billie Dee and Henry married. Their wedding plans have been held up long enough."

"Operation wedding is in full swing," Flint assured them. "Lillie is on top of it. Billie Dee's daughter, Gigi, is flying in Friday night. All the arrangements are made. Unless someone else in this family disappears… Billie Dee and Henry will be wed Saturday afternoon at the saloon with family and close friends."

"Good job, Lillie," AJ said. "Please tell her that I'm sorry I haven't been around to help."

"You two have been through so much," Flint said. "I'm glad you've both agreed to talk to the hospital psychiatrist."

They'd agreed to appease him. Cyrus knew what he needed more than anything was AJ and his Montana life back. He was a cowboy and when not on a horse, he liked both boots planted firmly on the ground—or kicked off at the end of his bed with AJ waiting in it.

Just then the family poured into the room. Lillie ran to her brother and threw her arms around him. "You remember me?"

"How could I forget *you*?" he asked with a laugh.

They all gathered around AJ and Cyrus, anxious to hear about everything that had happened. Cyrus looked at each of them, amazed how blessed he was. Even when he hadn't remembered his family, he'd felt their love. They were the bedrock that he'd depended on and would in the future. Together they were a force to be reckoned with, he thought with a smile.

"Dad's heart finally gave out, huh," he said finally.

"Massive heart attack," Darby told him. "We had to go ahead with the funeral under the circumstances."

He nodded around the lump in his throat knowing he'd never see his father again.

"The whole county turned out," Hawk said, quickly filling in the silence as he saw his brother's distress.

"They wanted to see if aliens flew over to give him a send-off," Lillie joked.

"Did they?" Cyrus asked, only to have his sister playfully slug him.

"So when can I start planning your wedding?" Lillie asked.

"Knowing you, it will be at Billie Dee's wedding reception," Cyrus said with a laugh. He looked over at AJ. She was so beautiful it took his breath away. "Also we don't want to steal Billie Dee's thunder." He looked at Flint. "I need to get the annulment first."

His brother nodded. "With Juliette's arrest it should be fairly easy to push through the paperwork." Flint could see that AJ and Cyrus needed their rest. "Come on, everyone. Let's get out of here before the doctor kicks us out." He herded them all out the door, stopping in the doorway to look back at Cyrus. "I'm so glad you're back. You were missed."

BACK AT HIS OFFICE, Flint called Deputy Harper Cole in. "Please have a seat."

Harp took off his hat and sat down in a chair across the desk, his head down. For a moment, the sheriff didn't speak.

"Harp, what am I going to do with you?"

The deputy raised his head. "But I—"

"Saved the day again." Flint nodded. "That's the problem. You use your own judgment, which is often questionable. However, you get results and those results have saved people's lives. Members of my family."

Harp turned his Stetson in his fingers and kept his head down.

"Maybe you've heard that Mark left to take a job down in New Mexico where his family is from."

The deputy's head came up fast, his eyes lighting up. Mark Ramirez was the local undersheriff. "I had heard that. I just assumed..."

Flint didn't have to ask what Harp had assumed. Since Flint's brother Tucker had joined the sheriff's department, everyone probably assumed that Tucker would get preferential treatment. Which meant they didn't know Flint at all.

"I need someone in that position who uses his head, who thinks before he acts, but that also uses his instincts," he continued. "I've seen how you've changed over the past year. You've become a family man. You've taken on assignments that you thought were beneath you, but you didn't complain. You have good instincts and you're smart."

Harp was sitting up, his expression anxious.

Flint chuckled. "I know you probably think you should be sheriff, rather than undersheriff, but I'm afraid the only job open—"

"Really? You're considering me for the position?" The excitement in the deputy's voice made him smile.

"Harp, I'm offering you the job."

The deputy let out a whoop, caught himself and sobered. "I appreciate your faith in me."

That was just it. Harp scared him by being impulsive and often not thinking of the consequences before he acted. But when it came to following his instincts, Flint couldn't fault him.

He rose and so did Harp. Flint came around his desk to shake the deputy's hand. "I'm glad to have you as my right-hand man, Deputy Cole."

"Thank you, Sheriff. I won't let you down."

Let's hope not, Flint thought, but smiled. "Did I hear that Vicki is expecting again?"

Harp's chest swelled. "Another son."

"Congratulations." As Harp left his office, Flint thought about how marriage and a child had changed the deputy. How it had changed him.

CYRUS PARKED AND climbed the hill, stopping at the foot of his father's grave as snow whirled around him. "Hey, Dad, sorry I missed your send-off. Sorry I couldn't have been here. At least you'll be getting your wish soon. All your sons will be married off."

He took a breath and swallowed the lump in his throat.

"You don't have to worry about the next generation, either. Everyone's working on that. I hope to get on that as soon as AJ and I are married. If I've learned anything, life is short even if we all make it to the ripe old age you did. I wish you could see how happy AJ and I are together. She's an amazing woman, but I think you already knew that. She says she wants a passel of kids." He laughed. "Not sure about passel, but I'd love three or four, for sure."

Cyrus looked out at the town below cemetery hill, his voice thick with emotion. "You have a nice view." He caught something out of the corner of his eye and turned a little to look back at the ranch and swore. "Looks like you've got a good view of our missile silo." He couldn't help but chuckle. His father had been keeping an eye on it for years—especially since that night he swore he was abducted by aliens near the spot.

"Guess you can keep on watching what's going on over there. If anything," he added under his breath. Most people still thought Ely was a crackpot. Cyrus reckoned they always would. They'd never know what happened that night or any other night when his father had been watching the silo. But Cyrus would have put his money on his old man being a whole lot smarter than people thought even before Flint had told him about their father's journal and the government taking it. They certainly believed the old man knew something.

The wind had picked up and the snow was falling harder now. He could barely make out the town in the distance. He tucked his chin into the collar of his coat, not quite ready to leave. He thought of his father spending all his time up in the mountains after he'd lost his wife. He'd never imagined that kind of love and devotion—until AJ.

"Well, Dad, I wish you were here for my wedding, it's going to be in the summer, up in the mountains. I know you would have loved that. But I suspect you're happier now that you're with Mom. Rest in peace. We're all going to miss you."

AJ HAD NEVER seen a more beautiful bride as Billie Dee said her vows to Henry and he put the ring on her finger, pulled her into his arms and kissed her. She and Gigi were both in tears. It was a small wedding, family and a few friends only. As the pastor introduced Mr. and Mrs. Larson, a cheer went up. Then everyone was hugging everyone else.

Gigi insisted on cooking the after-wedding meal at the saloon. "You aren't cooking on your wedding day," she'd told her mother. "Anyway, you've never had anything I've cooked. Don't you think it's about time?"

Billie Dee had hugged her. "I'm so glad I waited to get married so you were here. I can't wait to eat whatever you make."

"Well, you're a tough act to follow," Gigi had said. "I'm going to have to step up my game."

As congratulations died down, AJ followed Gigi into the kitchen. Gigi had flown in Friday night to get everything ready.

"It isn't every day that your birth mother gets married," she'd said.

AJ breathed in the amazing scents filling the kitchen. Her friend had been cooking almost from the moment she'd arrived. "You're making my stomach rumble."

Gigi grinned. "I just hope Billie Dee likes it."

"Are you kidding? You could feed her dirt sandwiches and she would rave."

"Not helpful," her friend joked. "She did make a beautiful bride, didn't she? Proves we're never too old to fall in love."

AJ caught something in Gigi's voice. "You met someone. Oh my gosh and you haven't told me?"

Her friend grinned. "I was going to tell you."

"Well?"

Gigi laughed. "You're going to love this. He's a cowboy. A *Montana* cowboy."

"You're kidding?"

Her friend shook her head. "He walked into the restaurant one night in Houston. Our eyes met across the room..." She laughed. "I know, just like in the movies. He came back the next night and the next..." She shrugged.

"Where in Montana?" AJ asked, clapping her hands.

"About an hour away from here."

AJ felt tears rush her eyes. "Have you told Billie Dee yet?"

"No, it is going to be my wedding present. Along with this meal, which we'd better get out there. Sounds like the family is getting restless."

Darby and Mariah and Lillie came back to help carry out the food. There were Texas tamales, Gigi's famous green chili shrimp, her version of Mexican rice and a pot of fresh pinto beans seasoned with bacon—a real Texas meal in honor of the bride.

"Don't worry," Gigi told the crowd. "I held down the spices, Montana style."

As everyone gathered around the table, Henry led them in a prayer. But before they could dig in, Gigi said she wanted to give her mother a wedding present.

"This is enough of a wedding present," Billie Dee argued. "Look at this meal. Gigi, you have outdone yourself."

"I'm moving to Montana, about an hour away," Gigi said. "Following your example, I met a cowboy and he's asked me to marry him."

Another cheer went up. Billie Dee burst into tears as her daughter came around the table to hug her.

"Okay, everyone," Gigi said, her voice thick with emotion. "Let's eat."

The meal was beyond wonderful. AJ sat next to Cyrus and looked around the table at the family that had adopted her. She couldn't believe how blessed she was. Lillie had already started planning AJ and Cyrus's wedding in the summer. Gigi had agreed to be her maid of honor.

Her parents had even cleared their busy schedules for the wedding. Her father had accepted the news that she wouldn't be one of his company attorneys better than she'd expected.

"I just want you to be happy, Ashley Jo," he'd said. "That's all your mother and I have ever wanted for you."

"I'm deliriously happy. I can't wait for you to meet Cyrus."

"Why don't the two of you fly down for a weekend so we can meet him before the wedding?" her father had suggested.

AJ had laughed. "It's a little hard to get my cowboy out of Montana right now. You'll meet him in the summer and I hope you'll start taking a vacation in Montana each year so you can spend time with your grandchildren."

"Grandchildren?"

"Not yet, Dad, but soon. They're going to grow up riding horses. Wait until you see this country up here. It's a little bit of heaven."

"Sounds like you've fallen in love with more than just your cowboy."

"I've fallen in love with his family, as well," she'd admitted. "And Gigi is moving up and getting married to a Montana cowboy, as well."

"You girls," he'd said with a laugh. "You've been inseparable for years. Gigi told me why you went to Montana in the first place. I'm sure I haven't said this enough over the years, but, Ashley Jo, you've done us proud."

Now as she looked around the room at the people she'd come to love, she still couldn't believe it. She'd never dreamed when she'd come to Montana that her life could turn out like this. All she'd wanted to do was find Gigi's birth mother in the hopes that it would take away some of her best friend's pain after losing her adoptive parents.

She had never thought that she would fall in love with the Cahill family, let alone a handsome Cahill cowboy. And now Gigi was going to be close by, marrying a cowboy and living the ranch life, as well. After everything she'd been through, she still wanted to pinch herself as she looked over at her handsome, soon-to-be husband.

Dreams came true, she thought, even when they weren't ones she'd ever dared to dream. Cyrus smiled at her and pulled her over for a kiss. Sometimes a girl just got lucky beyond her wildest dreams.

★ ★ ★ ★ ★